EASY PICKIN'S

Also by Fred Harris
Coyote Revenge

EASY PICKIN'S

FRED HARRIS

HarperCollins*Publishers*

HarperCollins books may be purchased for educational, business, or sales promotional use. For information please write: Special Markets Department, HarperCollins Publishers Inc., 10 East 53rd Street, New York, NY 10022.

FIRST EDITION

Printed on acid-free paper

Library of Congress Cataloging-in-Publication Data

Harris, Fred R.
   Easy Pickin's: a novel / by Fred Harris
         p.   cm.
   Sequel to: Coyote Revenge.
   ISBN 0-06-018399-3
   1. Sheriffs—Fiction. 2. Oklahoma—Fiction. 3. Depressions—Fiction. I. Title.
   PS3558. A64455 E27 2000
   813'.54—dc21   00-039695

01 02 03 04 ❖/RRD 10 9 8 7 6 5 4 3

For Margaret S. Elliston,
the muse I choose

ACKNOWLEDGMENTS

Many thanks to Margaret Elliston, Kathryn Harris Tijerina, Laura Harris, and LaDonna Harris for reading the manuscript and offering helpful suggestions. I'm grateful, too, for the help of Dr. Tey Diana Rebolledo, on Spanish; Geneva Navarro, on the Comanche language; Bill Sexton and W. C. "Doc" Wiley, on airplanes and aviation; and Dr. Deborah McFarlane, Marilyn and Jim O'Leary, Dr. Dayton Voorhees, and Jim Belshaw, on other important and technical stuff. And, finally, my special thanks and gratitude to my superb agent, Elaine Markson, and my wonderful editor, Carolyn Marino, vice president and executive editor at HarperCollins*Publishers*. All these contributed to making the writing of this book a labor of love.

ONE

It was the Saturday morning before Easter 1938, which that year fell on April 17, that a human body hurtled out of a diamond-clear sky and slammed right down in the middle of a flat Oklahoma oat field.

The day'd been windy, but the local weekly, the *Vernon Herald*, couldn't have made a headline out of that. It wouldn't have been news. The wind always blew in southwest Oklahoma. Stud Wampler, my main deputy, liked to say that chickens in that part of the country had to carry rocks to keep from getting blown away.

The relentless "dirty thirties" wind of the awful Dust Bowl years, just earlier, had scooped up and hauled a lot of Oklahoma on down to Texas, dribbling out lives and dreams along the way. But 1938, itself, had not been a Dust Bowl year—like 1936 and 1935 had been. Thank God! And by Eastertime, we hadn't had any tornados, yet, in those parts.

So, you didn't have to be the Cash County sheriff—as I was, right then—to deduce that no diabolically fierce wind had suddenly snatched up the human body in question from somewhere else and then dumped it like a tree limb in the center of that wavy, green field of newly headed oats.

The field belonged to two uncles of mine, Uncle Joe Ray and Uncle Leroy Vanderwerth, bachelor brothers of my dead mother. The common saying around there about people like those two was that "their eggs got shook." They'd been all right, twenty-one years earlier, in 1917, when they'd left Vernon to go and fight in the Great War in Europe. But they'd come back from the hell-hole trenches "shell-shocked," as people said, never the same again.

The two brothers, slat-slim and all knees and elbows, were as poor as Job's turkey, as Mama would have said. They made a living the best they could on a 160-acre Indian lease, hunting and fishing, raising turkeys, selling cream and eggs, and making home-brew beer. Periodically, they sold dressed squirrels door-to-door in Vernon for the asking price of two bits, but now and then had to take fifteen cents because times were hard, and a lot of people didn't any more have an extra two bits to spare than my uncles did.

There was nothing addled about the uncles' report of what they'd found in their field that Saturday before Easter.

"Hit were one of our coondogs, that bluetick named Willie, that set up sich a ruckus out in them oats," Uncle Leroy said.

"That uz how we-uns got the idee somep'n other was out there," Uncle Joe Ray said.

They'd followed the coondog's baying and run out, bare-backed and barefooted, to the oat field in front of their old house to see what was the matter. Finding the dead body, they'd looked it over quickly, then turned right around and jogged back to the house and jerked on their shoes—without socks, I could see—and their wrinkled gray work shirts, outside the suspenders of their ragged Blue Bell overalls. They'd hitched up their mismatched team, a big bay horse and a little sorrel jenny, to their frail wagon and careened off, north, to the rented house where I was batching—the old Billings place on the east side of Vernon—to bring me the news.

Telling me about what they'd found, the two of them were as excited as coondogs that've run an armadillo into a hole. Spraying snuff juice through snaggled teeth and talking over each other in their high-pitched voices, they blurted out their story, answering, when I asked, that the victim was dead when first discovered.

"Dead as Aint Idy's cat, Okie, hon" is the way Uncle Leroy put it.

I'd been named after these two uncles. My real name is Ray Lee Dunn. But my dad had put the nickname "Okie" on me when I was little because I was born on November 16, Oklahoma statehood day. The nickname had stuck. I was going on twenty-seven that Easter weekend of 1938, Oklahoma going on thirty-one.

"Deader'n ol' Woodrow Wilson," Uncle Joe Ray said.

The uncles were puzzled about one thing, though, and when they mentioned it to me, both of them, like twins, ran their bony fingers through spiky gray hair, which looked to me like they'd whacked on it themselves, maybe with their pocketknives. They'd been unable to decide whether the victim's death had come prior to the fall, or as a result of it.

"Acourse, hit don't make a heap a difference to the corpse," Uncle Leroy said.

"Deadfall or fall dead, all the same to the faller," Uncle Joe Ray said.

And fall was sure enough what that body had done, no doubt about it. Right out of a cloudless sky. It had neither been blown nor, as it turned out, carried to where it'd landed in the Vanderwerth brothers' oat field, about three miles southeast of the county-seat town of Vernon, Oklahoma, twenty some-odd miles this side of Red River.

The train of events that led up to the body falling from the sky had begun two days earlier, though, on the Thursday before Easter. That's the day a small covey of three strangers showed up, separately, in our little town—all of them somehow connected, time would show, to the "Case of the Unknown Girl," as Stud Wampler would soon start calling it.

TWO

Good thing, stud, you other sweetie not comin' to eat with us, after all," Stud Wampler said to me as he and I and Crystal Boucher, another deputy of mine, stepped out of the west door of the limestone-cube Cash County courthouse that Thursday noon, headed for Marshall's Café on Main Street. "She and that lanky home-ec gal might not hit it off too good, might get in a hair-pullin' over you."

"Audrey Ready's not my sweetie," I said.

Audrey was the widow of Dub Ready, the county sheriff I'd been appointed to replace after he'd been killed, back in November. The three of us—Audrey, her deceased husband, and I—had been best friends at Vernon High School, graduating together in the class of 1930. Since Dub's death, I'd escorted Audrey to a Christmas program and a box supper, and I'd twice taken her to a picture show in Vernon.

Not a whole lot of activity. But I knew that Stud Wampler

wasn't the only one trying to make something of it. And the truth was that I *was* attracted to the petite widow, who was also my longtime friend. She was fun to be around. She was attracted to me, too. I could tell. But each of us, it seemed to me, had ghosts on our shoulders—for Audrey, the live memory of her dead husband; for me, that of my old girlfriend, my only girlfriend ever, Juanita Ready, Dub's sister, no longer among the living, either. And Dub Ready's ghost was on my shoulder, too. I'd felt guilty, held back, about taking up with his widow so soon after his death—even though I'd wanted to.

"Darling home-ec teacher after you now, too, stud, not just Audrey Ready," Stud Wampler went on. "You 'bout to catch 'em faster'n you can string 'em!"

"Stud" was what my chief deputy called everybody, whatever their real names. So, people called him that in return. He was fifteen years older than me, my dad's best friend and as loyal and good-hearted as a brother. But he was as bad to tease as a sixthgrader. He was punching me about the two women because both had separately telephoned me that morning at the one-room sheriff's office—a room where nobody could avoid knowing all the other occupants' business.

First, Audrey, who was a practical nurse, had called me to say that she couldn't, after all, have lunch with us—"dinner" was the word she used, like everybody else, for the noon meal. Audrey had to deliver a baby out in the country, she told me.

Then, not ten minutes after her call, the high school home-economics teacher, Janeaster Parnell, had telephoned to say that she'd like to meet me during her noon hour. I didn't know her all that well, but I'd seen her several times at local functions, once when she'd brought a number of her students to put on a special program at the Vernon Lions Club. I wasn't alone in thinking that she was the sharpest-looking young woman in town. Janeaster had telephoned me, she said, because she wanted to talk about the upcoming Easter Parade program at the high school auditorium. That local event was sponsored every year by the Vernon Lions Club to raise money for the annual Cash County sunrise Easter Pageant, out at Kraker Park, north of town.

I wasn't in the market for a new girlfriend. That was for sure. But I didn't want to turn down the chance to be around an attractive young woman a little more, either.

"No reason why a man and a woman can't just be friends," I said to Stud Wampler as we were leaving the courthouse.

Stud assumed his W. C. Fields voice, another one of the occasional peculiarities he was known for. "You may remember, my boy," he said in the nasal whine so familiar to everybody from the appearance of the funny man with the bulbous nose in picture shows—say, as the Great McGonigle in *The Old-Fashioned Way*—"those were precisely the words, 'Let us just be friends, honey,' that Bathsheba once lovingly vouchsafed to the unsuspecting King David."

"Aw, she just wants me to *do* something—Janeaster," I said, a little irritated.

"The exact point I would have made myself!" Stud Wampler said, still talking like W. C. Fields. He raised his head toward an imaginary judge. "I rest my case, Your Worship," he said.

I'd told Janeaster to join us at Marshall's Café. It was the choice eating joint in Vernon, a place, as people liked to say, where you could always count on getting the best hamburger in Oklahoma, big as a plate, for a nickel.

My two deputies and I marched down the courthouse

sidewalk, west, to Main Street, then headed the block and a half south toward Marshall's. It was in the second block of the five-block, one- and two-story central business district of the little town where I'd grown up. Vernon was what you might call a one-bank, one-picture-show, three-grocery-store, four-beer-joint, six-church kind of Oklahoma town.

Even as Stud, Crystal, and I sort of paraded three abreast, we wouldn't have been taken by strangers for a sheriff's posse, which we were, in a way. Nobody would have confused us with Wyatt Earp's bunch, say, striding toward the O.K. Corral. All three of us were new to law enforcement. Stud, a stout and raw-boned heavyweight, half a head taller than my five-ten, was on my right, toward the curb.

Crystal was on my left—"plain, but plucky," Stud called her, but not to her face. She was half a head shorter than me, thin, and, unfortunately, sort of gawky in the unusually nice blue rayon suit, with a near ankle-length skirt, that I knew she'd made herself. Crystal was only thirty-two, but her hair was already graying from the hard life she'd had, though you'd never know about that, she seemed so unreasonably cheerful all the time.

None of our shiny badges was out in the open. We wore them on our shirts, inside our jackets—Stud's a hip-length brown leather jacket, mine a black suit coat over a white shirt and iron-creased Levi's, Crystal's the top half of her homemade combination.

Stud and I were wearing cowboy boots, all right, like Western lawmen—my black ones better shined, though, than his of brown rawhide—and we both had on our worn Stetsons. But none of the three of us wore holsters or had pistols show-ing. Fact was, Crystal and I didn't even carry weapons. And while Stud *did* tote a gun, as people put it, he always kept it out of sight, in his pants pocket. Said it was less showy that way. He didn't like the .45 automatic I'd taken off a Lawton thug and given to him. Too bulky. Instead, he carried a smaller gun—a little Colt .38 police-special revolver with a checkered walnut grip—in the right-front pocket of his loose khakis. He'd traded a bolt-action .22 rifle to a local Comanche Indian guy for it.

And, of course, Crystal was the main reason we didn't look like three lawmen. She *wasn't* a lawman. She was a law*woman,* and the first anyone around there had ever heard of, so far as I knew. She was raising a ten-year-old girl by herself—her husband had died in a steam-engine accident—and was the sole support of her parents, who weren't able to work, *if* they could have found work in those hard times. The Depression was still on. When I'd come in as sheriff, Crystal'd been the office receptionist and record-keeper, getting fifty-two dollars a month. I'd since talked the county commissioners into actually making her a deputy, so she could draw more, but they still wouldn't go above seventy dollars a month for her. Stud got ninety.

"Stud's right, Okie, 'bout you havin' two women on the string," Crystal said as we continued to walk south along Main. "And you know what they say 'bout two birds in the bush."

"No, what's that, Crystal?" I asked, teasing her.

She didn't respond for a couple of steps, apparently not quite remembering how the saying she had in mind applied—or maybe even how it went.

Stud filled in, heckling her. "Can't put salt on their tails when they're in the bush, ain't that what you mean, Crystal?"

"Naw, Stud, you know that's not how it goes," Crystal said and punched him lightly on the arm. "Okie, you know what I mean." She often tangled up adages she tried to use, and words, too, sometimes.

I changed the subject. "Your daughter doing all right?" I asked Crystal.

"Loretta taken sick, runnin' some fever," she said. "I'm kindly afraid of typhoid, a little, since I set up two nights with Miz Palmer that passed away from it, you know. But it's probably some kind of cold or something."

Crystal didn't have a high school diploma, just an eighth-grade education, which was as far as the country school she'd attended, Lincoln Valley, went. But she had a good brain and a notably compassionate heart. She was always helping out people who were less well off or in trouble, carrying over some green beans she'd canned, say, to a family down on their luck, or doing the milking for a sick neighbor who couldn't make it out of bed. Her favorite hymn, which she sometimes even sang under her breath while she was working in the office, went: "In the highways, in the hedges, I'll be somewhere working for my Lord." And, a good part of her spare time, she nearly always was.

At Parnell Dry Goods, on the southeast corner of Main and Kansas, the three of us crossed Vernon's asphalt Main Street, toward the vacant two-story sandstone building on the opposite side, where the failed Cooper Credit Furniture had once been located. We turned left, past the hole-in-the-wall Carl's Radio Repair, and stopped in front of Marshall's Café.

A bank of big thunderhead clouds was building up in the northwest. The wind was, for the moment, unusually still, like before a storm. I felt too warm in my suit coat to stand out front in the sun and wait for Janeaster Parnell. I opened the door to Marshall's. Stud and Crystal stepped inside the crowded eating joint ahead of me. I followed. A noisy electric fan stirred the hamburger grease and smoke that was heavy in the air in the large, tin-ceilinged room, but it cooled things off some, too.

The café was packed. We saw a vacant table against the south wall and took it, saying hello, here and there, as we made our way through the noontime diners.

We'd barely sat down, and Marshall's wife, Rita, had yet to bring us some water and take our order, when Janeaster Parnell and a fellow teacher showed up and walked over to join us. Stud and I stood up, again, when the two of them got to our table.

"This is my friend Eileen Sargent," Janeaster said after she herself had shaken hands with the three of us. "She teaches typing, and she's working with me on the Easter Parade program."

The young women pulled out cane-bottomed chairs and sat down at the rectangular oak table, Janeaster across from me, Eileen across from Stud. Crystal was at the end of the table, to their right.

You couldn't help noticing the remarkable difference in the appearance of the two teachers. It was almost as if Eileen, the one who taught typing, went around with Janeaster Parnell just to show off, by comparison, Janeaster, the prettier of the two, to greater advantage.

Eileen Sargent was short and chunky, dressed in a small-figured cotton dress and a heavily worn gray sweater that looked like it needed a shave. The too-white skin of her face was roughly pitted with what must have been scars from a bad case of teenage pimples. Janeaster, by contrast, was basketball tall, maybe as much as five-seven, lithe and graceful in a fitted beige silk suit, its skirt coming stylishly down to mid-calf. Her smooth, olive-toned face was free of makeup—and suffered not at all from the lack, I thought. The typing teacher's hair was a kind of dishwater blonde, bobbed short and waved. Janeaster's was black and shoulder-length, fluffed out on the sides and curled under at the ends.

If Eileen Sargent could have been taken for a kind of homely young English or Irishwoman, Janeaster Parnell might easily have passed for a Mediterranean or a Latin one. In fact, when Marshall's wife, Rita—herself, I knew, from the Valley, in south Texas—came over and took our order, she even, at the last, addressed a friendly question to Janeaster in Spanish, just before she left the table.

"*¿Eres Mexicana, verdad?*" she asked. You're Mexican, right? I knew Spanish myself, and understood what Rita'd said.

So did Janeaster, apparently. But she answered in English.

"No, just an American, through and through," Janeaster said. The young teacher then turned back toward us as the waitress acknowledged the response and left to place our order at the grill behind the counter. I was a little surprised that Rita didn't know Janeaster Parnell, since Janeaster's parents owned a store, I knew, right across the street. But Rita'd only moved to Vernon when she and Marshall married, which had been fairly recently, after his first wife died.

"Studied Spanish at Southwestern," Janeaster told us. "Eileen, too. We both got our teachers' certificates at Weatherford, you know."

Weatherford was the town, about fifty miles northwest, where Southwestern State Teachers' College was located. I knew that you could get an associate degree there, and be certified to teach in Oklahoma schools after only two years of study. Apparently, that's what the two young women had done.

"Let me just get right to the point, Sheriff Dunn," Janeaster said, the food-ordering over. "Eileen and I are here to ask you to serve as the master of ceremonies for this year's Easter Parade."

"Did Judge Dowlin die, and it didn't make the *Vernon Herald*?" I asked. That lovable old veteran of the War was not only the regular master of ceremonies for Vernon's annual Easter Parade program at the high school auditorium, he was the master of ceremonies for practically every other event that took place in Cash County, too, from box suppers to high school alumni banquets.

"Too old-timey," Janeaster said. "Embarrassing. That blond wig. Those war songs. If I have to hear 'Over There' again, I'll puke."

Eileen spoke up. "You're trained to be a lawyer, and—"

"Never finished law school," I said.

"Doesn't matter; you express yourself well, you're young, and you're modern," Janeaster said.

"Well . . ." I said.

"Don't say no," Janeaster said. She was kind of pleading. "Don't. We've worked so hard on this year's production—the modeling contests, the singing, the music. The more we've thought about it, the more we feel that Judge Dowlin would just ruin things."

Rita appeared with the food, then, and rapidly dealt the plates around the table like she was about to call out, "Jacks or better to open." I didn't have to give Janeaster an answer right away.

Crystal and Eileen started in on big hamburgers. Stud and I had the special—chicken-fried steak, mashed potatoes with cream gravy, fried okra, greens, and iced tea. A lot of food for lunch. A lot of food for thirty cents. Janeaster had the sliced turkey breast and English peas.

"Wait'll you see the great dresses Janeaster's made and what a knockout she is in the Easter Parade, modeling and singing," Eileen said, after a time, glancing over at her fellow high school teacher with obvious admiration. "She wrote the whole show, you know."

"You did?" Crystal asked, impressed.

"Had a lot of help," Janeaster said.

"You can't believe how talented she is," Eileen said. "Doubt we'll keep her long, here in Vernon. She's going to be a model."

"A model what?" Crystal asked.

"Fashion model, I hope," Janeaster said. "That's what I've always wanted to be. People who show off clothes, like in the Montgomery Ward catalog, for instance."

"They pay for that?" Crystal asked.

"Good money, ma'am," Eileen said. "Especially posing for magazine photographs. Janeaster studied fashion design at college, too. She sent pictures of herself last week to the Connor Model Agency in Dallas."

"Good for you!" I said.

"Hoping I'll get a call to Dallas for an audition," Janeaster said. "There's a chance, too, the Connor agency might send a scout to the Easter Parade. I invited them."

"They'll at least call you, I bet," I said, intending to be encouraging.

"You coach girls' basketball, too, I heard," Stud said to Janeaster matter-of-factly. The way he said it made me wonder if he didn't disapprove of that game for young women.

Janeaster said the season just ending was her first, as coach. "I played basketball, myself, in high school," she added. "Too fat, now, though."

"That's not true!" Crystal said. "Bestiality is no problem for you."

Janeaster and Eileen turned to look at each other, puzzled.

"Obesity, she means," I said.

Crystal reached over and touched Janeaster's arm. "That's no problem for you," she said.

Janeaster smiled. "Thanks. And the good thing is that you don't have to be in shape to coach."

"You're getting the job done, too," I said. "Those girls are *aggressive!*"

Janeaster's face lit up. "I don't think young women have to just giggle and act silly and wait for good things to happen to them," she said. "Like men, they have to go after what they want."

"Amen!" Crystal said, with feeling.

Stud and I both looked at her. We'd never seen her so animated.

"So, now, you want Okie—right?" Stud asked Janeaster. "What about hurting pore ol' Judge Dowlin's feelings?"

"We figure on asking the judge to handle the flag salute and the national anthem, before the curtain opens," Janeaster said. "We won't just drop the old guy." She leaned across the table, toward me, and put a delicate, thin-fingered hand on mine, the one with the fork. I held it steady. Our eyes met. "So, you'll do it, won't you, Sheriff Dunn?" she said, her voice sweet and persuasive.

"Okie," I said.

"Okie."

"I'll do it."

What else could I have said?

THREE

After we'd all finished eating and paid up at the cash register in front, the five of us stepped back out onto Vernon's Main Street. A swirl of the Marshall Café's griddle-grease air seemed to fog out the glass-front door behind us.

The wind had picked up again, and it swirled up toward my nose the stout aroma of dill pickles, onions, mustard, and fried hamburger that had apparently seeped into the fabric of my clothes.

"Smells like I'm wearing about as much as I ate," I said.

"Hamburger hounds gonna be on our trail for sure, stud," Stud Wampler said and pulled down his Stetson.

Just then, Sore-eyed Cecil and one of his raggedy little girls approached us from the recessed entrance to Modine's Hardware, next door, where they'd been standing in the shade of a blue awning.

"Christ is risen!" Sore-eyed Cecil said in a hoarse voice.

"Happy Easter to ya, Okie." He stuck out a bony hand, palm up, in my direction.

"How could you tell it was me?" I said. I'd been sheriff for only about five months, back in Vernon for not much longer.

"Knowed you voice, Okie, when y'all was a-talkin', comin' out," he said. "Same voice you always had."

I'd been away from my hometown nearly ever since my high school graduation, most of the last six years in classrooms. I'd finished college and, then, made it two-thirds of the way through law school.

On the sidewalk in front of Marshall's, I fished two nickels out of the right-front pocket of my tight Levi's and put them in Sore-eyed Cecil's palm.

"Take that girl in and buy her a hamburger, yourself, too," I said to him. The little girl's chapped face lit up.

"Much obliged, Okie," Sore-eyed Cecil said huskily. "Hope this year treats ya real good."

"Can't be worse than the last one," I said. That was true. Maybe I ought to take up cards, I thought to myself. I hadn't been too lucky in my choice of girlfriends in 1937. My old high school sweetheart, whom I'd been trying to hook up with again, had killed herself to keep me from arresting her for murder.

Sore-eyed Cecil heard the airplane before any of the rest of us did.

"Somethin' in the air," he said and looked up, northeast-ward, as if his red-lidded eyes still worked all right.

"Easter's in the air, stud, what it is," Stud Wampler said, laughing a little to soften the mild sarcasm.

Sore-eyed Cecil was insistent. "Naw, listen, it's a airplane," he said.

EASY PICKIN'S

We all caught the sound of the engine above the wind, then, and stopped and looked toward the direction the noise was coming from, Sore-eyed Cecil's little girl included. Out of a cloudless sky to the northeast, a little yellow airplane suddenly cleared the top of the three-story limestone-white courthouse building, a block and a half away. The plane, jerked and bounced some by gusts, zoomed toward us at what seemed like only about five hundred feet above the ground. At the last, it pulled up with a laboring bawl and banked south and east, evidently to go around and make another low pass at Vernon's Main Street.

The yellow craft was a small, high-winged monoplane, an enclosed and in-line two seater. I knew it for a J-2 Cub like I'd once been given a ride in, down in Mexico. That experience had further stimulated an early interest of mine in airplanes and flying, enough so that, later, when I was up at Norman for law school, I'd talked a guy I knew, a fellow law student, into giving me lessons. I'd soloed in an old Stinson, but never got a license, or put in many more hours to speak of, after that.

Sore-eyed Cecil and his small daughter, apparently more interested in eating than in the airplane, went into Marshall's as three other chicken-fried steak or hamburger addicts came out and joined Stud, Crystal, and me on the street. They'd apparently heard the plane and wanted to get a better look.

Across the street, we saw Janeaster's mother and father and a woman clerk emerge from Parnell Dry Goods, wave to Janeaster, then look skyward themselves, to find the source of the engine sound. Up and down Main, it was the same. Knots of other curious Vernonites showed themselves—just south of the Parnell store, in front of Carl's Confectionary and Monroe's

Variety store, and, on our side of the street, at the entrances to Modine's Hardware, Wheeler's Help-Yourself Laundry, and, even farther south, Skip Swyden's beer joint.

It wasn't every day, not even every week, that you saw an airplane in southwest Oklahoma in the spring of 1938—especially one flying so low.

It put me in mind of the time when I was a kid of a little over ten and my sister, Alene, was about twelve—that was about sixteen years earlier—and the two of us were much taken with a family story about how one of my mother's brothers had recently gone up in an airplane, down in Wise County, Texas, where he and his folks lived. So, anytime we heard one go over our house, back then, my sister and I would race outside and wave at it frantically, yelling in unison as loud as we could, "Hello, Uncle Leroy! Hello, Uncle Leroy!"

That childhood fascination with airplanes stayed with me, and I felt some of it, still, as the yellow airplane came around to buzz Vernon's Main Street again. This time, the pilot had folded down the top of the right-hand split-type door, and we could see his face quite plainly as he turned the plane a little on its side and leaned out. He waved to us and then pointed emphatically toward the southwest before climbing back up and banking again, apparently to make a third pass.

"Looks like that air stud wants somebody to come get him, out at the Moreland Dairy strip," Stud Wampler said.

"My dad picked up Wiley Post, once, after he buzzed Vernon the same way," Janeaster Parnell said. That was common aviator practice. "The Lawton field was closed—by fog or something, I think."

Wiley Post, the famous Oklahoma pilot with a patch over

one bad eye, had set an around-the-world flying record before he and Will Rogers were eventually killed in a crash at Point Barrow, Alaska.

"Y'all know what Will Rogers's last words were, don't you?" Stud asked.

Crystal bit. "What?"

"'Wiley Post, you one-eyed son of a bitch!'"

Janeaster ignored the joke. Maybe she thought, like me, that it wasn't very funny; Wiley Post had kinfolks in Vernon. Main thing, though, Janeaster was excited. "Let's go out to Moreland's and pick up the pilot, Okie," she said. "You want to? I'm off the first period after lunch. My kids are working on the Easter Parade."

"Nothing better to do," I said. "Crime's at low ebb at the moment." I was curious to see who the pilot was and why he'd come to Vernon.

Eileen, for her part, demurred. Had to get back to school. Crystal said she was going down the street for the twenty-dollar drawing that Vernon merchants put on every Thursday to get people to town to shop.

Stud wasn't interested in going with us. "Depart hence, my friends, without the trusty deputy." He was back in the nasal voice of W. C. Fields. "Myself, I have as much use for a flying machine as the proverbial hog does for a sidesaddle," he said.

"Don't want to go, Stud?" I said.

"My boy, I must hie myself to the courthouse and continue the fight against crime and/or evil," Stud said. He didn't have the bulbous nose of W. C. Fields, but he sounded just like him.

He turned aside, then, and stumped north on main in his cowboy boots. Eileen and Crystal both headed south.

"My sheriff car's at the courthouse," I said to Janeaster.

"We can take Mama and Daddy's," she said.

The two of us crossed the street. We said a quick hello to her folks, who were still standing out in front of their store. Mrs. Parnell was a plump natural-blonde woman in her early forties, smartly dressed in an expensive gray-worsted suit, but she seemed a little flashy to me. For one thing, I noticed that she was wearing a silver ankle bracelet. By contrast, the small and slope-shouldered, pink-faced and sandy-haired Mr. Parnell could have been a funeral-home operator. He was as formal and reserved in his manner as the white shirt and red silk tie he was wearing.

Janeaster told her parents that we were going to drive their car to the airstrip. Told them, I noted, not asked them. Mr. Parnell didn't seem to me to be the type to say anything much. And he said nothing at that moment. Mrs. Parnell did all the talking for both of them. I got the impression that she worshiped Janeaster and would have approved of her climbing water towers, or riding rodeo bulls, if that was what Janeaster took a mind to do.

All Mrs. Parnell said was, "Don't get your nice suit wrinkled, hon."

Janeaster and I hurried to the maroon Buick Roadmaster sedan at the curb.

FOUR

I folded into the passenger side of the heavy automobile as Janeaster, opposite, slid in under the wheel. She turned the key, already in the ignition, and pressed down on the starter pedal. The big engine roared smoothly to life. Janeaster put the gearshift in reverse, then backed the Buick away from the curb and headed north. At the next intersection, the southwest corner of the courthouse block, she wheeled the big car around in a U-turn, making the balloon white sidewalls screech, just as the yellow airplane came at us, then over us, to buzz Vernon a last time.

Janeaster headed the Buick back south on Main. We watched through the windshield as the little plane pulled up, then banked to the right in the direction of the grass strip at Moreland's Dairy, located at the southwest edge of town.

A block south of the Cash County National Bank, on the northwest corner of Main and Ice House Streets, Janeaster and I passed the two-story Kraker Building. Like the three-story

Luden Hotel, around the corner, on California, it was redbrick and had been built by old man Elmo Kraker in the same year, the big oil-boom year of 1919.

After that, the Depression that started in 1929 had hit Vernon as hard as the rest of the country—maybe harder, since it had come, locally, with a great drought, too. But by that spring of 1938, President Franklin Roosevelt's New Deal government had been in power for five years, and things were picking up a little. Still, I knew that half the offices in the Kraker Building were empty. Kraker Oil Company, itself, had moved out a year earlier, a little before I'd come back to Vernon, to concentrate its work, again, in its headquarters in Oklahoma City. A fourth of Vernon's storefront buildings stood empty because of the Depression. We'd made some headway against hard times, but we still had a long way to go.

Janeaster turned west at the Farmers' Gin, causing the balloon white sidewalls to squeal again. We began to bump across the railroad tracks. Up them, half a block to our right, was the tan-stuccoed and red-roofed Rock Island depot building. A southbound train waited there for passengers to board. White clouds of steam hissed intermittently from the lower sides of the big black engine, pointed toward us. The bell on top of it clanged back and forth.

"Old 'Try Weekly' is about ready to go," I said, plagiarizing Stud Wampler.

He called the Rock Island train the Try Weekly because he said it came one week and tried to get back the next. That was a joke. Actually, two passenger trains came through Vernon every day—and you could set your watch by them, as people said. A northbound train left the station at 6:23 every morning, headed toward Oklahoma City. A southbound train, the one Janeaster and I saw as we crossed the tracks, left Vernon at 1:05 every afternoon, headed toward Dallas.

Janeaster drove on west through Snuff Ridge for a couple of blocks, before heading south again on the gravel highway to Wardell. After about a quarter of a mile, we turned off, west again, toward Moreland's. The small yellow airplane had circled the strip by that time and was making its final approach, pointed in the same direction we were. I watched as the pilot slipped the plane sharply against a north crosswind, which had the grass strip's cloth windsock standing straight out from the pole, and dropped down rapidly.

Janeaster pulled the Buick up to the pasture gate behind the dairy barn. Ahead of us, the yellow craft flared out as it neared the ground and, straightening its nose at the last minute, touched down in a good three-point landing on the short-cropped, spring-green grass.

Janeaster and I got out of the car and walked up to the wire gate as the airplane rolled out, toward the west end of the strip.

"Sheriff—Okie—I really appreciate your agreeing to emcee the Easter Parade Saturday night," Janeaster said. We were standing very close. There was a fresh, lilac-soap scent about her.

"Beats sitting at home, listening to Amos and Andy on the radio," I said.

"You weren't planning on coming, before?"

"I probably would've. *Sure* would've if I'd known you were in it."

Janeaster turned, then, and moved around slightly, so that she was facing me, her dark eyes focused on mine. "My folks want me to complete college, somewhere, but I've had this lifelong ambition. Okie, you think I could model clothes professionally?"

"I think you could model refrigerators," I said.

"What?"

"Janeaster, I think you can do anything you put your mind to.

"Another thing," she said, then hesitated.

"Yes?" It was a question on my part, but I would probably have been willing to make it an answer, too, whatever she was about to ask.

"I was wondering if the two of us might go together to the sunrise Easter Pageant, out at Kraker Park, after the Easter Parade's over," Janeaster said. "I'd like it if you'd take me."

That certainly seemed to me to be a little bold on her part. Janeaster and I hadn't known each other well—or long. I knew I should have turned her invitation aside. But I hated to embarrass her after she'd put herself out to ask me. "Sounds okay to me, if it wouldn't bother you being seen with an old guy," I said.

"You're not *that* old," Janeaster said, flashing a Colgate smile up at me and pushing a fallen black curl off her forehead with her right hand. "I hope you don't feel I'm too forward, asking you, and all."

I said, "Forward march!"

The little yellow plane had taxied back. The squall of its engine cut off further conversation between Janeaster and me. The pilot pulled up to the near end of a metal, one-plane hangar, close to the gate. There was a cabin-model, white Waco biplane with red trim behind the hangar, tied down against the wind to three wafer-like rocks. I recognized the Waco as Jeff Moreland's. I'd been up in it with Jeff, a guy about my age whose dad had started the dairy that Jeff ran.

The pilot gunned the engine of the yellow plane and turned the craft to face south, swirling dirt and grass bits every which way in the prop wash. A black-stenciled sign on the fuselage said: "Rides $1. Flying lessons $4 an hour."

Janeaster and I waited outside the gate as the pilot killed the engine, opened the fold-down, hinged-in-the-middle door, then stepped heavily to the ground. He reached into the backseat and brought out a scuffed leather suitcase, then lumbered over to meet us. I opened the gate for him, and he walked through.

"Tobe Satville," he said in a gravelly voice, extending his right hand. "Much obliged for coming out to get me."

He was big and doughy, middle-aged, a kind of Wallace Beery–looking guy, but weaker and softer, and his eyes were shiftier, too, behind thick, wire-rimmed glasses. He was wearing a brown wool cap and a scruffy hip-length leather jacket, belted around a fleshy waist. His run-over brown work boots looked like they'd been through some hard living, and so did his splotched and bloated face.

"Okie Dunn—sheriff, here," I said, shaking his mushy hand. "This is my friend Janeaster Parnell."

"Glad to meet you," Satville said to me. His lens-magnified eyes looked Janeaster up and down. "How friendly is she?" he said. He took her hand and held it a little too long.

"We'll give you a lift into town," I said. I touched his elbow so that he'd let loose of Janeaster's hand, and to move him toward the car.

We started in that direction. Janeaster wiped her right palm on the hip of her skirt—out of Satville's view, but not mine.

At the Buick, the man threw his suitcase into the backseat before climbing in after it. Janeaster and I slid into the front seat from opposite sides. She started the engine and backed the car around, then headed toward town.

"That's a Taylor J-2 Cub you're flying," I said, turning my head a little toward Satville, in the back.

"Yeah, bought 'er used—old November Charlie triple-three niner." Satville recited, aviator-like, the yellow plane's call letters, which I'd seen stenciled in large figures on its wing. "They call 'em Piper Cubs, now. Made up in Pennsylvania. I doped some cotton patchin' on mine for repairs, and it's good as new. You fly?"

"Not solo, lately," I said. "I got a ride in an airplane just like yours, once, down in Mexico."

"Doing what in Mexico?"

You writing a book, nosy? That's what I wanted to say, as we did when we were kids. There was something about this guy that I didn't like.

What I *did* say was, "Found out after I got out of high school that I could make more money by prizefighting than roughnecking in the oil fields. And more by fighting south of the border than up here. What brings you to Vernon?"

"What weight did you fight?" Satville asked.

"Welterweight."

"Looks like you could make that hundred and forty-seven pounds, right now," he said. I knew it was an attempt to ingratiate. But Satville was right. I still could have made the weight. I'd stayed in shape, running.

"Who owns that white-and-red Waco biplane?" the man asked.

"Jeff Moreland—runs the dairy here," I said.

"Got money?" Satville asked.

"Some oil on his old man's place," I said. "And sells milk."

Satville changed the subject. "Any idea where a guy might find a car to rent around here?" he asked.

"Rent a car?" Janeaster asked. Satville's was not a question we'd had to deal with very much in Vernon.

"Yeah, sweetie, four wheels and a motor," he said. "Used one'd do."

"Might try Bart Suder, catty-cornered across the street west from the courthouse," I said. "Sells new and used cars."

"New and used horses and mules, too," Janeaster said. That was correct, though irrelevant.

"I'm huntin' somebody," Satville said, finally getting around to my earlier question. "It's a gal."

"She disappeared?" Janeaster asked.

"Not exactly," Satville said. "Kind of complicated. Lucky you picked me up, Sheriff. Courthouse's right where I need to go to. And maybe you could help me find this gal. I could make it worth your while."

FIVE

Why you lookin' for her, stud?" Stud Wampler's tone was unfriendly. He made quick judgments about people, I knew. You could tell he didn't have any more use for Tobe Satville than I did, though he'd met him only minutes before.

We were in the large, high-ceilinged one-room sheriff's office—my office, since the preceding November—located on the third floor of the Cash County courthouse. A big framed picture of President Franklin Roosevelt hung on the west wall of the room. A black-and-white print of Old Ironsides and a large Scott Blacksmith calendar, featuring a color view of the snow-capped Rockies, decorated the wall opposite.

Janeaster had dropped us off in the parking lot on the north side of the courthouse, then hurried on to her teaching duties at the high school.

Satville had huffed and puffed his way up the three flights of stairs behind me, let his suitcase drop to the tiled floor of the office, and then sagged into the prison-made oak chair I'd motioned him to, next to one of the three matching desks that were there. I'd introduced Satville to Stud. Crystal was out of the office to investigate a couple of overnight break-ins, Stud reported.

Stud sat up straight at his own oak desk. I was in a wooden chair to Stud's left, facing the out-of-towner. Satville had explained again that he wanted our help.

"Her mother wants me to," Satville said. He took a thin, black-and-red Prince Albert can out of the right-hand pocket of his jacket and shook out a cigarette. From the look of things, with tobacco sticking out unevenly from each end of the cigarette's paper, I figured that Satville rolled his own smokes—probably on one of those little table gadgets you could buy—and carried them around in a Prince Albert can. Putting the can back in his pocket, he lit the homemade smoke with a kitchen match that he dug out from the left-front pocket of his rumpled khaki slacks. After a drag, he exhaled, then spit out a couple of tobacco bits that'd come loose in his mouth.

"What's the girl's name, stud?" Stud asked.

"Don't nobody know that," Satville said. Smoke curled up from the cigarette that dangled from his fat lips, and, behind the thick glasses, he squinted his eyes against it.

"Her mother don't?" Stud asked.

"No."

I stood up, impatient. "What's she look like, then?"

"Don't nobody know that, neither," Satville said. He seemed uncomfortable. "Know how old she is. Born right here in Vernon, nineteen years ago, Easter day 1919."

I cut him off. "This is like a picture show that's commenced in the middle," I said. "Start at the beginning. What do you do for a living? How come finding this girl's so important?"

Satville began again. He lived in Oklahoma City, he said, and worked at different things there, mostly as a bounty hunter for a bail bondsman. "Finding people that don't want to get found" is the way he put it. On the side, he said, he gave airplane rides and flying lessons for hire—when he could snag a customer.

Satville said that he was a close friend of an Oklahoma City beauty parlor operator named Lily Morgan. Pregnant and unmarried, she'd come down to Vernon almost nineteen years earlier, when she was, herself, seventeen. She'd wanted to have her baby where nobody would know about it. She'd never held the child after it was born. She'd seen it for only an instant, but knew it was a girl. The baby was taken away at once and must have been given up for adoption locally, Satville said.

"Now," he finished up, "Miz Morgan's desperate to find her daughter and make amends."

He reached into his right-front pants pocket and pulled out a roll of bills. Not a big enough roll to set a wet mule afire, as Stud Wampler was later to say, but still impressive. Satville counted out two tens and a five, folded them over, and tried to hand them to me. He peered through his wire-rimmed glasses to look me in the eye for the first time.

"Here's twenty-five y'all can split between you," Satville said. "A kinda down payment. Be twice that much at the end, you help me find this little gal after I check some courthouse records for leads."

"The county pays us," I said, not moving from where I stood or putting out my hand to take the money.

"Suit yourself." Satville put the bills back in his pocket. "Point me toward the court clerk's office and the county clerk's office."

"Both on second, down one floor," I said.

"I'll be back," Satville said.

"It'll be a thrill," I said.

Satville pick up his scuffed leather bag and left.

"Best thing about fightin' crime," I said after Satville was gone, "you get to mix with such a fine class of people!"

"Ask me, that bird's not just trying to help a poor mother find her long-lost child," Stud said. "Crooked as a dog's hind leg. They's money in this, some way."

"Bounty hunter, by his own words," I said. "On the old *dinero* trail again, my guess."

As things turned out, Stud was soon to say that I'd been wrong; that, really, the best thing about fighting crime was not that you got to mix with such a fine class of people, but that somebody was always coming around trying to give you money.

It was the very next morning that Stud and I were to be offered cash a second time. And for the same "Case of the Unknown Girl."

SIX

On Good Friday, I got up at my usual time of five-thirty in the morning. It was not yet light when I pulled on a pair of faded-blue Hercules overalls and a gray work shirt. In the kitchen, I lifted off the glass chimney of the coal-oil lamp that sat on the little table, there, and lit the wick with a kitchen match.

The house had a quiet and lonesome feel to it. I'd kept on living at the rented Billings place, alone, after my dad died. On the east edge of Vernon, just outside the city limits, it was a small, two-bedroom house, set on forty acres, and had almost none of the modern conveniences that a majority of the homes inside the city limits had—no indoor toilet, electricity, gas, or water. I *had* put in a telephone, after becoming sheriff. That was the only thing up-to-date about the Billings place, and even it was behind the times, being a party-line phone where several subscribers could listen in on each other's calls.

The morning was cool when I stepped outside. My dad's old

mixed-breed, muckledy-dun dog, Scooter, came running from the barn, ready to go with me. Stumbling a little in the dark as the dog ran excitedly alongside me, I trotted to the section-line road in front of the house and then broke into a steady jog for my usual two-mile morning run. It was something I'd been doing ever since my boxing days. My dad had always thought I was crazy to keep it up. Work enough, you wouldn't need any other exercise, he'd always said.

The hard leather soles of my work shoes pounded a steady cadence on the packed-dirt roadbed. I headed east to the school-route road, then south. I would turn around at the barbed-wire gate that led, east, to old man Nahnahpwa's house, built on a 160-acre allotment when the Comanche Indian reservation was broken up. The house was down close to the leafy-green pecan, oak, elm, and hackberry woods of East Cash Creek. The old man and his wife, Lucy, were the parents of Marvin, another boxer, who I'd trained with in high school. I'd spent a good deal of time, back then, at their house. Along my route, the dog, Scooter, scared up a field lark, now and then, along the fence rows and, once, flushed a covey of bobwhite quail into the crisp morning air.

We started back from Nahnahpwa's gate. By the time I was home, the sun was half up, and it was getting to be daylight. I went in and got some meat scraps and a bone that the butcher had saved for me and threw them out to Scooter. The dog occupied, I turned to my morning ritual. As a boy, I'd once accidentally stumbled on to old man Nahnahpwa's devotional exercise, early one morning, and he'd tolerated my staying. I'd soon adopted something like his ritual for myself, back then, and, since my dad had passed away, I'd revived the practice.

EASY PICKIN'S

I faced the sun, just risen over the East Cash tree line, a quarter of a mile away, and opened my arms to receive the first rays. "You've been good to me, Lord," I said. "Help those in need. Thank you." I smiled broadly. Look happy, and you'll feel happy. I'd learned that somewhere, and had found it to be true. Then, as usual, I recited a psalm in Spanish. Somehow, it seemed more magical to me, that way. *"Alzaré mis ojos a los montes, de donde vendrá mi auxilio. Mi auxilio viene del Señor."* I will lift up my eyes unto the hills, from whence cometh my help. My help cometh from the Lord.

Off a ways, in a mesquite tree, a dove called, once, and, then, again—the lonesomest sound in the world.

There were morning chores to do. I mixed ground feed and water in the trough for the hog and threw several double handfuls of grain in the dirt for the laying hens. I put out cottonseed meal and hulls for the white-faced steer, hayed and watered the two riding horses, mine and my dad's, and milked the old Jersey cow. I gathered the eggs and then carried in a can of coal oil for the lamps and the cookstove and a fresh bucket of water that I'd pumped for the kitchen.

By the fence on the east side of the house, I picked up my hoe and went to work in the garden. I hadn't planted anywhere near as much ground as my dad always had, but I couldn't *not* have a garden of some size. Every spring, all my life, I'd had one, even a little one, outside my garage apartment, when I was in law school at Norman.

That morning, I manicured the dirt in the English-pea rows and around the potato hills. There'd soon be new peas and new potatoes in the pot. I liked the smooth feel of the hoe handle and the swishy sound of the well-filed blade as it sliced away at new weed sprouts and grass shoots. My dozen tomato plants were dotted with yellow blooms. I picked several bugs off the squash plants and crushed them under my boot. The cucumber plants were uninfested and had made good vines. Grandma Dunn would come out in late summer to help me can my vegetable surplus and put up some dill pickles. A few of the green onions I'd bordered the plot with, to help keep out insects, were trying to make flowers. I went along, breaking the stalks over so that the energy would go to roots, not seeds.

Finished, I went back in the house and lit two smelly front burners of the coal-oil cookstove, setting a kettle of water to boil on the yellow-and-red flame of one of them. I put an iron skillet on the other and fried myself two thick strips of home-cured bacon and a couple of eggs, sunny-side up. I sliced a slab of the light bread that Grandma Dunn had baked for me and got out some of her hand-churned butter and homemade currant jelly from the icebox.

I switched on the battery-powered Philco radio to the early morning farm program on WKY, out of Oklahoma City. Sitting down at the little kitchen table, I ate my breakfast and listened to Wiley and Gene crack corny jokes, sell Superior Feeds, and sing country songs. Afterward, I quickly cleared the table, then poured hot water from the steaming kettle into a wash pan and shaved. The cattle-market report came on the radio, and I paused between swipes of the straight razor to catch the details. The county let Stud Wampler and me continue to trade cattle on the side, like my dad had done.

I peeled off my shirt by the kitchen sink and sponged off with a wet washrag—gave myself what my mother would have called "a lick and a promise." After coming home from work the night before, I'd jogged east, crossed through old man Nahnahpwa's barbed-wire fence, then gone on down and bathed in East Cash Creek—a bit cool, but an invigorating experience. That was my favorite way of taking a bath, which I usually did two or three times a week. Much better than trying to sit down in a number-ten washtub filled with water heated on the stove.

I brought my clothes to the kitchen—a clean pair of pressed Levi's, a starched gray work shirt, and black cowboy boots—and dressed as I listened to the WKY news headlines: "The president's wife, Eleanor Roosevelt, yesterday visited a coal mine in West Virginia. General Motors has finally recognized the United Auto Workers union after a yearlong sit-down strike. The union is asking for the same five-dollar-a-day wage that steelworkers recently won. Nothing yet from the new Pacific search for Amelia Earhart and her downed plane. And, on the home front, eighty thousand needy Oklahoma children will get free, hot school lunches provided by the state board of welfare at a monthly cost of eighty cents a child."

When I got to the sheriff's office that Good Friday morning, Stud said Crystal had sent word that she'd be late coming in because she'd had to take her little girl to Doc Watson. Stud'd already brought the breakfast tray from the Truckers Café, which had the county contract. He'd fed the only prisoner we had, half a floor up in the attic jail, a Devol kid who was charged with stealing a saddle and bridle. The boy was going to spend Easter behind bars because his folks couldn't make the bail.

Stud and I poured ourselves a couple of cups of coffee, brewed on the hot plate in the corner of the office, and sat down at our desks. That's when Em Hoffer showed up.

"Looking for the law," she said as she came through the open door. Her voice was husky and assured. A little irreverence in it, too. Stud and I both stood up.

"You're looking at all the law there is, west of East Cash Creek," I said. I put out my hand to her. "Okie Dunn, county sheriff."

The grip of her long-fingered hand was strong. She appeared to be a year or two older than me. There was no wedding band on her finger, I noted. Not that I made a point of looking.

The woman said her name and sized me up. "Em Hoffer. You the high sheriff, are you?"

"High and mighty," I said.

It was a surprise to me that Hoffer was a woman. She'd earlier written our office a letter on lawyer's stationery—"Em Hoffer, Attorney"—saying that the writer intended to drive down to Vernon from Oklahoma City and would like the help of the sheriff's office on a matter of importance. But I'd had no idea that she would turn out to be a woman. I'd never met a woman lawyer before.

I'd never met a woman as *tall* as Em Hoffer, either—tall enough, I thought, if she'd been the right sex, to win herself a basketball scholarship up at Oklahoma A&M. She was well-built, too, and well-proportioned, so that, if you hadn't seen her next to something you could measure against, you wouldn't have guessed that she came to pretty near six feet. She was red-headed—and it didn't look like the kind of red that came out of a bottle.

Her eyes were the same color green as the tailored wool slack suit she wore. And the slack suit was a remarkable thing in itself. Mostly, it was the men who wore the pants in Oklahoma, as they said.

I nodded toward Stud. "This is my chief deputy, Stud Wampler," I said.

"They call you Stud, do they?" Em Hoffer said. There was a kind of Mae West air about the way she eyed Stud, but she was better-looking than Mae West and more refined, too, I thought.

"A nickname, nothing descriptive," Stud said. The two of them shook hands.

"Take a seat," I said and motioned her toward the one in front of my desk. She laid the tan-wool army-style raincoat she was carrying across the back of the chair and then seated herself. I eased into my own chair. Stud sidled around and stood on my right.

The redhead opened her saddle-bag-size brown leather satchel purse and took out two business cards from a little suede folder. She handed one to Stud and one to me.

"I got your letter." I looked down at her card and then back up at Hoffer. "But—"

"You figured I was a man," she said, cutting me off before I could say that. "I use Em on purpose. It's Emma, but I let people think it's Emmett or some other man's name. Better response that way."

She did another man thing, then. She took a combination silver cigarette case and lighter from her purse, selected a cigarette, and, without waiting for any help we might have proffered and without the slightest hint of embarrassment about smoking in public, lit up. She took a long drag as she put the case away and then let the smoke drift slowly out through rich red lips and white teeth.

"My dad's where I got both my size and my ways from," she said, as if answering a question that she knew was on our minds. "He sent me to law school in Kansas City because he didn't have a son to send. I was the only child. Dad was a captain in the Army Air Corps during the war. Raised me like one of his soldier boys. I even wear his raincoat." She motioned toward it with her head.

"Nobody would take you for a boy now," I said. "Go to Pace Law School, then, in Kansas City?"

"Yeah," she said. "How you know about law schools?"

"Went to one myself—University of Oklahoma," I said.

"You a lawyer, then, are you?" she asked.

"Not quite," I said. "Slapped a professor, my final year—a nutty thing to do—when he put his hands on me during an argument we were having, after he'd made a bad remark in class about President Roosevelt. Law dean frowned on that kind of student behavior. Suspended me for two years." It was probably more information than the woman wanted.

"Slapped?" she asked.

"Okie'd coldcocked him, the man'd still be gittin' up," Stud said.

"You going back—to law school?" Hoffer asked me.

"Like to," I said. "I could read law and pass the bar, I guess, but I'm appealing to OU's president to get the suspension cut to one year. I'd rather finish law school."

Stud spoke up. "So, Miz Hoffer," he said, "you're a lawyer, then. What brings you to Vernon? Want us to help you sue some widows and orphans?"

She laughed, and I laughed with her.

"I'm the lawyer for a woman in Oklahoma City, Lily Morgan," Hoffer said.

"The beauty parlor operator," I said.

Hoffer was surprised. "You know her?"

"Not hardly," Stud said. "But you're the second person in two days to mention her name to us. Don't tell me you're lookin' for her long-lost kid."

"Who else is?" she asked. We had her attention.

"Lumpy sack of potatoes named Satville," I said. "In here yesterday."

"Money-grubbing bastard!" Hoffer stood up as she said this. Pretty rough talk for a woman.

"Great friend of yours, huh?" I said.

"Like shit!"

"Said he works for a bail bondsman and gives airplane rides and flying lessons, some," I said.

"*I* sure wouldn't want to ride with him," Hoffer said. "Bounty hunter—that's what he is."

"Said he was a friend of your Lily Morgan," Stud said.

"He went with her a little, that's all," Hoffer said. "Found out about her lost daughter. But Lily Morgan never asked for his help, I promise you that! He's a freelancer." She leaned over and angrily ground out her cigarette in the unused glass ashtray on my desk, then sat back down again. "What'd he want from y'all?"

"Same as you, I expect," I said. "Offered us twenty-five dollars to help him find Miz Morgan's daughter."

"I'll give you twice that, if that's what it takes," Hoffer said.

"Relax," I said. "We didn't take his money, and we don't need yours. Why's everybody trying to find this girl, anyway?"

"Imagine Satville told you the girl was born out of wedlock," she said.

"He did," Stud said.

"Mother-daughter thing," Hoffer said. "Woman wants to find her baby. I'm trying to help the woman do that. I don't think she's got long to live."

"What's wrong with her?" I asked.

"TB."

Just then, the upright black telephone on my desk rang, making us all jump. I grabbed the earpiece from the holder and put it to my right ear, then spoke into the mouthpiece. "Hello, sheriff's office," I said.

It was Lulu Crabbe, the county clerk, calling from one floor below.

"Okie, you better come down here," she said. "We had us a break-in last night, and I think it was that guy, Satville, you sent to see me yesterday."

"Be right there," I said.

I told Stud and Em Hoffer what Lulu had said, and I mentioned Tobe Satville's name.

"I'm going with you," Hoffer said and grabbed up her air corps raincoat and satchel purse.

I asked Stud to stay and hold down the office. He looked like he wasn't totally thrilled about my taking off with the tall, redheaded lawyer without him.

SEVEN

Em Hoffer and I found Lulu Crabbe waiting in the hall, just outside her office. She was a thin, pitchfork-handle of a woman, as free of cosmetics as a holiness preacher's wife. Severe in dress and manner, she was nevertheless a pleasant person, and she'd been getting herself elected county clerk for as long as I could remember. Lulu was an old maid, as people said, the sole support of a chronically sick mother and a father who hung out all day at the domino parlor. "She needs the job" had always been her word-of-mouth campaign slogan—and it'd always worked.

I introduced Em Hoffer.

"Now, aren't you a big one!" Lulu Crabbe said to her.

I spoke up. "Lawyer."

"*Big* lawyer," Lulu said.

She turned to show us how the door to her office had been jimmied. It was a metal door, like all the main office doors in the courthouse, painted a government green, with a frosted-glass top half. Black lettering on the glass read: LULU CRABBE—COUNTY CLERK.

"He must have used a crowbar, Okie," she said. "Look how he boogered up my door, breaking the lock loose."

"What was he after, you think?" I asked.

"This way, and I'll show y'all," Lulu said. We followed her into the office, nodding to a young female secretary who was wearing enough lipstick and rouge to more than make up for her boss's total lack of cosmetic adornment. Lulu led the way around the front counter and back into the record stacks.

"Your man Satville—" Lulu said.

"Not *my* man," I said.

Lulu went right on. "Your man Satville said you sent him down here to me."

"Told him where your office was, that's all," I said.

"Anyway, he came in, said he wanted to see the county birth records for 1919," Lulu said. "We record the information that the doctor or midwife fills out on the certificate they bring us, and, then, we mail it on to Vital Statistics in Oklahoma City."

"And these are public records?" Em Hoffer asked.

"No, ma'am, that's just the point," Lulu Crabbe said. "Only the very person, or a next of kin, can get their own record, and, of course, there's no way they're going to get to look at somebody else's record."

"So you turned Satville away," I said.

"Law's the law," Lulu said. "He left madder than a wet hen."

She pulled a record book from the shelf to our right. It was bound in red leather and was about an inch and a half thick and twice as wide and long as a Big Chief school tablet.

"This, right here, is the 1919 book, the very one Satville tried to get me to show him when he was here in the office," Lulu said. "Now, this morning, I found it laying on the floor, down here, as soon as I came in. When I picked it up and went over it, there was a page torn out. He evidently found what he was looking for."

"What page was it, Miss Crabbe?" Em Hoffer asked.

"The week beginning Sunday, April the twentieth," Lulu said. "Here, I'll show you—just you, Sheriff. Young lady, I'll have to ask you to stay back."

Em Hoffer remained where she was. Lulu carried the record book to a table at the end of the stack. I followed. She put the book on the table and switched on a brass lamp over it. When she opened the volume about a third of the way through, I could see, just as she'd said, that a page had been ripped out.

I leaned down and flipped pages back and forth to examine the ones just before and just after the missing page. I looked at the entries for the week beginning April 13 and the week beginning April 27 of 1919. Right away, something jumped out at me.

"How come so many of these new parents shown here were from someplace else—a lot of them from way off?" I asked.

"That's old Doc Askew for you," Lulu Crabbe said. "People came to Vernon from nearly everywhere, seem like, to have their babies, here, at his clinic."

"Doc Askew's been practicing a long time," I said.

"Lots of babies," Lulu said. "Lions Club gave him that award a couple of months ago, for all his good works." I thought I heard a note of irony in her voice when she said this last. "Mostly retired, now, I understand," Lulu added.

I turned my attention back to the 1919 record book. "Quite a few of these births weren't to people from Cash County," I said. "Just in these two weeks I'm looking at, there are two to couples from Lawton, one to a couple from Oklahoma City, and one to a couple from Wichita Falls."

"Don't know anything about that." Lulu seemed uneasy and looked away as she spoke.

"Is there an index for births, by year?" I asked her.

"Front of the book, under the mother's last name."

I turned there and then leafed to the letter "M." Nothing whatsoever under Morgan for 1919.

"Sure hope you find that Satville and lock him up for busting in my door and tearing up my record book," Lulu Crabbe said as she and I rejoined Em Hoffer and walked back through the stacks to the front counter.

"You pretty sure it was him, then?" I asked.

"Had to be," Lulu said. She left us at the front door.

I figured she was right. And it turned out that Lulu's wasn't the only office that Satville, apparently, had broken into.

EIGHT

Out in the hall, Em Hoffer told me that she'd heard what Lulu Crabbe had said to me.

"And Dr. Askew—Milford Askew—that's the right name," Hoffer said. "Lily Morgan came to his clinic, here in Vernon, to have her baby. No doubt about that. No doubt, either, that it was April of 1919."

"Why isn't Lily Morgan's name in the birth index, then?" I asked.

"I don't know that," Hoffer said. "But I do know this. That bastard Satville found out something or he wouldn't have ripped the page out of the county clerk's record book. Must have found the right birth under a different name."

"How would he know?"

"Easter," Em Hoffer said. She took out and lit a cigarette. "I doubt there was more than one child born in Vernon on that day."

"Satville told me and Stud that the girl was born on Easter

Sunday," I said. "But would he have known which Sunday in April that Easter fell on in 1919?"

"April the twentieth," she said.

"How do you know that?"

"Looked it up," Em Hoffer said. "Satville would've, too."

"Let's go to the court clerk's office, now we're down here," I said. "We might as well check out the adoption records while we're at it."

Em Hoffer and I were pretty close to each other as we walked down the hallway, west. She was wearing Evening in Paris, a sweet and heavy perfume that reminded me of gardenias. I knew the scent well, and it always had a strong effect on me.

Within a few yards of the court clerk's door, we could see that it had suffered greater damage than the county clerk's. The door had been so twisted by a break-in jimmy that it couldn't even be closed completely.

Mollie Traynor, a wholesome-looking, young, and chubby brunette in a middy blouse and pleated navy skirt, was standing inside at the front counter. She was the court clerk. This was her first term. Her daddy was a county commissioner and a friend of mine. He'd talked me into taking the sheriff's job.

"Okie, I just called you, and Mr. Wampler said you were already down here," Mollie Traynor said. "We were broken into, last night. Lulu was, too, I heard."

"Probably by the same guy," I said.

"Big guy, didn't look right out of his eyes, shifty?" the young court clerk said.

"Tobe Satville," I said.

"That's the name he gave me, all right."

"Wanted to see the 1919 adoption records?" Em Hoffer asked.

Mollie Traynor looked Hoffer up and down. "And you, ma'am—you a part of the investigation, some way?" she asked.

I intervened quickly to make the introduction. "Em Hoffer," I said to Mollie. "She's a lawyer from Oklahoma City."

"A lawyer?" the court clerk asked, glancing quickly at me. Then she went on. "You're exactly right, Mrs. Hoffer. He wanted to see the 1919 adoption records. Ugly about it, when I told him that they're sealed, here, the same as the central records are at Vital Statistics in Oklahoma City. Tried to offer me money. I turned him down flat and escorted him to the door. He took off in a huff, down the hall toward Lulu's."

"What's missing?" I asked.

"Funny, but it seems like nothing's missing, thank goodness," Mollie Traynor said. "He got out the adoption book for 1919, looks like, and left it on a table over yonder. But nothing's gone, far as I can tell."

"No pages missing?" I asked.

"Nope," she said.

"I know you can't show us the book, Mollie," I said, "but is there any way you could check a name for us? Is there an index?"

"By year and by the last names of both the natural and the adoptive parents," she said.

"This may be a little out of line," I said, "but could you see your way clear to check 1919 for me—and see if the name Morgan shows up as the natural mother of a child put up for adoption that year, particularly in the month of April?"

"It *is* irregular, Okie, but I can do that much, I think, for an officer of the law. Wait here, please, y'all." She turned and walked back into the rows of metal record shelves.

Em Hoffer had time to smoke another cigarette while we waited. She asked me if I wanted one. When I said I didn't smoke, she asked if her smoking bothered me. It did, but I said it didn't. Tobacco smoke had been one of the worst things about my prizefighting days. Arenas were always fogged with it. You could see it like a pyramid cloud under the central ring lights. And, especially in the later rounds, if a fight lasted, you could feel it burning your lungs, too. My dad had died from smoking—lung cancer. I'd never taken up the habit. It hurt your wind.

"Nothing," Mollie Traynor said when she came back. She glanced over with a reproachful expression as Em Hoffer put out her cigarette in a metal, government-issue ashtray. "No Morgan, or anything like that, as a natural mother of a child put up for adoption—not in April and not in any other month of 1919."

Hoffer ignored Mollie Traynor's look of disapproval. "No wonder Tobe Satville didn't tear out a page; nothing he wanted," Hoffer said.

I thanked the young court clerk, and Hoffer and I left. Halfway down the hall, Hoffer stopped at the broad stairwell. She wasn't going back up to the sheriff's office. I was. We shook hands. She said she'd be back in touch.

"I think I'll nose around town awhile," Hoffer said. "Back in 1919, when Lily Morgan got pregnant, she was working in Oklahoma City as a receptionist for Kraker Oil Company."

I was a little taken aback by Hoffer's use of the word "pregnant." Women didn't normally use that term when talking to men.

But if I showed any shock, Hoffer ignored it. She went right on, "Kraker Oil had an office, here in Vernon, then. I saw the building on Main Street when I drove in, yesterday afternoon."

"Closed, now, the Vernon office," I said. "I think old man Elmo Kraker built the office building as an investment, mostly. That was 1919, the big oil year in Cash County. Kraker got filthy rich. Gave the town Kraker Park the same year. But after the old man died a few years back, Elmo Junior, the son and heir to the whole fortune, moved everything back to the main office in Oklahoma City."

"I know all that," Hoffer said.

I went on, anyway. "They say Elmo Junior looks like the old man—they're Lebanese or Syrian, or something—but the boy's a lot meaner," I said. "Canned a bunch of people and closed the Vernon office because the oil workers' union tried to organize his refinery, I heard. He had some union men beat up. There was even supposed to have been a killing, but nothing ever came of it. They said the Kraker Oil guy that probably did it went off to Mexico. How sure are you, Miz Hoffer, that—"

"Em," she said.

"How sure are you, Em, that Miz Morgan had a baby, here in Vernon, on Easter day of 1919?"

"Sure as old Hoover got us into this Depression," she said.

"Why's there no record of any adoption?" I asked.

"Something funny about that," she said. "But I'd be willing to bet that Tobe Satville's found out the girl's name—and he's looking for her, right now. We find him, we find her."

"We'll find him," I said. "Not many places a guy can go, here in Cash County."

"I noticed that, myself, soon's I drove into Vernon, yesterday," Hoffer said.

"Stud Wampler and I'll be on Satville's trail like Stanley after Livingston," I said.

Em Hoffer smiled.

I changed the subject. "Bored, last night?"

"Nothing to do," she said. "I sat in my room, down at the Busy Bee Tourist Cabins, next to the Truckers Café. There's not even a radio in my cabin, couldn't even listen to *Fibber McGee and Molly.* Got any suggestions for tonight?"

"Picture show, maybe," I said.

"What's showing?"

"You choosy?" I asked. "It's Sonja Henie and Tyrone Power in *Thin Ice.*"

"Not sure I can stand that much excitement, Okie," Em Hoffer said. "But I'm stuck, here, in Vernon. I don't want to drive back home until I get this all cleared up, and I'm not likely to get a better offer for tonight. So, what the hell!"

She said I could come by and get her at the Busy Bee Tourist Cabins, at the foot of the hill on the north end of Main Street. She didn't have to tell me where it was. We agreed on six-thirty.

NINE

Stud Wampler was on the phone when I got back upstairs to the sheriff's office. Crystal had come in and was at her desk. As I walked in, Stud put his hand over the telephone mouthpiece and spoke to me in a low voice: "Old lady Askew, Doc Askew's wife."

I said hello to Crystal and went over to pour myself a cup of coffee.

"How's your daughter?" I asked.

"Loretta's still got this high fever. Doc Watson don't think it's typhoid. Said to watch her and bring her back tomorrow. Mama's lookin' after her."

"Take off all the time you need," I said. "I wouldn't mess around too long. And I don't have much confidence in Doc Watson. Maybe you ought to think about taking her up to Crippled Children's Hospital in Oklahoma City."

"Thanks, Okie," Crystal said. "Around the office, here,

Good Friday's pretty dull, so far. No stabbings reported, no dog-fights—nothing today, since last night's two break-ins, downstairs. Stud told me about Lulu's, and I talked to Mollie Traynor on the telephone about hers."

I filled her in a little more on the courthouse crimes. "Had to be that Oklahoma City guy, Tobe Satville, looking for records on the girl he's trying to find," I added.

"Got the word on him from Stud, too," Crystal said.

Stud said good-bye and hung up the telephone earpiece. "Mother of pearl!" he said, leaning back in his desk chair and affecting his nasal W. C. Fields voice. "A breaking-and-entering attempt was perpetrated last evening, in the waning hours of the morning, at the offices of the good Dr. Milford Askew, his aging spouse has just informed me, per the electric telephone."

I walked over to Stud's desk with my coffee. "What'd the burglars take?"

"Burglar, singular," Stud said, still in his W. C. Fields role. "Surprised in the act by the good Missus Askew herself—the which, I'm confident, appeared more than a little menacing in her night mud pack and hair curlers—the intruder fled thence, taking nothing for the nonce, or so it is reported to your servant."

"Connection between the three break-ins, you think, Stud?" I asked. I walked back to my desk.

Stud answered in his Cash County voice. "Can't hardly see how *not*," he said. "Things have a way of hookin' together, been my experience."

"Satville's looking for the records on Lily Morgan's lost daughter, and Doc Askew is the one who's supposed to have delivered her," I said. "The connection's got to be trying to find out her present identity—who she is and *where* she is."

Stud changed the subject with a question to me. "You gonna give us a report on the powerful redhead, Okie?"

"Redhead?" Crystal asked.

"Big redheaded Oklahoma City lawyer of the female persuasion came acalling before you got here this morning, Crystal," Stud said. He got up and walked over to her desk. I sat down at mine. Stud took Hoffer's business card from his shirt pocket, and handed it to Crystal. "Em Hoffer's the name," he said.

Crystal looked at the card, then looked back up at Stud. He returned to his desk and perched on its front edge. "A woman lawyer?" she asked.

"Licensed," Stud said. "A mite taller than Kate Smith, but definitely thinner and on the less homely side. Woman proceeded to offer Okie and yours truly, the gentle lawman, twice what old Satville offered—and that was pretty good—for us to solve the Case of the Unknown Girl."

"Y'all take the money?" Crystal asked, looking toward the hulking Stud Wampler, first, then shifting her glance to me. "I wouldn't put it past the two of you. Both probably suckers for a pretty face."

"Naw, Okie told her we'd find the girl for nothin'," Stud said.

"You're a black-headed Easter bunny, Okie," Crystal said to me.

"Main thing, right now, you two," I said, "are these courthouse break-ins. How're we going to track down this Satville guy?"

"Maybe that woman lawyer, Miz Hoffer, maybe she'll find him for you, you blink them dark eyes at her," Stud said.

"Crime fighters need all the help they can get," I said. "Why don't we see if Tobe Satville rented a car from Bart Suder and start looking for it, if he did?"

That seemed like something we ought to do. None of the three of us in the sheriff's office had been in law enforcement long. We had no established investigative routine.

"Me and Crystal'll split up and ask around the tourist cabins and some stores, here—and maybe down in Wardell," Stud said.

"We could check the filling stations, too, see if anybody's seen him," Crystal said. "We got to stop him before he does something else bad. Like they say, 'A stitch in time saves a dime.'"

"Tonight, though, I cain't do nothing," Stud said. "I told old lady Askew I'd come and stake out the doc's office, if it'd make them two feel better, case the burglar comes back. That's what she wanted."

"Call her back, Stud," I said. "We've got to work on everything at the same time—finding the girl, finding Satville. Ask Mrs. Askew about a baby the doc delivered on Easter Sunday, April the twentieth of 1919. Get the baby's name and the names of the natural and adoptive parents."

"Yessir, boss stud," he said and reached to jiggle the earpiece rest to get the operator.

I turned toward Crystal. "You call the *Vernon Herald*, ask them to look up their old newspaper for the week following that same Easter Sunday of 1919 and give you the names and parents of any and all babies born on that day."

She went to work. So did I. When the operator answered my signal, I said, "Central, could you ring Bart Suder's dealership for me?"

"The number's twenty-four, Okie," the woman said in a bored voice. "One moment, please, and I'll connect you."

Bart Suder himself answered. We said hello, and I asked him if he'd rented a car to a Tobe Satville. I described the man.

"Sure did, Okie," Suder said. "Said you sent him. Green '35 Chevy coupe, white sidewalls. Paid me cash, and I filled 'er up with gas, free. What's the deal, Okie? Guy not on the up-and-up?"

I told Suder I had my doubts and asked him to call me if Satville came back. He said he would. We hung up after mentioning that we'd see each other at the noon meeting of the Lions Club. Both of us were members.

I passed the rented car's description along to Crystal and Stud.

"What about Satville's airplane?" Stud said.

I made another telephone call, this one to Moreland's Dairy. I figured that all the milking and bottling were done for the morning and that Jeff Moreland would be back at the house. He was.

"Jeff, that little yellow J-2 Cub still out there?" I asked him.

"Sure's hell is, Okie," he said. "Ain't moved an inch since it first come in."

I told Moreland that we were looking for the owner, to call if he saw him. Then, I listened to the reports that Stud and Crystal were waiting to make.

"No luck with old lady Askew," Stud said. "'All our records are confidential,' she said. Doctor-patient relationship, or something like that."

"Maybe we ought to get a search warrant," I said. I turned to Crystal. "You do any better?"

"Gonna take a few days, John Perkins at the *Herald* told me," Crystal said. "All their old papers are at the public library. Haven't been put in order or indexed, yet."

"Well, in the meantime, let's get on with finding Tobe

Satville," I said to her and Stud. I reported to them that the Oklahoma City man's airplane hadn't left the grass strip.

"Satville's still someplace around here, then," Stud said. "How 'bout me checkin' out the Luden Hotel, then the south side of town and the Conoco station, find out if anybody's seen him or the green Chevy coupe?"

"I can take care of the Luden, myself, Stud," I said. "Lions Club meets there at noon. Go ahead and do the other stuff."

"I'll go down to Essaquahnadale store, too," Stud said. "Maybe on to Wardell from there, while I'm at it."

"For my part," Crystal said, "I can check out the north side and the tourist cabins. The two filling stations on the highway. After that, I can drive up to the two country stores, toward Geronimo."

"Be careful, you two," I said. "Satville could be dangerous. Don't try to do anything by yourself, Crystal."

"I won't," she said.

"Me, I've got my little thirty-eight police special," Stud said. He patted the bulge in his right pants pocket. What about you, Okie?"

"Developing leads tonight," I said. "May be skating on thin ice, more ways than one."

Crystal looked up at me, puzzled. "What?"

"Sonja Henie movie," I said. "*Thin Ice.*"

"Oh," she said. Pause. "What?"

TEN

The three-story Luden Hotel was a half block off Main Street, on the north side of California, around the corner, west, from the Kraker building. Both redbrick structures had been built with Kraker money, but the old man had sold his interest in the Luden soon after it'd opened.

The sign out front read: *NEW* LUDEN HOTEL. But the sign, itself, was the only thing new about the place. Everything else was out of date. Hotel bathrooms were down wallpapered halls. Fire escapes for the upper-floor rooms were coiled ropes by the windows. And there were no guest-room telephones.

A guy named Ketchum, who had a pencil-thin mustache and hair shellacked down with brilliantine, was the desk clerk. He doubled as the redcap, too, and he liked to tell that he'd once shown a fancy-dressed salesman up the broad stairway to his room, and the man had said, when handing him a tip, "I'd like to have a wake-up call at seven-thirty tomorrow morning."

"Told him I'd give him a call, all right," the desk clerk said, "but it'd have to be loud and from the bottom of the stairs."

Coming into the hotel for the Lions Club luncheon meeting, I stopped at the reception desk and asked Ketchum if he had a Tobe Satville registered. The man didn't have to look. No such guest, he said. I gave him Satville's description. No such person had been around, he said.

The side room next to the coffee shop was where the Vernon Lions Club met every Friday noon. It was nearly full when I got there. Most of the twenty or so members were already seated at round tables, each with a basket of colored Easter eggs as a centerpiece.

As two pink-uniformed waitresses hurried back and forth, slapping down plates of food, the meeting was in its usual uproar. Marsh Traynor, built like a wrestler and bald as a balloon, was that year's Tail Twister, as well as my banker and friend. He was also an elected county commissioner and my boss, in a way, at the courthouse. Traynor had talked me into accepting the appointment as sheriff, after the incumbent, Audrey Ready's husband, was killed. And he'd also persuaded me to join the Lions Club, said it'd help me get elected to a full term. To please Traynor, I'd agreed to become a Lion. I'd filed as a candidate, too.

As I came in, Traynor was hovering over a flustered Ducky Herschel, a druggist and an avid hunter of winged things, demanding payment of a fine for one of the usual horseplay charges, all to a lot of group merriment. Fines went to pay for eyeglasses for poor kids, so there were always a lot of inventive charges.

The burly Tail Twister held a fur-lined porcelain pee pot in

Ducky's face until the druggist finally gave up and dropped in his quarter. Traynor squeezed a series of irritating honks from the rubber air bulb of a metal horn that was screwed to the pot, causing another burst of laughter from the crowd.

Moving toward a back table, patting car-dealer Bart Suder on a muscled shoulder as I passed, I quickly sat down at a vacant place next to Earl Munson, the fussbudget Rock Island depot agent. I wanted well out of the forced hilarity.

No such luck. Across the room, beanpole Clifford Branch—everybody called him Twig, no lie—stood up and fished a coin from his pants pocket, then pointed at me. "Here's a happy quarter," he shouted. "Two bits to hear Okie Dunn sing the official Oklahoma state song." Cheers went up.

The Tail Twister collected Twig's quarter in the pot, then hurried to me, honking the horn as he came.

"Okeydoke, Okie!" Traynor hollered.

I stood up. "Oklahoma, I've been a roamer, but I'm coming back to you." I sang that first line and quickly sat back down.

"Not enough!" Twig Branch shouted.

"Fine him! Fine him!" other members called out.

"Two bits for shortin' us, Okie," Marsh Traynor bawled. He brandished the fur-lined pee pot in front of my face. I paid up.

Ducky Herschel, the song director, took over and led the group in "There's a Long, Long Trail Awinding," "In Your Easter Bonnet," and, finally and more seriously, "Christ Arose!"

The club president, an optometrist who everybody called Speck, stood up in front of the round purple-and-gold Lions banner and announced that it was time to get on with "the serious eating," as he put it.

The food should have been called "seriously lacking."

Undercooked ham with a sweet sauce and a canned pineapple slice on it, cold mashed potatoes with watery brown gravy, and hard English peas, a bilious green. Dessert was a jaundiced cube of Jell-O with little cherry chunks and other fruit pieces trapped in it, like insects preserved in amber. No wonder the Luden Hotel coffee shop was said to be going under, I thought.

I tried a little conversation with the fastidious, no-nonsense Rock Island railroad agent next to me. "Everything on track at the depot, Earl?" I said. Probably not the first time he'd heard that line. "Any famous passengers come in?"

"Nobody famous, I reckon, Okie," Earl Munson said, soberly. If he got the joke about everything being on track, he didn't show it. "Did have a kind of odd lady-killer guy arrive on the 7:23 yesterday morning."

"Lady-killer?"

"Real jelly bean—looked like he'd just stepped out of a band box," the depot agent said. "High-priced, double-breasted suit with a silk handkerchief in the pocket. Spit-shined alligator slippers, with spats. Came up from Mexico, by way of Dallas, he said."

"A Mexican?"

"Didn't look like a Mexican. Blond, blue-eyed. But he talked Mexican. Talked it to ol' Solly Tamale, so Solly told me."

"Solly Tamale" was what some people called the pecan-brown old man, a native of Chihuahua, who pushed a two-wheeled cart around town and sold homemade tamales from its hot pots, mostly at the depot and the bus station. His real name was Salvador Soto.

"Buy tamales from Solly?" I asked.

"Didn't buy anything. Just talked—in Mexican."

"What's the lady-killer in Vernon for, I wonder," I said.

I'd stopped trying to eat the food, after more or less playing with it for a while. I particularly liked nudging over the Jell-O cube with my fork, then watching it bounce right back when I took the fork away.

"Never said. He hired Reeves Martin to haul him around town. Reeves's got that old-model Packard, you know. Hauls light freight, delivers telegrams that come in, and, ever now and then, gets a passenger that'll pay. Lady-killer hired him full-time. Said he might need him two or three days. Wanted to know where the airport was. Asked about Doc Askew's office, too. I told him next door, west, here, of the Luden."

"Doc Askew?" I said.

"Yeah. Didn't say why he wanted to know."

Dr. Milford Askew's home/office was in a rambling yellow-frame residence that fronted California Street. The office part was at the back of the house, down a long driveway that ran between the house and the west side of the Luden Hotel. Hardly anybody went to Askew anymore, since he'd pretty much shut down his practice.

"The man came in last night, Thursday night?" I asked Munson.

"Last night."

"Have a name?"

"Introduced himself to me as John Carter."

The Lions Club speaker for the day was a visiting preacher from the First Christian Church in nearby Chickasha. His theme was that the teachings of Jesus were the only cure for what ailed America and the world and the only way to deal with the growing menace of Adolf Hitler of Germany. The preacher wound up his remarks by saying, finally, "It may take a hundred more Easters, but in the end these teachings will conquer."

Good luck to us, one and all, in the meantime, I thought.

The speaker sat down to strong applause. There was the usual backslapping and handshaking, and another weekly Lions Club meeting was over.

I wanted to learn more about the lady-killer who'd come up from Mexico the day before, asking about Doc Askew. Leaving the Luden after saying good-bye to other members, I walked east to Main Street, crossed it, then walked half a block south to the bus station. I stopped to let a Lawton bus pull out, then turned up the driveway, looking for Solly. He was just putting his stuff up and closing the lids of the tamale cart.

"*Salvador. ¿Qué tal?*" I said. "*¿Qué de nuevo?*" How're you doing? What's new? I'd studied Spanish, some, in high school, then had a chance to practice it more, when I was prizefighting for half a year, down through Mexico. That was before I'd come back to Oklahoma to go to college and law school.

Solly looked up and jerked off his frayed straw hat. He smiled broadly. Two of his top left teeth were missing.

"*¿Cómo está, Señor Dunn?*" he said, pronouncing my last name as "doon." He put out his hand and shook mine vigorously.

I inquired in Spanish about the well-dressed man who'd come in on the Dallas train the day before, Thursday, the one who'd told the depot agent that his name was Carter. I described the lady-killer.

"*No, señor, me dijo Leo Castor,*" Solly said. No, sir, he told me Leo Castor—the name sounding out as "lay-o cah-store." Not Carter.

"*¿Se llamó Castor?*" He called himself Castor?

"*Sí, señor.*"

Solly said the man had asked him about the location of Dr. Askew's office—the same, I knew, as he had the depot agent. Making conversation, Castor, or Carter, had asked where Solly was from in Mexico, and, when Solly answered Chihuahua, the man had volunteered that he himself was from Oklahoma City, but was working in Mexico, in the state of Veracruz.

I asked how Castor's Spanish was.

Like a gringo's, Solly said, then quickly apologized for using that derogatory term.

"*No hay ningún problema,*" I said. No problem.

I thanked the old Mexican and headed back toward the courthouse.

I rolled everything over in my mind as I walked. Now there were three new people in Vernon—Satville, Hoffer, and Castor, this last one giving out a made-up name. All of them had arrived on the preceding day, Thursday. All were connected in some way to Dr. Milford Askew—and, more than likely, the Case of the Unknown Girl.

ELEVEN

At six-thirty on Good Friday evening, driving the blue sheriff car, I pulled into the gravel lot at the Busy Bee Tourist Cabins, down at the foot of the hill on north Main. I got out and stepped inside the office door. Busybody old lady Barkley, squat in a wraparound cotton housedress, was pressing a man's shirt at an ironing board, set up behind the counter. I asked for Em Hoffer's cabin.

"She's in number three, Okie," the woman said. She motioned toward the north with a head full of curlers and at the same time raised her bushy, unplucked eyebrows in a kind of questioning look of disapproval. I didn't know whether this was of me or Em Hoffer, or both of us. "Don't slam the door 'cause Ernie's roughneckin' evenin' tower, and he ain't up yet," she said, and turned back to her work. The Barkleys lived in a couple of rooms in the back part of the office.

I started to leave, then thought to ask about Satville. "Been a kind of bloated guy named Tobe Satville around here? Driving a green Chevrolet coupe."

"The answer's still 'No, ain't see him,' and I'm gittin' a little tired of givin' it," old lady Barkley said, not looking up from the ironing board.

"Who else asked you?"

"That woman you're here to see—Hoffer—and, since then, that Crystal that you made a deputy of yourn."

I shut the door quietly and crunched my way three cabins north in the loose gravel to number three. In front of it sat a 1936 blue, four-door Chrysler Airflow sedan. Its black-and-yellow 1938 license tag began with the number one, which meant it was from Oklahoma County—where Oklahoma City was located. Em Hoffer's car, I figured. I knocked on the cabin door.

"It's unlocked," she called from inside.

It was. I was a little uneasy about going into a woman's tourist-court room. But I did. And I closed the door behind me because of the wind. The air inside was heavy with the scent of Evening in Paris.

Em Hoffer turned. She was seated on a stool in front of a cheap veneer-wood vanity with a lighted mirror. She'd been putting on what looked like some of the red lipstick that had been so heavily advertised in magazines: "Natural lips of Tangee Red win with Dick Powell!" Hoffer was wearing a dark-khaki slack suit. A fluffy, green satin bow was tied at the collar of her white linen blouse.

The only women I'd ever heard of who wore pants were in moving pictures—Marlene Dietrich and Katharine Hepburn.

Em Hoffer was better-looking than either one of them, and she filled out a slack suit a whole lot better than they did, too, especially Katharine Hepburn.

I glanced around. The room was plastered white and had thin, red cotton curtains on the only window, next to the door. Em Hoffer's soft, brown leather suitcase was open on the floor, under the window. On a nightstand next to the bed, its varnished-pine top scarred by a decade's worth of careless cigarette burns, was a lathe-turned wooden lamp that looked like somebody's boy had made it in high school shop. A straight, hardback chair was pulled up toward the rumpled bed, loosely covered with a pastel-green chenille spread. Hoffer's tan air corps raincoat lay along the foot of the bed. A faded color print of the familiar Indian-on-horseback *End of the Trail* hung on the far wall. There was no bathroom. A common one was outside.

"You had supper?" Em Hoffer asked before turning back to the mirror to rouge her cheeks a little. They didn't need it. She already had plenty of healthy color.

"Just ate," I said. After milking the Jersey cow and doing the evening chores at the Billings place, I'd gobbled down a light-bread sandwich of sliced bologna and cheddar—what my dad had always called "dog meat and rat cheese."

"Me, too," she said. "Went next door to the Truckers Café. Good chicken-fried steak and a friendly waitress named Irma who thought your dad hung the moon. You want a drink?" She stood up and turned to face me, and I was made aware again of how tall and full-bodied she was.

"What you got? To drink, I mean."

"Seagram's and Coca-Cola." She motioned toward the right

side of the vanity, where I saw there was a half-pint of whiskey, as well as two open bottles of Coca-Cola, and a couple of empty glasses. "You're not a Holy Roller, are you?"

"I could confiscate that liquor, you know," I said. Prohibition was still the law in Oklahoma, and the only thing legal was 3.2 beer.

Em Hoffer's voice took on a mock-formal tone, like she was testifying before an arraignment judge. "I swear it's for medicinal purposes only, Your Honor," she said.

"Okay then," I said.

"Throw your hat on the bed and take a seat," Hoffer said and turned back to the vanity. "There's no ice. But the Coca-Colas are cold. Carried them over from the café."

"Bad luck," I said.

"Whiskey and Coca-Cola?"

"That, too, probably," I said. "But putting your hat on a bed is, for sure." My dad had been superstitious about that, the same as he was about opening an umbrella in the house, or moving on a Friday.

Em Hoffer stepped my way from the drink fixings, took my Stetson, and pitched it on the bed. "Bad luck's better'n no luck at all," she said.

It gave me a momentary twinge to leave the hat there, but I did, anyway, and sat down in the hardback chair. "Speaking of luck, you had any—trying to find out who, and where, Miz Morgan's daughter is?" I asked.

Em Hoffer came over and handed me one of the two drinks she carried. "None so far," she said. "And you haven't found that bastard Satville, either. Right?"

"We'll find him."

"But you haven't, yet."

"Nope."

She stepped carefully past the tips of my black cowboy boots and sat down on the bed, facing me, making the springs squeak. Our knees were almost touching. She lifted her glass toward me. "Well, here's to motherhood," she said.

We drank. The sweet brown mixture gave me little, sickening chills. My experience had been that if you ever woke up with a hangover from whiskey and Coca-Cola, it made you want to swear off and take the cure.

Hoffer leaned over and picked up her large satchel purse from the nightstand. She fished out the silver combination lighter and cigarette case, opened it and took out a cigarette, closed the case and tamped the cigarette on it, then lit up. She turned her head to blow the smoke away from me.

"Why did you want to be a lawyer?" I asked her.

"To help people, I guess. The kind of people the law doesn't usually care much about. My dad got behind on his payments after he got sick, and the bank took his airplane. He was a barnstormer pilot—putting on shows for people—after he came home from the war. What about you, Okie? How come *you* wanted to be a lawyer?"

"One time, a guy from Lawton came to talk at our high school assembly," I said. "Didn't look like much, sort of cowboy looking. Told us about a lawsuit he'd filed for the Comanche Indians, to win back some of their land and get them better paid for the rest. Their reservation was broken up by the government, each tribal member forced to take a one-hundred-sixty-acre allotment. Hearing that lawyer, I thought to myself, 'Now, that's the kind of job I'd like to have.'"

"Why in the world did you slap that law professor?" Hoffer asked.

"Instinct. Reflex. I'm a counterpuncher, by training. Guy hits me, I hit him back, automatically, without thinking. Can't help it. Dumbest thing I ever did."

"Chance the president at OU might cut your suspension to a year?" she asked.

"Should hear this month. Can you make a living, Em, representing the kind of people you do?"

"You can't get rich," Hoffer said. "But I pay the rent and buy groceries—sometimes barely."

"And representing Lily Morgan—money in that?"

Hoffer frowned, then took a slug of her drink. "I don't have any deal with her, if that's what you mean," she said. "I feel sorry for the woman, that's all. Want to help her find her daughter. Hope we can do it while Lily's still around. I'm afraid she's not going to be around, much longer. Her TB's getting real bad."

I changed the subject. "Tobe Satville's driving a green '35 Chevy coupe with white sidewalls," I said. "Rented it from the dealer. Keep your eyes peeled for him or the car. But don't try anything on your own. I wouldn't be surprised if the guy carried a gun. Just let me know if you see him or the car, and I'll take care of it."

"Don't worry, Okie," she said. "I know Tobe Satville's kind—yellow as baby dookie, and that's about what he'd do in his pants if I even so much as looked at him cross-eyed. You stepping out with the widow of the former sheriff?"

"What?"

"Her name Audrey?"

"Irma say something?"

"Irma's not the only one," Em Hoffer said. "Sweet on your dead predecessor's wife pretty quick, aren't you? That bother you any?"

"Some. You married?"

"Was. Ain't. I've thought about finding another town to move to. It'd be good to live somewhere away from my ex-husband. I made the mistake of marrying just about the first man I met after I got out of law school. He's a lawyer, too."

"Still gives you trouble?" I asked.

"Parks in front of my house, sometimes. Tries to talk to me. Begs me to take him back. Cries and says he's sorry for what he did to me."

"What was that?" I asked.

"I don't know why I'm telling you all this. I hardly know you."

"Naw, go ahead," I said. "I want to hear your story."

"Beat me up a lot, for one thing, my ex-husband. There were days when I couldn't go to the courthouse without caking the makeup on my face to hide the bruises. Felt really ashamed about it all. Lily Morgan was the only one I could talk to. She was so good to me. I went to her regularly to get my hair fixed. She saw the bruises, from time to time, and figured it out. Let me cry on her shoulder. And she kept telling me I oughtn't to put up with that kind of treatment."

"How'd you ever let him get away with it in the first place?" I asked. "You look big enough to take care of yourself."

"My growth came late—and fast. I didn't know my own strength for a long time. That's the truth. Besides that, I was raised, like every other girl, to be a good wife, to put up with whatever your man wanted to do to you."

"What changed?"

"Bastard hit me one time too many, I guess," Hoffer said. "Something just snapped. I thought, I don't have to take this shit. I slapped the tar out of him. He went to whining, said how sorry he was. I said, 'You're pretty damned sorry, all right.' I said, 'Get your stuff and get the hell out.' I helped him carry it and throw it in his car. He started in begging some more. I acted like I might haul off and hit him again. I said, 'You better get your sorry ass out of here.' He took off like a scolded dog."

"Good for you!" I said.

"It'd be a relief to get away from that guy. Maybe someday. And a smaller town than Oklahoma City would give a person a chance to be more a part of a community, too."

"Vernon interest you?"

"Could."

We downed the rest of our drinks without saying anything more and put the glasses on the floor. I stood up.

"We better get moving toward the picture show," I said.

She stood up, too, then. We faced each other, inches apart, hemmed in, held together, in a way, by the bed right behind her and the hardback chair right behind me. My boot heels made our lips almost level with each other, though hers were still slightly higher. Our lips were close, too. And then they got closer. I don't know which one of us first moved forward.

We fell into an embrace, pressing tightly against each other. The kiss was tender and hot, and lengthy.

Hoffer ended it, finally, and pulled back. "What do they call you—'The Cash County Flash'?" she said and laughed.

I reached awkwardly around her and picked up my hat from the bed, glad to have something to do with my hands and my eyes.

Em Hoffer moved to gather up her raincoat. I helped her on with it. We'd earlier heard thunder outside.

"You ready, Flash?" she asked.

"Ready to go, if that's what you mean," I said.

"Devil!"

I took her arm and guided her out the door, then across the gravel to the blue sheriff car, over next to the office.

At the Murray Theater, downtown, I bought the popcorn, greasy and heavily salted, just the way I liked it. I bought two sacks. I'd always hated to share—a feeling left over from growing up poor, maybe. Inside, Em Hoffer chose a row on the right, about halfway down. I guided her in, first, then took the aisle seat.

The comedy short was a Laurel and Hardy hitchhiking piece called *On the Wrong Trek*. During one early, funny scene, Hoffer leaned forward suddenly and laughed out loud, real hard. I took the occasion to slide my right arm around her, letting my hand rest on her far shoulder. She didn't seem to mind. It was like high school, I thought, and I'd never been much good at it—back then, or since.

The comedy ended. The weekly serial started, the second chapter of *Tim Tyler's Luck*. In the episode, as the two boys, the main characters, emerged at one point from their armored "jungle cruiser" and were suddenly charged by an angry lion, Em Hoffer jerked back in her seat slightly, like she was, herself, shying away from the big cat on the screen. I let my hand glide slowly down from her shoulder. Hoffer deftly took hold of it, checking the movement—but smoothly, as if she'd hardly noticed.

Thin Ice, the main feature, was thin-*plotted*, obviously made, I thought, just to show off Olympic ice-skating champion Sonja Henie, her famous dimpled smile and celebrated pirouettes on the ice, with lots of twirling legs and flashing tights. I wasn't very interested at that moment, though, in whether it was a good picture show or not.

Back at the Busy Bee Tourist Cabins, afterward, Em Hoffer was still friendly enough, but she didn't invite me in, either. I thought it was just as well. Old lady Barkley was at the front desk and on the alert, watching through the glass window of her office, as we got out of my car and walked together toward Em Hoffer's cabin. At the door, Hoffer gave me a kind of sisterly peck on the lips and a pleasant "Good night."

Before turning away, I said, "Want to get a bite of early breakfast with me in the morning at the Luden Hotel coffee shop? Tired of my own cooking."

"Sure, I could stand to pass up the Truckers Café," Hoffer said.

"Seven."

"Seven?" Hoffer asked.

"Early to bed, early to rise—"

"Makes Jack a dull boy," Hoffer said.

"You met Crystal, my deputy?"

"What?"

"Nothing. See you in the morning."

Em Hoffer put the key in the door and opened it, then stepped inside.

I headed home to the Billings place. But, as it turned out, my night wasn't over yet.

TWELVE

I'd only been asleep for close to three hours, when, a little after two in the morning, my party-line telephone began to ring. The phone was on the kitchen wall, and I couldn't hear it well in the bedroom. Even after I began to wake up, it still took a couple of minutes more for me to realize that it was *my* ring— a long and a short.

I hurried to the kitchen and grabbed the receiver from its cradle and pressed it to my ear. Leaning close to the mouth-piece, I said, "Yes?"

Calls at that hour were never good news.

"This is Mrs. Askew," the voice said in my ear. "Better get over here. It's Mr. Wampler, your deputy."

"What's happened to him?" I asked.

"Struck on the head and rendered unconscious," Mrs. Askew said. "Doctor's looking after him, and he's coming around. He was watching the office and got knocked out by a burglar. The burglar got away. Can you come?"

I suddenly remembered that Stud had agreed to stake out the Askew office. "Be there in a minute," I said.

I hung up and pulled on a gray work shirt and some Levi's, then jerked on my boots. I dashed out the back door and down the steps in the dark, toward the blue 1936 Ford sedan with the enlarged sheriff decals on the front doors. Scooter came running up, looking a little tentative, like he thought it was early to go running, but ready. I patted him on the head, then jumped in my car, slammed the door, and took off for town.

At the sprawling, yellow Askew home/office, next door to the Luden Hotel, I swerved into the long driveway and pulled all the way back to the patients' entrance. Up the concrete steps, I jerked open the back door and charged inside the glassed-in porch that had served as the doctor's reception room. Mrs. Askew was waiting there. She was wearing a pink robe over her nightgown, her gray hair in a hair net.

"This way," Mrs. Askew said. "He's doing better." She led me down a short hall, past a patient room with an empty bed in it, to the doctor's sizable office and clinic.

Following Mrs. Askew in, I saw Stud Wampler sitting up on the edge of the doctor's examination table, Askew standing beside him. The doctor, slight and stooped a little with age, was still in his pajamas. A sheaf of white hair that he normally combed from his left temple to cover a bald spot was standing straight up.

"Looks like he's going to be all right," Askew said, peering at me through rimless spectacles. "Hard blow to his head, though. Concussion."

"How you doing, Stud?" I said to my chief deputy, moving closer to put my hand on his big shoulder.

"'Speck I'll make it, Okie stud," he said. His voice was a little weak. He was holding a wet cloth to the back of his head. "My ol' head sure hurts. It was dark, and somebody blackjacked the hell out of me from behind."

Dr. Askew spoke again to me. "Sheriff, Mrs. Askew surprised a prowler here Thursday night, trying to pick the lock and come in the back door," he said. "The prowler ran off, and she couldn't see who it was in the dark. We asked Mr. Wampler to sit up here tonight, in case there was a repeat attempt. Good thing!"

"You see what the guy looked like that hit you?" I asked Stud. "It was a man?"

"I reckon," Stud said. "Couldn't make out whoever it was. I'd turned all the lights off. And, to tell the truth, Okie, I dozed off, sometime after midnight, out there in that waitin' room. Pickin' the lock didn't rouse me. But the sound of them filing cabinets openin' in here did."

Stud stopped talking for a minute and closed his eyes. I looked around and noticed that some of the drawers to two oak-wood filing cabinets, in a far corner, next to the doctor's desk, were standing open. What appeared to be patient files were strewn on the white-tiled floor near the cabinets.

Stud put the wet cloth to the back of his head again.

"He's still a little woozy," Dr. Askew said.

"Why don't you wait, Stud, and tell me the rest, up in the day, when you feel better," I said. "I'll drive you home."

He opened his eyes again. "Naw, that's okay," he said. "So, hearin' them filing cabinets openin' here, I roused up. Pulled my little police special out of my britches pocket and snuck over here to the clinic door. Floor squeaked, though, like a nest of mice. Reckon the burglar heard me, 'cause I just got a couple a steps in here when—blam!—I got hit from behind, and my lights went out."

I turned toward Askew. "Doctor, what would the prowler have been after?"

Mrs. Askew answered. "Narcotics, don't you imagine?" she said.

"You keep narcotics in the filing cabinets?" I asked.

"No, over there in that locked upright cabinet by the wall," Dr. Askew said, motioning.

"Why were the filing cabinets rifled, then, do you think?"

"Who knows what criminals will do?" Mrs. Askew said.

"Anything taken, that you can tell?" I asked.

"We haven't tried to put all those patients' files back together, yet," Dr. Askew said. "We can do that in the morning. You'd better get your deputy home." He turned his attention back to Stud. "Mr. Wampler, I wouldn't go to sleep for a couple of hours after you get home, just to be sure everything's okay. Take two more aspirins, if you need them. You're going to be all right."

I helped Stud stand up and steady himself. Mrs. Askew picked Stud's worn Stetson off the floor by the door where, evidently, it had landed earlier. She handed the hat to him. Stud didn't put it on, but held it.

"Wait a minute!" he said. He patted his right pants pocket. "My gun! I don't have it."

Dr. Askew, his wife, and I began to scour the room for it. Stud watched. The little revolver with a checkered walnut handle was not to be found.

"Not only puts a knot on my noggin, son of a bitch runs off with my gun, too," Stud said.

Outside in the sheriff car, Stud said he'd left his own car a block north on Main Street and had walked over. He hadn't wanted to warn off the prowler by parking out front or in the driveway of the Askew place.

"Leave my car where it is, stud, and carry me on home," Stud said to me. "I'll get it tomorrow—well, later today. It's already Saturday, I reckon."

I backed out of the Askew driveway and headed toward Stud's house on the west side of Vernon.

"No doubt about it, now, Okie, stud," Stud said. "This here's all tied together with the Case of the Unknown Girl."

I was thinking that, too, I told him.

"Prowler, whoever it is, lookin' for Lily Morgan's file, wantin' to find out where the baby girl went," Stud said.

"Tobe Satville, you think?" I asked.

"Him—or maybe even your new redheaded girlfriend."

"Not my girlfriend, Stud. And I don't think she's the one that hit you."

"*Big* enough," Stud said.

"Wrong trail," I said. I hoped that I was right. "This just means that we've got to work harder at finding Satville."

THIRTEEN

Em Hoffer was already seated at a table next to the big corner window on the west side of the room when I got to the Luden Hotel coffee shop that same Saturday morning at about seven.

Clangled awake an hour earlier by my wind-up alarm clock, I'd instantly regretted having made the breakfast appointment with Hoffer. With little sleep after getting back home from Doc Askew's in the early hours, I felt like I'd been on a two-day drunk—or, as Stud Wampler might have put it, like I'd been "shot at and missed, shit at and *hit*." I'd rushed through my morning chores—and skipped my morning run, altogether, much to Scooter's obvious disappointment.

By contrast, Hoffer looked fresh. She was wearing a tailored, dark-gray gabardine slack suit with a light-gray taffeta blouse. Her red hair was well-brushed and loose, down to her shoulders. Her face was as sunny as the Oklahoma morning, shining on her through the expanse of glass to her left.

She looked up from the local weekly, the *Vernon Herald*, that was open in front of her. "Pull up a chair, Flash," she said.

I did and sat down facing her across the table for two, a porcelain vase of fresh red tulips between us. Out the window, down and to my right, was the long driveway and yellow Askew house/office that I'd been called to, a very few short hours before.

The Luden coffee shop's middle-aged waitress, Gladys, had followed me over to the table, and I asked her to bring me a cup of coffee.

"How you want it, hon?"

"Intravenously," I said. She didn't smile, but went away to get the coffeepot.

Out at the Billings place, dressing fast, after chores, I'd grabbed on the clothes nearest at hand—worn Levi's and a red-and-white OU sweatshirt. I could tell that black sprigs of my barely combed hair were sticking out a little on each side of the green-and-yellow John Deere ball cap that I'd clamped down on my head.

Hoffer folded the newspaper and dropped it in my lap. She looked me over. "Off work today, I see," she said.

"No crime on weekends."

"You look terrible," she said. "Eyes all bloodshot."

"Ought to see them from *this* side," I said.

"You didn't go straight to bed, like I did. Either that, or didn't sleep well."

"I had to get up in the middle of the night and go see about my deputy, Stud Wampler—you met him," I said. "He got blackjacked by a prowler, right over here at Dr. Askew's office." I motioned out the window with my hand.

"Lord!" Hoffer said. "How is he?"

"He'll make it," I said. "Tough as a badger, that guy."

"Prowler caught?" she asked.

"Got away."

"What did he take, the prowler?" Hoffer asked.

"Not sure, yet, but looks like he was after patients' files."

"That bastard Satville," she said.

"Same thing I was thinking," I said.

The waitress came and poured my coffee and refilled Em Hoffer's cup. The two of us ordered—Hoffer, dry toast, a poached egg, and orange juice; me, a short stack, scrambled eggs, and bacon.

"How'd you get full-grown, eating like a field lark?" I asked.

"How come you're so lean, eating like Coxie's army?"

"May have to go up one weight class, if I ever take up prize-fighting again," I said. "Anything in the paper?" I hadn't had time to read that week's edition.

"Doings at the high school auditorium, tonight," Hoffer said.

"Easter Parade, they call it. Big deal, every year."

"You going?" Hoffer asked.

"I'm the emcee, matter of fact," I said. There was silence for a moment, then I noticed that Hoffer was waiting for me to say something more. "You want to go?" I asked quickly.

"Wouldn't put you out?"

"Naw, come on and go," I said.

"Okay," she said.

I hesitated a minute. "It'd be best for us to just meet at the entrance, if that's all right," I said. "Take separate cars. I've got some stuff to do, afterward."

The afterward "stuff" I had to do, of course, was to take Janeaster Parnell to the annual sunrise Easter Pageant at Kraker Park. But I didn't feel like passing this information on to Em Hoffer, right then.

Hoffer said there was no problem about our going to the program separately. I told her that it was to begin at 7:45. She said she'd read that. I told her she could park her car in the gravel lot, across the street south of the auditorium.

The waitress came and set down our breakfast orders, and at that moment something out the window caught my eye. I turned away from my food to look.

What I saw was Janeaster Parnell, walking briskly down the sidewalk from the west, toward the Luden Hotel.

Em Hoffer's eyes followed mine. "Nice-looking girl," she said. "Know her?"

"Janeaster's her name, high school home-ec teacher," I said. "Matter of fact, she's in the Easter Parade program, tonight."

"Janeaster, huh?"

"Janeaster Parnell," I said.

"Calls herself Easter, I guess," Em Hoffer said.

"I don't think so."

"Right here in the paper," Hoffer said. She got it from her lap, turned the bottom half of the front page up, and handed it to me.

I scanned the two-column story. Sure enough, it listed "Easter Parnell" among those to be featured in the 1938 Easter Parade program at the school.

I handed the paper back to Hoffer. "Kind of a stage name, I imagine. She wants to be a professional model."

The two of us looked again at the young woman. She had

come along the sidewalk to the purple-blooming lilac bush at the front of the Askew house, almost to the hotel. She didn't raise her eyes toward the hotel window, but glanced both ways quickly at ground level, then turned to her left and walked down the long driveway to the back of the Askew place.

"Furtive," Em Hoffer said. "What's she up to?"

"Hope she's not sick," I said. "Knock her out of the Easter Parade."

Janeaster Parnell disappeared into the doctor's office. Em Hoffer and I turned our attention to our breakfast.

We ate for a while without talking. Then, Em Hoffer said, "So, if you do go back to law school, what then? What would you like to do?"

"Have my own law practice, if I could," I said. "But I don't know if I could make a go of it by myself."

"Maybe you'd have to take in a partner who'd split the costs with you."

"Maybe," I said. "People say, though, that finding a good partner is as hard as making a good marriage."

"Don't look at me; you know I've tried both without notable success," Hoffer said. She glanced out the window. "Here's your home-ec girl, again."

I turned, too, to watch as Janeaster Parnell strode back up the driveway toward the lilac bush at the sidewalk in front. She was just beneath us. I felt like knocking on the glass to get her attention, then waving to her. But something about her manner stopped me. Her glance shifted back and forth at ground level as she walked, as if she was afraid she'd be seen coming from Doc Askew's office. And she seemed upset.

"Appears she's been crying," Hoffer said.

It was true. Janeaster's eyes were clearly reddened. We watched her as she turned to her right at the sidewalk and headed back west, pretty soon disappearing around the corner to where, I thought, she'd probably parked her car.

"What in the hell would that young woman want with Doc Askew?" I said, not so much to Em Hoffer, but wondering out loud to myself, really. "I don't think he even takes patients, now."

"Whatever she wanted from him, she came away disappointed, looked like," Hoffer said. "Okie, it's interesting to me that the girl's name is Easter and that she's just come from the office of Dr. Askew—Easter, Askew. See the connection? How old's that girl?"

"Around nineteen, I'd guess." I hadn't, up to then, seen any connection.

"See!" Hoffer said. "Nineteen from 1938 gives us 1919—the year Lily Morgan's daughter was born, on Easter Sunday. I'm more interested than I was, now, in going with you to tonight's Easter Parade program. I'd like to look that girl over, talk to her."

"Janeaster's a Parnell, though, Em," I said. "These things you're fixing on are just coincidences. Unless you know something I don't know. Do you?"

"Pretty dern strange coincidences, if they *are* coincidences," she said. "I'm just putting two and two together, that's all."

We finished our breakfast, Hoffer well before me. At the cash register, I said I'd pay, since I'd eaten the most. She didn't protest. I repeated for Hoffer the evening Easter Parade time and the parking directions, mentioning, again, that she and I would just meet at the entrance to the high school auditorium.

"Yeah, yeah," she said. "In the meantime, I'm going to pick

up my stuff, move over here to the Luden. Hate to leave the beautiful Busy Bee Tourist Cabins, but this'll be more convenient. After that, I'm going to drive around town to see if I can spot Tobe Satville or his car before I take off for the high school auditorium."

"More urgent, now, we get our hands on that bird Satville after last night," I said. "I'm gonna take a quick nap or I won't be worth a damn to anybody, then I'm on Satville like a chicken on a June bug. We gotta find him today, before he does something else bad."

Hoffer and I said good-bye, and she took off while I waited for my change at the cash register. Afterward, crossing the hotel lobby toward the front door, I stopped a moment, thinking about Leo Castor, the lady-killer, then turned back toward the hotel desk to inquire about him.

"We ain't got no Castors," the desk clerk with the pencil mustache said, sure of it.

"What about John Carter, then?"

"Got *him!*" the man said at once.

I described the visitor's jelly-bean clothes and appearance. They matched perfectly with the hotel guest the desk clerk knew as Carter.

"Still here," he said. "Comes and goes a lot. Didn't have no breakfast this morning. Left real early."

"By car—how?" I asked.

"Reeves Martin left his old Packard car out front last night and his keys, here at the desk, for Carter," the man said. "He drove himself."

*　　*　　*

The minute I got to the Billings place, I went to the kitchen and cranked my wall telephone for one long ring. Central came on the line, and I had her get me Lulu Crabbe, the county clerk, at home.

"Sorry to bother you, Lulu," I said when she answered.

"That's all right, Okie," she said. "Not doing anything but sitting here shelling some new peas."

"Lulu, when we talked about Doc Askew, Friday, after your office was busted into, you seemed to show some displeasure at the mention of his name," I said.

"Yes, I did, Okie," she said.

"Why was that?"

"Well, I never want to run anybody down," she began.

"This could be important, Lulu," I said. "What do you know or what have you heard, negative, about Doc Askew?"

"Abortions, for one thing, Okie," she said, "if you must know."

"You mean what I think you do, Lulu?"

"Lots of people say that he used to perform abortions, right there in his clinic, next to the Luden Hotel," she said.

"Abortions," I said, mulling over this information, not sure if it meant anything.

"Don't do 'em, now, for sure, since he's old and his hand's got palsied," Lulu said. "And I ought to make clear to you, Okie, that I can't swear to this. I never saw anything with my own eyes."

"I know, Lulu," I said. "But you said abortions were *one* thing. Was there something else?"

"I can only tell you what people say and what I, myself, suspicioned," she said.

"And what is that?"

"More than likely, he used to sell babies," Lulu said.

"Sell babies? How'd he do that?"

"Unwed mothers came to him for deliveries that their folks back home wouldn't know about," she said. "Other people who were desperate to adopt a baby heard, some way—the word got around, I guess—that they could get a baby from Doc Askew."

"Selling babies out of his clinic, then," I said.

"Okie, you said it, not me," Lulu said. "Hearsay won't hold up in court, you know as well as I do."

"I know, Lulu, but I appreciate your frankness, and we'll keep it between us, for now," I said. "Talk to you later."

I hung up the telephone earpiece. A lot of pressing thoughts that I needed to make sense of were rattling around in my head. But, for the moment, I was too sleepy to sort it all out. I lay down for a nap.

FOURTEEN

When I woke up, later that Saturday, it was close to noon. In the Billings place kitchen, I warmed up some leftover corn bread and red beans. I had just sat down to go to work on them, after pouring myself a glass of sweet milk from the icebox, when my two uncles drove their rickety wagon, pulled by the mismatched bay-horse-and-sorrel-jenny team, into my yard to bring me the report about the body that'd dropped out of the sky into their oat field.

Scooter, the dog, didn't make any racket because he knew Uncle Leroy and Uncle Joe Ray. So, I didn't realize that they were around until they hollered to me.

"Okie, you in there?" Uncle Leroy yelled.

I went out at once. "How you doing, Uncle Leroy, Uncle Joe Ray? Get down, y'all."

"Nawsir, hon, we-uns just come to bring you some right peculiar news," Uncle Joe Ray said from the wagon's spring seat, where he and his brother continued to sit. He was excited. "Body done fell out of a clear sky into that oat field a ourn. Hit's a man."

Engaged, I moved closer to the front wagon wheel nearest me, looking up at those scraggly, grizzled two, snuff juice dripping out of the corners of their mouths. "You know who he is?"

"No idee in this here world," Uncle Leroy said. "We didn't wont to disturb nothin' by looking for no papers. Don't do that, them true-detective magazines say. Face weren't one mite familiar to neither one of us, Okie."

My two uncles were what people called "bless their hearts." Grandma Dunn, for example, never uttered one of the uncles' names without immediately adding the modifying words: "Your uncle Leroy, bless his heart . . ."

Not a week went by that they didn't gather up, and save, all the newspapers and magazines they could get their hands on in Vernon. They tied the publications in bundles with binder twine, then stacked the bundles to the ceiling, in dust-gathering rows, in the living room of their unpainted, tin-roofed shack until they'd packed that room full. Then, they started in on the kitchen. The uncles saved string, and baling wire, too. The ball of string on their shaky back porch had grown through the years until you couldn't have fit it into a number-ten washtub. And a dung beetle would have had to be bigger than a billy goat to roll the balled-up baling wire they kept out by the side of their teetering old barn.

"How'd he get to where you found him, the dead man?" I asked my uncles.

"Wadn't drug there," Uncle Leroy said. "Nawsir!"

"Wadn't carried there, neither, nor throwed out a no wagon or automobile," Uncle Joe Ray said.

"Nary a track of no kind 'round the corpse," Uncle Leroy said.

"Wadn't blowed there," Uncle Joe Ray said. "Weren't no wind that stout. Man plumb dropped out'n a blue sky."

"Sure'n hell did," Uncle Leroy said.

They told how their coondog had led them to the body and, then, how they'd rushed to bring me the news.

"Y'all see an airplane about that time?" I asked.

"An airplane? Nawsir," Uncle Leroy said. "Didn't hear none, neither."

"Acourse, we-uns was in the house, listenin' to W. Lee O'Daniel and them Light Crust Doughboys on the radio," Uncle Joe Ray said. "Statticky and all—we never heard nothin' outside."

"Okay, you two—and much obliged for going to all this trouble," I said. "Y'all go on back. I'll get Stud Wampler to come out here, and the two of us'll follow you down to your place, directly." I hoped that Stud'd recovered from the blow to his head.

Uncle Joe Ray was driving. He popped the black-leather lines on the team's rumps, and they jerked forward in the trace chains. "Get up there, Barney," he said. "Come around, Jude." He pulled on the left line, on the little sorrel mare-mule's side, and the team began to make a wide turn in that direction.

I went back in the house, to the wall telephone in the kitchen, cranked up central, and asked her to ring Stud Wampler, at home. Stud said he was feeling better after a little sleep. I told him about my uncles' report, and he agreed to drive right out to the Billings place and go with me to investigate. I had central connect me, then, with Stigler-Martin Funeral Home. I told Greg Martin to send a hearse down to my uncles' place. I gave him the details and the directions.

Stud must have stepped out his door the minute he hung up the telephone after talking with me, because he was at my place in little more than fifteen minutes.

"Your head better?" I asked him, coming out to my yard when he drove up.

"No better'n it ever was," he said.

"I mean after getting knocked on the head at Doc Askew's last night."

"Feel like Braddock when Joe Louis got through with him," Stud said. He lifted his Stetson with one hand and rubbed the back of his head with the other. "Still got a knot. Head's my toughest part, though."

"Let's take my sheriff car," I said, "and I want to go, first, over to the airstrip at Moreland's, check on whether Tobe Satville's plane's still there. The dead body dropped out of the sky—no tracks."

"See if Satville's left town," Stud said.

We got in the blue Ford. I went down to South Boundary Street, then followed it all the way across Vernon, from the east side to the west side, which, no bigger town than Vernon was, didn't take long. We saw the little yellow Piper Cub as soon as we drove up to the grass strip's gate, behind Moreland's Dairy. The plane was on the north side of the hangar, headed west and on the other side of Jeff Moreland's white-and-red, south-pointed Waco biplane. The Piper Cub's door was oddly open.

"Satville's airplane's here, but not where it was when he came in," I said. "Been moved."

"Main thing, means that derned bounty hunter ain't got away—still around, somewhere," Stud said.

"And he's been out in his plane lately," I said.

No person or car was in sight. I turned the blue county Ford around and headed west, back across town. At the corner with the Pomoceah place, where South Boundary dead-ended into the gravel school-bus route, I turned south on it, toward my uncles' farm.

Off to our left, less than a quarter of a mile, was the tree line of East Cash Creek. Stud motioned in that direction with his left hand. "Guy gonna grabble, stud, ain't no better place than right down there," he said. "Bet you ain't done that in a long time."

Stud was talking about catching big catfish in the creek by hand.

"You're right," I said. "Never was much good at it, either, like you and my dad."

"'Member that time me and you dad caught that hellacious Appaloosa catfish, right over there, back under the roots of that big oak on the north end of old man Nahnahpwa's place, close to that old wagon crossing? You were on the creek bank."

"I remember," I said.

"Hudge had to go way back up in a hole, this side, under the bank, to get him. Rammed his hand down the old Appaloosa's throat and pert near drownded before he brought that sucker up. Any drunker'n he woulda drownded. Catfish weighed thirty-one pounds at Hubert's Grocery."

It was a familiar old story.

"That's my bathing hole, now, down by that old crossing on the creek," I said. "Haven't run into any catfish, though."

Three-quarters of a mile farther south along the road, with pasture and oat and wheat fields on each side, we came onto a WPA work gang, grading and regraveling a stretch of the school route road, north of old man Nahnahpwa's gate. They were putting in a new culvert for the old Comanche, too.

"I see my brother-in-law, there," Stud said as we approached the road workers. The brother-in-law was backed up with his wagon, ready to unload some gravel. He and Stud nodded to each other. "Government's givin' him a dollar thirty-five a day, for him and his wagon and team."

"Buys groceries," I said.

A little past those workers, we saw three others, working on the new culvert at the entrance to Nahnahpwa's place, as the old Comanche sat, bareback, on a little black pony, watching them. I pulled the car over and turned off the key.

"Let's ask old man Nahnahpwa about an airplane," I said.

Stud and I got out of the car and walked over to him, saying hello to the nearby workers as we passed them. The Comanche was wearing a big, unblocked gray hat, his long braids, on each side of his head, hanging down from under it. His face was smooth and coppery, totally hairless. In the Comanche way, he plucked out all his whiskers, eyebrows, eyelashes—everything.

I knew Nahnahpwa, having grown up with his son, both of us boxers in high school. I'd trained in the old man's barn, and I'd stayed overnight a lot at his house. I'd picked up some Comanche, back in those days.

"*Hah, matsai,*" I said in that language. Literally, take hold of it. I put out my hand to him.

"*Hah, mahduahwe,*" the old man said in greeting. He leaned over from horseback to shake my hand, making his dangling peyote-bird earrings wobble as he did so. He was wearing loose, blue overalls and high-topped black shoes.

"You know Stud Wampler," I said.

He did. The two of them shook hands.

How to pose my question to the old man? I couldn't remember the way you said "airplane" in Comanche. Nahnahpwa spoke some Spanish, I knew. His father had been a native Spanish speaker, captured as a boy in the early days by the Comanches, down around San Antonio, then raised as a member of the tribe. From the father, old man Nahnahpwa had learned a little Spanish. But I didn't figure he would know the Spanish word for airplane, "*avión.*"

So, I decided to try the question in English, a language the old man understood, some, though he didn't speak it. "You see an airplane early this morning?" I asked him. I flattened my right hand and flew it slowly around in the air, by way of illustration, my makeshift sign language.

The old man caught on at once. "*Hah!*" he said energetically. "*Puhetskuh nuh ohapti yuhtsuh ah punii.*"

"*Ohapti?*" I asked. Yellow? I'd caught that, easily, and the word for airplane, "*yuhtsuh*"—something that flies.

"*Hah, oor sa yuhtsuh tuhweh oha whyahkootauh nee nabunii,*" the old man said and used his hand to show how it'd flown, something like I'd earlier done.

I interpreted for Stud. "He says, yeah, he saw a yellow airplane in the sky, this morning, like a butterfly."

I shook hands with the old man again and thanked him. Stud and I walked around the workers, went and got in the car again, then headed on south.

FIFTEEN

The wire gate at the entrance to my uncles' place, a mile or so farther south from old man Nahnahpwa's, was already open. I turned in. Their old shack was down a rutted pasture road, east, about a quarter of a mile from the gravel school-bus road. It was backed up against the woods of East Cash Creek—but we wouldn't go that far. The fenced, twenty-acre oat field where the uncles had found the body was a little bit north of the pasture road, midway between the school-bus road and the uncles' old house. I cut over in the short grama grass of the pasture and drove to the field.

Stigler-Martin's black Packard hearse was already pulled up to the field gate, waiting there. Uncle Leroy and Uncle Joe Ray were standing beside the hearse, chattering like young squirrels to Greg Martin and his helper, a boy named Tyler. I drove up and parked next to the hearse. Stud and I got out. I'd gone to school with Greg Martin, a deacon-mannered undertaker with slicked-down hair—a pretty good guy, really. He and the boy crawled out of the hearse. I told Greg that he'd need a stretcher for the body because you couldn't drive into the oat field without knocking down too much of the crop. The young helper went around and opened the back door of the hearse and took one out.

"We-uns shut them hounds in the house, Okie, hon—keep 'em from botherin' nothin'," Uncle Leroy said to me.

"Good thinking," I said.

Uncle Joe Ray was anxious to get going. "This way to the dead man," he said, like he was a picture-show usher with a flashlight and proud to be in charge. He stepped over and took down the wire gate to the field, then stood aside so that Stud and I could go first into the field of swaying green oats, fully headed out, in the direction that he motioned. "Hit's out yonder—the corpse is—in the middle of them oats," Uncle Joe Ray said. He pointed down at the ground at our feet. "These here'n are the tracks that Leroy and I made. Ain't no other'ns."

We proceeded into the field, Stud and I out front, my uncles, Greg Martin, and the boy Tyler lagging back.

I made out the body when we were still ten yards away, and what I saw was a shock.

"Tobe Satville!" I said.

Stud and I moved closer to the dead man.

"Shit for breakfast!" Stud said. "Sure's hell Satville, all right, stud."

"Sure's hell dead, too," I said, kneeling down by the body.

There was quite a bit of blood around Satville's lifeless mouth. It was already dried and turning brownish. His left leg was bent above the knee at a crazy and unnatural angle, obviously broken—maybe, I thought, when the body hit the oat-field dirt a yard to the east, then bounced to where it lay.

"I figured, all right, before we got here," I said, "that we'd find out that the dead guy was pushed out of an airplane. No other explanation works for how he got where my uncles said he was without any tracks around."

"'Less he was brought by the Easter bunny," Stud said. He was still standing, looking down at the corpse.

"The Easter bunny doesn't fly," I said. I stood back up and looked around. "Even *he* would have left tracks."

"Ain't no tracks in any direction, except the ones your uncles made," Stud said. That was true.

I knelt down, again. "I figured, too, that the guy who dropped somebody out of an airplane would be Satville," I said.

"Now, turns out he was the *droppee*," Stud said. "We gonna have to earn our money, looks like, stud—go to sleuthin'.'"

"Big knot on the right side of Satville's head, here," I said, indicating. "Skin's broken."

Stud stepped around and squatted on the other side of Satville's body. "He didn't get that hittin' this red dirt," he said.

"Funny thing," I said. "I don't see his glasses around here."

"He wore thick glasses," Stud said. He patted the pockets of Satville's scuffed leather jacket, then turned the body back and forth. "Not here," he said.

We stood up and looked all around to see if the glasses might have bounced somewhere nearby. They were nowhere in sight.

"Y'all come on up," I said, motioning to my uncles and the funeral parlor guys, who'd all been hanging back—so as not to get in the way of our investigation, I supposed. They stepped forward. "Dropped out of an airplane—his own, most likely," I explained to them.

"Then, the airplane flew its own self away from here, Okie?" Uncle Leroy asked. "That don't make sense, hon."

"No, I meant that somebody had to dump him out," I said.

"Who do you think?" Greg Martin asked.

"Who knows, Greg?" I said. "That's what Stud and I've got to find out. But we're through, here. Y'all carry the body back to town and call Doc Watson, as usual, to come over to the funeral parlor and make out a death certificate." I turned back to Stud. "We oughta run back by and take a closer look at that yellow plane."

"Righto, Mr. Eversharp stud," he said.

We didn't wait for the funeral-home people to load the body. Stud and I said good-bye to my uncles and hustled on back and got in the sheriff car, then turned around and headed toward Vernon.

On the road into town, we were quiet for a while. Then, Stud said, "So, you're going to emcee the Easter Parade program at the school, tonight, are you, stud?"

"Yep," I said. "You going?"

"Thought I would, me and my wife," Stud said. "Nothing good on the radio, Saturday night. See you there, stud. Going with Audrey Ready, I reckon? Be honest, I'm kinda glad y'all are gittin' together."

"Em Hoffer invited herself to sit with me," I said.

"The big lawyer woman," Stud said. "What about the Easter *Pregnant*, down at the park—hope you two ain't goin' to that, afterwards?"

The sunrise Easter Pageant at Kraker Park was the "Easter

Pregnant" to a few irreverent locals like Stud. Every year, a goodly number of young couples rolled out their blankets on the grounds, there, and whiled away the night hours before the start of the pageant with something other than Christ's crucifixion and resurrection on their minds. And the claim was made by some Vernonites that a larger-than-usual number of local babies came into the world each January, exactly nine months after the sunrise pageant event—but this was never proved.

"Guess you could say I've got religion on the brain, Stud," I said.

"The big lawyer woman, too?"

"Not going to the pageant with her."

"The home-ec girl, huh?"

"What made you think of her?" I asked.

"Stud, I didn't think she come to eat with us the other day just to get you to emcee the Easter Parade program."

I didn't say anything.

At the southeast side of Vernon, I turned west on South Boundary and, before long, we were back at the little airstrip behind Moreland's Dairy. The yellow Piper Cub was still where it had been when Stud and I had stopped by earlier. We got out and walked through the gate, and, as we got closer to the plane, we saw something on the other end of the tin hangar that we hadn't seen before.

"The car Satville rented from Bart Suder," Stud said.

He was right. The green 1935 Chevrolet coupe had been pulled in close to the west end of the hangar. It hadn't been visible from outside the airstrip gate.

"Better take a look," I said. We walked over to the car.

The right-hand door was hanging wide open. Satville's

beat-up leather bag, some of his clothes, a few papers, and a pair of low-top brown shoes were strewn in the grass on that side.

"Somebody's cleaned this thing out," Stud said.

"Whoever pushed Satville out of the plane must have landed it right back here this morning and then rifled through Satville's stuff," I said. "Looking for the birth-record page Satville must have taken from the county clerk's office, more than likely, and, if Satville was the break-in guy at Doc Askew's office, too, for whatever he took there."

Stud agreed. I picked up the scattered papers from the ground and looked them over. Nothing from the county clerk's office. Taken already, I figured. But there was something that caught my eye.

"Look at this, Stud," I said. "Satville's diary, or calendar, or whatever you want to call it." I began to flip through the little book. Nothing appeared remarkable, except the name, "Kraker," famous in Vernon, that I noticed on one page. "Here," I said. "This past Tuesday. Satville's scribbled that he was meeting Elmo Kraker Junior at Kraker's office on Western Avenue in Oklahoma City. What do you suppose that was about?"

"Satville came down here to Vernon, right after that," Stud said.

He picked up the leather bag and looked inside. "Nothing in here of any use," he said.

"Somebody's already got what they wanted from all this stuff," I said.

The two of us gathered up all the litter and packed it into Satville's bag, to carry away with us. I got in Satville's rented car and put my hand under the front seat. I immediately found a crowbar under the driver's side and brought it out for Stud to see. He looked at it closely.

"Let's take this, too," Stud said. "Two bits says it matches the marks on the boogered doors at the courthouse."

"I believe it," I said. I closed the car door. "I'll call Bart Suder to come pick up his car. Let's take a look at the airplane."

Stud carried Satville's bag, and we walked back to the Piper Cub and circled around to the right side, to the open, fold-down door.

"Whoever pushed Satville out would have been in the back-seat," I said. The plane was a two-seater, one seat behind the other. Each seat had its own set of controls—throttle, joy stick, and rudder pedals. I leaned in.

"See anything?" Stud asked. He was standing behind me, under the high wing.

"Nothing in the backseat," I said.

I straightened up, then turned my attention to the front. Nothing out of the ordinary. I ran my hand beneath the seat. "Here's something," I said. I brought out a pair of thick, metal-rimmed eyeglasses. "Here we go, Stud," I said.

I stepped back from the plane. Stud and I looked at what I'd found.

"Satville's glasses, all right," he said.

"Right lens cracked, right earpiece bent in," I said. "That's where he got hit. That knot with the busted skin was on the right side of Satville's head. Blackjack."

"Backseat driver surprised that bounty hunter, all of a sudden, looks like, 'bout like I was at Askew's office," Stud said. "Coldcocked him upside the head."

"Knocked him unconscious, then folded the door down, banked the plane on its side, and dumped him out," I said. "Must not have been dead until he hit the ground."

"We're looking for an aviator, stud," Stud said.

"Somebody, probably, that got Satville up in the air by making a date with him, like a customer wanting a flying lesson or a ride." This was pure speculation on my part, but I was willing to bet that I was right.

"Last ride of all for Satville, way it turned out," Stud said.

When we got out of the sheriff car, back at the Billings place, Stud said, "Hope, tonight, all your women don't find out about each other, stud."

SIXTEEN

Admission was fifteen cents for students, a quarter for adults. The Easter Parade program, the annual Lions Club fundraising event to finance the sunrise Easter Pageant, was always a success. Entertainment competition in Vernon wasn't overly stiff.

I had to search for a parking place. The big blacktop lot, across Nevada Street, south from the high school auditorium, which served as the community meeting place, had been built as a project of the WPA, the federal public works program. I finally found a spot on the back side of the lot. I got out of the blue sheriff car, careful to take with me the black loose-leaf notebook laying on the passenger seat. Janeaster Parnell had earlier sent a high school girl to deliver the notebook to me at the sheriff's office. It contained my master-of-ceremonies script.

I crossed the street and walked quickly to the auditorium entrance, saying hello on the way to a couple of men I knew.

Em Hoffer was waiting, just outside the entrance door. "You spiffed up since morning, Flash," she said.

I was wearing my gray gabardine suit—"graveyard gray," Stud called it—and flowered tie. Later on, I planned to exchange my suit coat for the leather jacket that I'd stashed in my car.

"You look pretty good, yourself, miss," I said. She was wearing the khaki slack suit she'd had on that morning.

Hoffer said, "I bought the tickets already, before they were all sold out." She handed me mine.

"You're one of the cheapest dates I ever had," I said.

"How many have you had?"

"You're the first this year, matter of fact," I said. "Good baseline, though, to judge the others by when the rush starts."

She turned to go in, but I stopped her with a hand on her arm. "Em, I've got to tell you something. We found Tobe Satville this afternoon—dead."

"Dead? Where, Okie? How?" Hoffer sounded shocked.

"Out in the country, south of town," I said. "Early this morning, somebody talked Satville into taking him up in his airplane, looks to me like, then knocked him in the head from the backseat and dumped him out in the air. Two uncles of mine found him in their field. Stud and I went out there and identified the body, then checked out Satville's plane. It'd been landed back at the airport. Papers and stuff in his rented car had been gone through."

"Find anything important?"

"Crowbar," I said. "Probably what Satville broke into the courthouse offices with. But not the page he tore out at the county clerk's. My guess is that's what whoever pushed him out of his airplane, and killed him, was after. It was gone. His little calendar book was there. Nothing in it important, but there was a kind of interesting thing. Tuesday, before he came down here to Vernon, he had an appointment in Oklahoma City with Elmo Kraker Junior."

Hoffer seemed to think about that for a moment. "So, the bastard went to see Kraker, huh?" She went on, then, "Okie, who do you think killed Satville?"

"Somebody, a pilot, who was after the documents Satville stole that might reveal the identity of Lily Morgan's daughter, that seems pretty clear," I said. "Whoever it was probably also wanted to stop Satville, himself, from finding the girl, which he may have been about to do. You got any ideas, Em? Wouldn't be surprised if my deputy Stud Wampler doesn't suspect you, a little."

"Okie, surely *you* don't suspect me," Hoffer said. She seemed genuinely indignant. "I didn't like Tobe Satville. You know that. But I wouldn't have killed him."

"We're looking for a pilot," I said. "Your dad, you said, taught you everything, like a son."

"Not everything," she said. "Please don't think I did this, Okie."

I studied her eyes. "Okay, Em," I said after a moment. "But where's the money in this? That's what I don't get—unless it has to do with who the father of Lily Morgan's daughter was."

"You're on the right track, there," Hoffer said.

Just then, I saw Audrey Ready and another woman I knew coming toward the auditorium entrance—and Hoffer and me. I'd figured that I'd probably run into Audrey at the program, and I was kind of dreading it. I should have called her, earlier.

"How you doing, Okie?" Audrey Ready said warmly. I bent to

give her a hug. She was tiny, smartly dressed in a blue-twill suit with a calf-length skirt, her short hair neatly permanented. "This is my neighbor, Mrs. Bates." I shook hands with the middle-aged, heavyset woman. "I thought maybe you weren't coming tonight, you hadn't called," Audrey said to me.

"I meant to, but we've been working on a strange case at the office," I said. I felt self-conscious and a little ashamed about not calling her. I hoped that Audrey's feelings weren't hurt. I liked her. And I felt guilty about showing up at the Easter program with Em Hoffer, guiltier about the later plan for going with Janeaster Parnell to the sunrise pageant.

Audrey Ready turned to look at Em Hoffer, taking in the fact, I noticed, that Hoffer was wearing a slack suit. "And this is . . . ?"

"Excuse me," I said hurriedly. "Mrs. Em Hoffer of Oklahoma City, a lawyer, part of the case we're working on." I was aware that I'd emphasized, the "Mrs." Then, to Hoffer, I said, "Audrey Ready, the widow of my predecessor in the sheriff's office."

The two women shook hands, Hoffer extending hers first.

"What an attractive suit," Hoffer said.

"Your . . . slack suit, too," Audrey replied. She turned to the woman with her. "Well, Mrs. Bates, we'd better go in and get a seat. Call me, Okie. Don't be a stranger." The two women went into the auditorium.

I gently pulled Hoffer a little way over to the side of the entrance door. "You haven't been totally square with me, Em, about whether there's money, some way, in finding Lily Morgan's daughter."

"That's not right," she said. "I haven't held out on you. I would have answered any question you asked me. Lily Morgan's daughter, born out of wedlock, was the child of old man Elmo Kraker Senior of Kraker Oil Company. He died intestate."

"Intestate?"

"He didn't have a will," Hoffer said.

"I know what intestate means."

"Elmo Kraker Junior was held to be his only heir," she said.

"Good lord!" I said, letting this news sink in. "Whoever the girl is, then, if she's alive, she has to be rich, worth millions," I said.

"That's right, Okie," Hoffer said.

"No wonder Tobe Satville was looking for her," I said. "He must have planned on showing up with her in Oklahoma City and charging a percentage of her inheritance for finding her."

"That's what I figure, too," Hoffer said. "No doubt in my mind that Satville went to meet with Elmo Kraker Junior, like you said his diary shows, to try to shake Kraker down. Satville's a bounty hunter, after all—or was."

"Em, Stud Wampler might say that that was your motive, too."

Hoffer's tone, when she spoke up very quietly, seemed more sad than indignant. "Okie, I told you why I'm doing what I'm doing—trying to help a dying friend. The very reason I hadn't told you, before now, that Elmo Kraker Senior was the father of Lily Morgan's daughter was that I was afraid you'd think that I was just like Satville—that I was only after a share of the daughter's money. Looks like, now, I was right to worry about that. This hurts, Okie. First, you entertain the outrageous thought that I might have murdered Satville, myself. And, now, you hint that I might be no better than a bounty hunter like him."

"Take it easy, Em," I said. "Not saying I believe those things." I'd always thought of myself as a good judge of people and their motives, and I didn't want to think that I'd been wrong about Hoffer. "Come on, we gotta go in," I said. "I'm the emcee. But we have to talk some more about all this."

Hoffer started in with me, but she pulled away when I tried to take her arm.

"I'm sorry," I said to her in a low voice.

She didn't respond.

The Vernon High School auditorium was also the school gym and basketball court. There were five rows of fixed seats, like bleachers, on each side of it, north and south, with movable metal chairs set up in rows on the rectangular floor in the middle. The raised stage was on the north end. A heavy, blue velvet curtain was closed across it. On the curtain, in white, was the outline of a devil's leering face and, above that, the words "Vernon Blue Devils." The fifteen-member high school swing band, the Moonlighters, all dressed up in black bow ties and white jackets—handed down, I knew, from one year to the next—was seated down front, just below center stage.

The auditorium was packed for the Easter Parade program, nearly every place taken. But there were a couple of reserved chairs ribboned off, first row, left. A high school girl, apparently on the lookout for Hoffer and me, escorted us to those seats, then straight-pinned onto my lapel a white carnation that she carried. I took the seat on the aisle, so I could quickly get to, and up and down, the stage steps on that side to do my duty as the master of ceremonies. Stud Wampler and his wife, Ethel, matronly looking in a flowered dress, were just behind us, in the second row. I said hello and introduced Hoffer to Mrs. Wampler before I sat down.

"Wanted to be right close, stud, so I could fill in for you if you get tongue-tied," Stud said.

The program began. Good old Judge Dowlin, with his blond wig a little off center and wearing his green suit, probably his only one, went up on the stage from the opposite side and led the crowd in the flag salute and the "Star-Spangled Banner."

Afterward, when everybody had settled back down, the judge said, "Ladies and gentlemen, it is a great pleasure and a signal honor to present to you our fine master of ceremonies for this year's Easter Parade program, Cash County's own up-and-coming young sheriff, Mr. Ray Lee Dunn! Let's give him a big hand."

Black script-notebook in hand, I hurried up the stairs to the lectern at stage right. As the applause for me died down, the Moonlighters began a kind of swing version of "In Your Easter Bonnet." After a few bars, the music went softer, and slower.

I was nervous. In law school, we'd had to stand up when we recited in class. But I still wasn't accustomed to public speaking. I felt lucky I had the script to read that Janeaster, the kind of person, I'd found, who took care of every detail, had prepared for me.

I read, over the background music. "Welcome to tonight's annual Easter Parade program, sponsored by the Vernon Lions Club. Ladies and gentlemen, the Vernon Blue-Devil Glee Club."

The heavy blue curtains opened to reveal, at the back of the stage on semicircular risers, about twenty blue-and-white-robed young men and women, already in place and swaying slightly to the music. They took up the words: "In your Easter bonnet . . ."

They were good, I thought. But it was taking me a while to

get into the spirit of the program. The Lily Morgan girl was still on my mind.

Band music and choral words softened. Still at the lectern at the side of the stage, I began to read what had been written for me. "And, now, ladies and gentlemen, the first of tonight's two great style shows.

"These beautiful gowns you are about to see have all been designed and made by the young ladies who'll be wearing them. Leading off our first style-show contest is the Vernon High School home economics teacher who, we're all expecting, will receive a call, any day now, to Dallas for an audition with the Connor Model Agency there."

I figured that Janeaster Parnell, herself, had written my script. A little self-promotion never hurt anybody, I thought.

"Ladies and gentlemen," I continued reading, "how appropriate it is that the young lady who will begin this year's Easter Parade was actually born on an Easter Sunday, herself—tomorrow is her birthday—and, thus, the professional name which she has adopted for her modeling career. Ladies and gentlemen, Miss Easter Parnell."

The stage lights dimmed, the band music swelled as the chorus began to hum the Easter bonnet tune, and Janeaster Parnell—Easter Parnell, as she apparently wanted it—glided gracefully onto stage from stage left.

I'd read the script over, earlier. But the fact of Janeaster's Easter birthday, taken with her new professional name, suddenly hit me harder than it had before, when Em Hoffer had first tried to connect certain things at our Luden Hotel breakfast. I ran over everything in my mind as I watched Easter and waited to read my next lines.

EASY PICKIN'S

She was stunningly beautiful in a lavender off-the-shoulder, floor-length satin gown. Her shining black hair, crowned by a wide-brimmed white straw hat with a great lavender satin ribbon and bow, framed, I thought, a perfectly lovely olive-toned face. She carried a small bouquet of spring flowers. Out front, there was a low hum of murmured approval in the large crowd.

Easter Parnell took up the words of the song in a sweet soprano voice as the band played and the glee club hummed harmonically behind her.

She curtsied to the crowd when she finished. There was an exploding ovation, spiked through with loud cheers and sharp whistles of approval. Janeaster bowed and, while the applause died down, moved back and stage right, positioning herself to the side and in front of the glee club.

The group hummed, the band played. I read the introduction for the second of the young women contestants.

There were six of them in all, each in a self-designed and self-made evening gown of different style and color, every girl carrying a pretty bouquet of flowers. Three of the contestants wound up on one side of the stage, three on the other. At the last, they walked downstage and took a group bow as the crowd awarded them an enthusiastic and long round of applause.

There followed a dance number, an operatic duet, and songs from both a men's and a women's quartet. Then, I presented the second of the two style-show contests—the young women, again, showing their own dress creations. Once more, Easter Parnell was to be the star.

The lights went down, the Moonlighters struck up "Alice Blue Gown," which I'd read somewhere had been written for Teddy Roosevelt's daughter. Easter came out from stage right,

119

wearing a blue silk cocktail dress that buttoned in back and flared down to mid-calf. Her blue pumps matched the attractive dress, as did the blue purse she carried. She began to sing in her clear, fresh voice, moving across the stage with the same graceful poise as before. "In my sweet little Alice blue gown . . ."

I got goose bumps, or, as the Mexicans put it, "*El piel del pollo*," skin of the chicken.

The other five young women followed, in turn, each in a blue outfit of a different shade that she'd designed and made and each taking her place, stage left or stage right, as before. All six of the young models then joined the glee club in the final chorus of the song.

The heavy blue velvet curtain came down, then twice had to go right back up again at the insistence of a standing and cheering audience.

The Easter Parade program was a great hit. But things got even better for Easter Parnell. To a fanfare from the Moonlighters and fervent applause from the crowd, Judge Dowlin took the stage to report that the judges had awarded her both prizes of the night—the prize for the best dress or gown, as well as the one for the best performance.

But was Janeaster—or Easter—Parnell the long-lost daughter of Lily Morgan of Oklahoma City? We could hardly wait—Em Hoffer, Stud Wampler, and I—until we could get outside, to ourselves, to chew on that question. The minute we exited the auditorium, the three of us and Ethel, Stud's wife, bunched up in a little knot to talk, off to the right of the auditorium's entrance door. Every now and then, one or the other of us Vernonites spoke or nodded to someone we knew, coming out, but mostly we concentrated on the question before us about the Case of the Unknown girl.

"Is she the one, y'all think—Janeaster?" I asked.

Hoffer finished lighting a cigarette. "I'm persuaded. I haven't seen any documents, of course, but she's got to be the one. Calls herself Easter. Too many coincidences. Born, here in Vernon, on Easter Sunday."

"In 1919, that's true," I said.

Stud Wampler wasn't convinced. "I never heard nothing about the Parnell girl being adopted," he said.

Stud's wife agreed. "I clean house for Miz Parnell. I can't believe that Janeaster's not her blood child."

I voiced the suggestion I'd earlier worked out in my mind. "What do y'all say we not worry Janeaster with this, right now? This is her night. But tomorrow, when she and the Parnells are back from church, let's show up at their house—she lives with her folks—and find out, once and for all. Look at her birth cer- tificate, question the Parnells."

"Where do they live?" Em Hoffer asked.

"They're the two-story stone house at the east end of Ice House Street," I said. "But I'll come by the Luden and pick you up, Em. You can ride there with me."

A black cloud was developing toward the north. Lightning flashed, still a good way off. The thunder that followed was yet a distant rumble. Maybe there'd be a break in the drought we'd been having. The welcome smell of rain was in the air.

"Most important thing, stud," Stud Wampler said, looking at me, "we gotta figure out who pushed Tobe Satville out of his plane and killed him. And what about the break-in at Doc Askew's? Who did that—and hit me on the head?" He shifted his gaze to Em Hoffer, then. "Any questions you wanna answer, Miz Hoffer?" he asked.

"Ask away," Hoffer said.

"Tomorrow'll be soon enough when we get together at the Parnells," Stud said. "Comin' up a storm, now. All of us better pull up stakes."

Just then, a well-dressed and good-looking blond-headed man in his forties came out of the auditorium. He was wearing a dark blue jacket with a yellow tie, gray trousers, and black alligator slippers and was by himself in the stream of people still leaving. The stranger's gaze was on the ground, as if he was pointedly trying to ignore our little group on his left.

I knew at once that the man had to be Leo Castor—the lady-killer. I stepped over quickly and put a firm lock on his left arm, which, I found, was lean and hard in my grip. The man stopped and deliberately turned his hard blue eyes on me in a poisonous stare.

"Who are you? What are you doing in Vernon?" I asked. People shied around us, regarding the two of us with obvious curiosity as they passed.

Castor was not intimidated by me. For degree of meanness, I'd always found that there were two kinds of men, like there were two kinds of dogs. Most dogs that'd bark at you were easily scared off. They'd turn tail and run the minute you bent over and acted like you were going to pick up a rock. But a really mean dog, by contrast, would take an action like that as a signal to attack. Leo Castor was a mean dog. With his right hand, he quietly peeled my fingers from his arm, all the while continuing the angry glare.

He spoke. There was a sharp edge to his low voice. "The answer to your first question is, 'None of your damned business.'

The answer to your second question is, 'None of your damned business.'"

I stepped back. I wasn't afraid of Castor, tough as he appeared to be. I'd dealt with tough guys before. But I didn't have enough proof to arrest the man, right then.

He tugged down the sleeve of the arm I'd had hold of, shrugged himself back in his blue jacket comfortably, then without another word headed on his way.

Feeling a little frustrated, I went back over and rejoined our little group.

"Who the corn bread hell's *that* pretty-boy?" Stud Wampler asked.

"Never saw him before, but I'm certain that he's a guy named Leo Castor," I said. "Description they gave me fits. Been in Vernon since Thursday."

"Description *who* gave you?" Stud asked.

"Earl Munson at the depot, for one," I said. "And Solly—Salvador—the Mexican that sells tamales. They both saw the guy when he came in on the train Thursday. Munson called him a lady-killer. And, if he *is* Castor, I think he's looking for the same girl we are. Maybe feels he's learned something, here, tonight, too, like some of the rest of us do."

"Okie, what makes you think he's trying to find Lily Morgan's daughter—and why would he be?" Hoffer asked.

"A hunch on my part," I said. "First thing he asked when he got off the train was where Doc Askew's office was. Can't be coincidence. He wanted to get his hands on the girl's birth record, my guess. Second thing he wanted to know was the location of the airport. Some way, I think, he knew Satville was in town, too, wanted to head him off—or get him out of the way."

Stud wrinkled his forehead. "I seen that guy someplace before," he said.

"Spoke Spanish with Solly when he came in, said he came up from Mexico—Veracruz," I said.

"Mexico—that's real interesting," Em Hoffer said.

"Why?" I asked.

"Because Kraker Oil Company's got an operation down there—or did," Hoffer said. "There was a big story in the *Daily Oklahoman* last week saying the Mexican government had taken over Kraker Oil, with all the other private oil companies in Mexico. Story in the paper's what activated Lily Morgan to try to find her daughter. Talked to me about it, probably Tobe Satville, too, I'm afraid."

"Kraker Oil!" Stud said. "That's where I seen that guy. Antiunion enforcer, here, for young Kraker before the company pulled out of Vernon for good. Hard character. Sure needs watchin'."

"Why would Castor still be in Mexico if all the American oil companies got taken over?" I asked Hoffer.

"How do I know?" Hoffer said. "Cleaning up the last of Kraker Oil's affairs down there, maybe."

"I wonder if he's a pilot," I said.

"Wouldn't be surprised," Hoffer said. "Kraker Oil's got a plane. It'd make a lot of things make sense."

Learning of Castor's connection with Kraker Oil put pieces of the puzzle together for me, though not yet for Stud Wampler, I knew. He hadn't heard Hoffer's earlier revelation to me that the dead Elmo Kraker Senior was the father of Lily Morgan's child. The oil company connection made me more sure that Castor had been summoned up to Vernon by young Kraker to find the daughter, himself—and for no good purpose. There'd be plenty of time to explain all this to Stud the next day, I figured.

For the moment, I said, "What about me and you, Stud, collaring Castor at the Luden Hotel tomorrow and putting the squeeze on him—as soon as you and Ethel get out of church— say, around a quarter to one? We could all get together at Easter's place, then, at about one-thirty."

"Good plan, stud," he said.

We split up. I hadn't wanted to mention my later Easter Pageant date with Easter. I made it look like I was going to leave, too, but after Hoffer and Stud and his wife had moved off toward the parking lot, I detoured around to Main Street and entered a side door that led to the rear of the auditorium. I didn't think of my actions as deceptive. More like discreet.

SEVENTEEN

"Yes, Okie, I was born on Easter Sunday in 1919, just like your emcee script put it," Easter Parnell said. "No, I'm not whoever you're thinking about. Look at my birth certificate, if you want to. I'm not adopted. My parents, the ones you saw again, just a while ago, they're my real parents. No use your going on about this."

She was quite emphatic.

"All right, then," I said.

I would meet Stud and Em Hoffer at Easter's house after church the next day, Sunday, unannounced. We'd clear things up, once and for all, I thought. But, right then, I had to deal with Saturday night.

The two of us, Easter and I, were sitting in the front seat of the blue sheriff car, still in the parking lot across from the Vernon High School auditorium. I'd started questioning her while we were walking to my car. But I wasn't getting anywhere. I decided it was time to drop the subject for the time being and get going.

Earlier, backstage at the auditorium, I'd had to wait a good while outside the women's dressing room until her proud and fawning parents, and all the other well-wishers, had finally cleared out. I'd waited some more, then, until she'd changed into a brown skirt and a sweater set and given her mother her other stuff to take home.

Easter told me that she'd brought along a grocery sack filled with some fried chicken, a couple of ham sandwiches, two Baby Ruth candy bars. Hearty provisions for the night.

"Starving to death'd be worse than getting crucified," Easter'd said.

"Try telling that to Jesus," I said, then added, "I thought models had to diet all the time."

"Not me," Easter said. "I think God intended some people to be jockeys or models. Eat all they want to and still stay slim."

I'd carried her sack of food and put it in the trunk of my car, where I'd already stashed two quilts, a lantern, and a small ice chest of Coca-Colas.

In the car, I started the motor and eased toward the exit on Nevada Street. The parking lot was dark and largely empty. The storm cloud that'd built up earlier in the north had since grown larger and more general. I turned right at the exit, east. A bright flash of lightning illuminated the area, and I got a glimpse of a dark, old-model sedan, half a block back, sitting at the curb, pointed in the same direction I was. I thought nothing of that, at first—could have been anybody's parked car—until I noticed in my rearview mirror, as I turned north on Church Street at the next corner, that the dark car had begun to move forward, with its lights off.

It, too, turned north on Church Street, behind me, about

two blocks back. The car's lights were still off, but at corners where there were streetlights, I could see it seeming to be following. Down at the highway, I turned west for a block, then north, again, on the dark gravel road to Kraker Park.

"Not as much traffic as I expected," I said.

"People probably worried about a storm coming up," Easter said.

The road behind us was unlit. There were other cars. I couldn't tell whether the dark car was still behind us or not. But who the hell would have been following us—and why? I decided I'd better keep my eyes peeled and my guard up.

EIGHTEEN

As I drove through the entrance to Kraker Park, you couldn't see any stars in the sky because dark thunderstorm clouds were all around us, and threatening, though there was still no rain.

Elmo Kraker Sr. had built the park as a generous gift for Vernon, the place where he'd made his first oil millions. It was situated on sixty acres of well-mowed Bermuda grass, shaded by great, native pecan trees, along the banks of East Cash Creek. The creek serpentined through the park and was crossed by several swinging bridges. The whole acreage of the place was beautifully laid out and landscaped—here, weeping willows around a duck pond, there, large green junipers flanking cement-bordered beds of yellow jonquils, farther along, a fountain surrounded by varicolored tulips. Vernon called it "A paradise on the plains."

Visitors could skirt around the west edge of the park on an

iris-lined gravel road and eventually come to a great, grassy amphitheater in the park's northeastern corner. The outdoor auditorium was partly natural, but had been improved and enlarged by crews with horse-drawn, dirt-moving fresnos. The amphitheater sloped east, down toward a big elbow in the creek. A poured-cement platform was at the bottom, as a stage, back-dropped by a wall of flowering redbuds. The religious-based sunrise Easter Pageant, sponsored by the Vernon Lions Club, was put on there each Easter Sunday morning.

I drove around to the pageant site, stopped, back a ways from the lip of the amphitheater, and parked among the large number of vehicles already there—cars of all ages and states of repair, and disrepair—from Model-T and Model-A Fords to new Dodges, and even a few wagons and teams. Easter and I gathered our stuff from the car trunk and started down the grassy, half-moon embankment. Couples and groups with kerosene lanterns were assembled, here and there, on their quilts and blankets, seemingly well-provisioned with food and drink for the long wait before sunup. We picked our way among these clusters, the great majority of them Christian pilgrims, I figured, though there were some in view who looked more like good-time picnickers.

Way off to our right about thirty yards, just coming into the amphitheater from the opposite side, a well-built, dark-headed guy, accompanied by some other young men and women, suddenly stopped and glared at us. He was wearing a maroon-and-black football jacket with a big white "C" on the front. The young man caught Easter's eye, the same as mine, but she glanced toward him for only a second, I noticed, then quickly looked away. The guy hollered something at us, but two young men with him handed him a bottle of beer, then dragged him along.

"That Kenny Partin, the fullback up at Cameron College?" I asked Easter.

"Yeah. Looks like he's already had too much to drink."

"What's the matter with him, why stare at us, and yell at us, like that?" I asked.

"Who knows?" Easter said, and shrugged.

She and I walked down and to the left. We found an unoccupied patch on the slope. "Good place to make a nest, right here," I said.

Easter and I spread one of my quilts on the grass. We'd use the other one for cover, if we needed it. Spring nights could get a little chilly. We put down our food and drink. I lit the lantern with one of the kitchen matches I'd brought.

I surveyed the groups scattered here and there around us. A few appeared to be hitting the beer pretty hard, already.

"Some of these people gonna be asleep by sunrise, when the pageant starts," I said to Easter. "Resurrection may not come for them until about noon. Reminds me a little of the five foolish virgins in the Bible who went to sleep on the job."

"May not be five left around here by morning," Easter said. I must have looked a little shocked because she laughed and said, "Just kidding."

She broke out two Coca-Colas for us, then, and some fried chicken. We sat close together, eating. In a little while, she unfolded the second quilt and put it around our shoulders. I felt good, comfortable.

But that didn't last. There was a sudden blinding flash of lightning, followed closely by a booming explosion of thunder, and the rain that had been threatening all evening began to come down, as Stud Wampler would have said, like a cow pissing on a flat rock.

"Uh-oh!" I said. I quickly blew out the yellow flame of the lantern to keep the cold raindrops from cracking the hot globe.

All around us, people began to squeal and yell as they grabbed up their quilts and things and ran for the cars, to wait out the storm. Easter and I hurriedly did the same, making it to the sheriff car before we were soaked. We jumped in the front seat and threw all our stuff in the back.

The rain beat down on the car roof. Easter shivered, then reached over the seat and got the quilt that we'd earlier covered with. "Here," she said. "Let's put this around us again until we warm up."

We did. She snuggled up to me. I pulled my right arm from between us and, because there was nothing else to do with it, put it around Easter's shoulders, under the quilt. She turned her head toward me and raised her lips to mine. We kissed. One thing led to another. Very tentatively, I put my free hand on the front of her sweater. She took it in hers, but, instead of moving it away, slid it *under* her sweater from the bottom. We arranged ourselves so that the length of our bodies touched. Our breathing became heavy. The car glasses clouded.

Bonk! Bonk! Bonk! A fist pounded on the top of the car.

"Hey, what's going on in there?" a man's voice yelled loudly from Easter's side.

Easter spoke to me quietly. "Kenny Partin," she said. We both sat up and adjusted our clothes.

"What's the matter with him?"

"He's an ex-boyfriend," she said. "Bad mistake of mine. We

broke up, but he's drunk, sounds like, and wants to cause trouble. Let's just be still and he'll go away."

Little chance of that.

Bonk! Bonk! Bonk! Heavy pounding on the car roof again, strong enough to shake it with each blow.

"Hey, Janeaster, open up!" Partin yelled.

"Go away, Kenny!" Easter hollered back, apparently abandoning her plan about keeping quiet. "You're drunk. Go away!"

Suddenly, the door on Easter's side was jerked open. Too late, I was sorry we hadn't locked it.

Kenny Partin, eyes glassy, stuck his dark head and thick neck in. Rain splashed on Easter. "You whoring around again, huh?" he said loudly, close to Easter's face and slurring his words.

I spoke up. "Partin, we don't want any static. Go on back to your friends, now, and leave us alone."

He reacted contemptuously. "This county business—propositioning girls in your sheriff car?"

Before I could respond, the stocky football player grabbed a wad of Easter's hair in one of his hands and jerked her toward him. "Come out of that car!" he yelled. She shrieked.

I blasted from my door and around to the other side of the car in the hard rain. But, by then, Partin had drawn back his head and shoulders from Easter's door and had squared himself, ready for me.

Confronting him, I said, "This has gone far enough!"

"You're the one who's gone far enough," Partin said. With that, he shoved me backward with a beefy hand.

That did it for me. I took a half step forward and hammered a crushing right to his nose. He roared from the pain and swung wildly. I took the blow on my right shoulder. It knocked me back a step and almost spun me around with its force. But I straightened myself quickly and shot a hard left hook to Partin's nose again. He recoiled with the renewed pain of that lick. I planted my feet and started a straight right that I meant for Partin's jaw, but the jab to his nose had made him sort of rear up, so my extra-heavy blow hit him directly over the heart. The man dropped, faceup, like he was paralyzed. I stood over him as the rain continued to pour down. But he didn't move for a couple of seconds. Then, he began to gasp hoarsely, trying to suck in air, like the breath had been knocked out of him.

By then, Easter had jumped out of the car. She grabbed me by the arm. "My God, is he okay?" she cried, rain beating down on her head, as it was on mine.

But before she or I could think of what to do next, two guys who'd been hanging around in the background lunged over. They grabbed Partin and stood him up. One of them shook him by the shoulders. The other clapped him on the back, as you would a person choking. Partin began to get his breath back. He was wobbly, head hanging down. It appeared he might be sick.

"Come on, Kenny, we'd better get you back home," one of the young men said. They slow-walked him away.

Beside me, Easter appeared about to faint.

"Here, let's get you in the car," I said. I opened the passenger door and pushed the quilt over, then helped Easter in, closing the door after her. My right hand hurt, some. I went around quickly and got in the car on the driver's side. I raised a corner of the quilt up toward Easter. "Dry yourself off," I said.

I felt shaky, myself. It had been an unsettling happening. I started the sheriff car up.

"We're through, here," I said. "I'll take you home."

Easter offered no objection. I backed around and headed out of the park. She rubbed her hair and face with the quilt.

"I regret that I hurt that boy," I said. I really did. The whole episode, from start to finish, had disheartened me.

Easter said nothing. Neither did I until I'd calmed down a little.

Then, I wanted to know about Kenny Partin. "What was between you and that boy?" I asked.

Easter waited awhile before she answered. Finally, she said, "He and I went together for a while—pretty heavy. Met at a Cameron College dance. I don't know what I saw in him. Big football hero, I guess. Then, something happened, and we busted up. He's still mad."

Another question I'd been wanting to ask Easter crowded into my mind next. "You went to see old Doc Askew this morning," I began. This got a quick and shocked reaction from Easter.

She pushed farther away from me until her back was against the door. She pulled the quilt over in front of her, like a shield. "Who told you? How'd you know that?"

"Never mind," I said, sternly, glancing over toward her as I drove. "Why'd you go see Askew?"

"He's our family's doctor. Why do you want to know?"

"I don't believe that—that Askew's your family's doctor," I said. "He hardly practices anymore. And I don't think you went to talk with him about something like teenage pimples, anyway. You came out very upset." Easter was silent, almost sullen, I thought. She obviously wasn't going to say any more, on her own. "Askew used to be known for abortions," I said. That had been on my mind. "You're not expecting, are you?"

Her eyes went wide. "Expecting?"

"You are, aren't you?" I reached over and gently squeezed her arm with my right hand. "Aren't you?" I repeated. "Kenny Partin the father? That what you busted up over?"

"Why is any of this your business, Okie?" she asked.

"Because I admire you, and I'm concerned about you," I said.

She cleared her throat. "Dr. Askew said he couldn't help, or wouldn't," she said, finally.

"Abortion?"

"He was awful. Made me take off some of my clothes. Felt around on me more than I thought he should. When I objected, he dismissed me, said something like, 'Little lady, find you a man who'll marry you, or go down to Mexico, where you can get things taken care of.'" Saying this last, she imitated the doctor's grouchy voice.

"Abortion's against the law," I said.

"I'm going to be a model, Okie, and a baby without a father would absolutely ruin me—and everything!" Easter said. "Nothing's going to keep me from my dream."

She was silent, again. I couldn't think of anything else to say, either. But I was ruminating on something. Had I almost taken advantage of her, back at Kraker Park, or had she almost taken advantage of me? The more I thought about it, the more it seemed to me that Easter'd been the more aggressive one.

In town, I went east on Ice House Street and drove to the end of it, then turned left into the driveway of her folks' two-story stone house. It'd stopped raining. Farmers would be disappointed that there hadn't been more moisture in that storm, I thought.

"Your friendship's a great help," Easter said as she opened the door. "I'm sorry about the trouble."

"See you tomorrow," I said, though she didn't know anything about the planned confrontation meeting. I reached over and patted her on the shoulder. She got out and went into the house.

Once, after I'd headed toward the Billings place, I thought again that I was being followed by a dark car, but when I slowed to check my rearview mirror more carefully, I didn't see anything.

NINETEEN

Back home a lot earlier than I'd expected to be, I was still too worked up about all that'd happened that evening to feel ready to go to bed. A fast dip in East Cash Creek seemed like a good idea. It wouldn't turn out that way.

I quickly changed into Levi's, an OU sweatshirt, work shoes, and my John Deere ball cap, then grabbed up a ragged towel and a white bar of P&G soap. Outside, I didn't have to whistle for Scooter. He was ready and waiting by the back door. The night sky was clearing. There were patches of stars beginning to show and some general glow from a cloud-shaded moon.

With the dog alongside, I jogged out to the dirt street in front of the house, intending to turn east, there, toward the dead end with the school-bus road. But Scooter stopped and began to bark, looking back west on the dark street. I commanded him to shut up and come on, and we trotted together to the east end of the street. I jumped the bar ditch, there, and was in the act of climbing through the four-strand barbed-wire fence at the north end of old man Nahnahpwa's pasture, when, a hundred yards behind me, I heard a car coming in the dark. Suddenly, its headlights went on. I stood a moment to look, but because of the glare couldn't make out the car or the driver.

The car came on faster, the lights getting brighter. On the other side of the fence, I turned and jogged off through the wet pasture grass, down toward the creek, Scooter running ahead. Behind me, I heard the car stop at the bar ditch and fence. There was the sound of a car door opening, and, then, I heard the blast of two close-together pistol shots—*blam! blam!*

Somebody was shooting at me! I had no idea who. I had no idea why. Kenny Partin? Leo Castor? Main thing was that I wasn't hit—not yet. And it wasn't far to the East Cash Creek woods. I kept on going, but faster. An incident like that, I thought, was almost enough to make me reconsider my practice of not carrying a gun.

Behind me, I heard the car jump the bar ditch and ram the barbed-wire fence. There was a loud crack as a fence post broke off at the ground, whines and snaps as fence strands stretched and jerked loose from a corner post. The car was through the barrier. Then, with a gun of the motor, it took after me at great speed, the beams of its headlights bouncing crazily behind me as I glanced back.

I ran in earnest. Scooter was still ahead of me. The lights and the roar of the car motor grew closer behind us.

At the edge of the trees, I bounded down the old crossing road, and, just then, heard the loud crack of another shot from the oncoming car, only forty yards or so back. I saw a burst of dirt explode from the ground, in front of me and to the right, and dropped my towel and soap.

Spotlighted from the back by the headlights of the onrushing car, I reached the big oak tree and the water's edge, sped past Scooter, who'd stopped there, and let my momentum carry me right on into the pool to the left of the rocky crossing. The last thing I heard before going headfirst into the creek, losing my green-and-yellow ball cap in the process, was the car sliding to a stop behind me.

Underwater, my first thought was to swim rapidly across the creek, jump out, and take off, south along the other bank. But I realized instantly that whoever was after me was too close behind, would shoot me the minute I surfaced. My dad's catfish-grabbling hole under the oak-tree roots flashed into my mind.

None of these thoughts came to me in an ordered sequence, nor did all of them together take even a full second. They were rapidly firing sparks in my adrenaline-jolted mind.

Holding my breath underwater, I vigorously kicked left. My hands found the hole, a small, watery cave. I started in and, doing so, touched the slick tail of a big catfish. It instantly whooshed past me, out of its hidden nest. I propelled my body forward and took the huge fish's place. I raised my head to the top of the cavity and found the air pocket that I remembered my dad'd said was there. Thank God for it! Lying on my back, head pressed upward and breathing in and out rapidly, I realized that I could see some dim light, up through tiny cracks in the tangle of close-growing tree roots at the top of the hole.

I could hear my attacker, too, though all outside sounds were partially smothered.

"Come up—and I've got you," the voice said, apparently at the water's edge, off to the right, slightly, from my wet hiding place. The voice could have been Kenny Partin's, or Leo Castor's, or anybody's. I couldn't make it out enough to recognize it.

I heard two loud shots—what at, I didn't know. My hat, maybe?

Scooter hadn't barked, at all. Intimidated by the lights and shots, I figured. But, all of a sudden, I heard him just above me, huffing and beginning to scratch at the roots and dirt that were my roof. Apparently catching my scent, the dog yipped excitedly a couple of times, then set frantically to scratching again, right over me.

The attacker's footsteps came closer.

"What the hell's the matter with you, dog?" the muffled voice said.

Scooter began to yelp, again, then to scratch with even more frenzy. A shot suddenly exploded right above me. It cut one of the dog's yelps in half, stopping it instantly. I could smell the cordite.

The attacker had shot my dog.

Footsteps receded. I heard a cough, down by the water's edge. Then, I heard the attacker walk back to the car, slam the door, and start the motor. There was the sound of the car backing around, then taking off.

I stayed in my hole for what seemed like another fifteen or twenty minutes. Then, I held my breath, dived down, and swam out to the bank. I hauled myself up and sloshed my way over immediately to see about Scooter. It was too late. He was shot in the neck, from what I could tell in the dark, and was dead.

"Poor guy," I said aloud. The dog was the last link I'd had with my dad since he'd passed away. Now, that link was broken. I pulled the poor, lifeless body over closer to some fallen tree branches and used a few of them to cover him up until I could come back the next morning to bury him. I was sad as I went about that task. I was mad, too. I was going to make somebody pay. Shooting at me was mean enough. Killing my dog was just real sorry, as Mama would have said.

I went up through the pasture in my wet shoes, back to the school-bus road. There, in the dim night, I quickly surveyed the ruined fence and broken post, all flat on the ground where the car had run over them, coming and going. The car, itself, was nowhere in sight. I stepped over the barbed-wire strands, then jumped the bar ditch.

I decided not to go directly west on my dirt street to the Billings place. Instead, I jogged south a ways on the school-bus road, then crossed a fence to my right and came up on the back side of my barn. I kept to the darkest parts of the yard—under the trees, past the chicken house. I went around the west side of my house and crept quietly out to the dirt street in front. The car was definitely no longer around.

I circled to the back of the house and went in. Too late to go out looking for my attacker. Better luck in the daylight. I latched the back door, which was unusual for me, stripped off my wet clothes without lighting a lamp, and soon slipped into bed.

Before I went to sleep, I thought pretty hard about what had happened. My attacker could have been Kenny Partin, all right, but he didn't seem the type to come after a person with a gun. More likely, I figured, it had to be Leo Castor, the lady-killer and Kraker Oil enforcer, who'd shot at me. Trying to kill me, or maybe trying to scare me off. I was in his way, a threat to his plans for Easter Parnell. But—and I smiled involuntarily to myself as I thought this—if Castor *was* the one who'd shot at me, he was going to be pretty damned surprised to see me, alive and mad as hell, when I got hold of him at the Luden Hotel the next morning.

TWENTY

I didn't wake up until ten on Easter Sunday, really late for me. And, when I did, I was not in a good frame of mind. My dog was dead. I'd been shot at and had narrowly escaped from somebody who wanted me dead. And it didn't make me feel good, either, to remember my near-seduction of Easter Parnell, earlier the same night—no matter that she'd seemed awfully compliant. Nor did I feel proud about having beaten up the Cameron College football player, Kenny Partin, though the boy'd certainly asked for it. Losing my temper or getting in a fight—aside from prizefights, of course—had always depressed me, afterward. I never liked losing control.

At the kitchen sink, I poured some water out of the bucket into a wash pan and splashed it on my face. I meant to find Leo Castor that morning, check out the front of Reeves Martin's old Packard for the fence damage I figured I'd find there, then, if I was right, collar Castor and throw him in the county jail.

But, first, I felt I had to go bury my dog. I put on a pair of worn blue overalls and a work shirt, then pulled on some high-top tennis shoes. My other clothes and my work boots were still wet from the night before.

Outside, the sun was halfway up in a clear sky. It was an Oklahoma spring morning. A hearty westerly wind bore the pleasing scent of wet, green pasture grass. My dad had always said that April was the best time to sell a farm in Oklahoma. Everything looked good and green, then, and that was when you could get the best price. July, he said, with its hot, dry wind and parching sun, was the best time to buy. Prices were down, then.

I rushed my usual devotional exercise—facing east and bathing in the sun's rays with outstretched arms, saying thanks, reciting my Spanish-language psalm words. My sense of uneasiness was not dispelled, this time. The lonesome calls of a dove, down by the barn, didn't improve my mood, either. I hurried through my morning chores.

I threw a shovel in the back of my dad's old gourd-green Ford pickup. I'd held on to the little truck. Thinking, then, about Nahnahpwa's ruined fence, I also pitched in a hammer, some staples, and a little fence-stretcher boomer. I jumped in the pickup and headed toward the corner where my dirt street dead-ended on the school-bus road.

Old man Nahnahpwa and his wife, Lucy, were already there. He was dressed the way I'd seen him last—overalls, high-topped shoes, unblocked hat. She wore an ankle-length, small-flower-print cotton dress, made with large butterfly sleeves in the style of an old-time buckskin outfit. Both of them wore their gray hair in braids, as usual. They'd apparently ridden over from their house, bareback, on a couple of their ponies, his the black one I'd seen earlier, hers a roan, both grazing nearby. When I drove up, the old Comanche couple were working a handheld posthole digger, making another hole, next to where the post had been broken off the preceding night. I pulled over in the bar ditch and got out of the pickup.

We greeted each other in Comanche.

The old man said something further in that language. I caught the word "*pimaroo*." Cow. Lucy translated. "Old man says he saw our cows in the road. Then, he found this break in the fence." The two of them had apparently driven the loose cows back in, earlier.

Nahnahpwa spoke again. "*Possa tiabo!*" he said, with anger, then something else I didn't get. Again Lucy translated. "Some crazy white man run over my fence last night. We heard shots."

It was my time to talk, then. I paused frequently so Lucy could translate for her husband. I reported what had happened the night before, said that I'd come back to fix the fence and to bury my dog.

The three of us worked together. We put what was left of the broken post in the hole that the old couple had dug. It wouldn't be tall enough to reach the top wire, but it would do, for the time being. Using the little boomer, we separately stretched each of the four barbed-wire strands and stapled them to the corner post, again, and, then, farther back, the lower three strands to the reset, shortened post.

I got my shovel out of the pickup and excused myself. I headed on foot down toward the creek with the shovel on my shoulder. As I got to the edge of the woods, a blue jay, high in a hackberry tree, let out a shrill alarm at my approach and fluttered into noisy flight. Off to the right, a family of crows picked up the jay's warning signal and repeated it with loud caws, but they stayed in the top branches of two pecan trees, watching me.

Poor Scooter's body was under the branches where I'd left it. Close by, in some soft dirt, I dug a good, deep hole, then dragged the remains over to it, and then in. I felt like I should say a few words, but couldn't think of what. I covered the body with the loose dirt and tamped it down with the back of my shovel. My dad's dog was now in the ground, too, like him. One loss after another. I'd miss old Scooter.

I turned to leave. A cardinal—redbird, people called it— flew in and settled onto the top limb of a little persimmon tree very close to me. I knew that was supposed to be good luck. I felt I could use some.

I *was* lucky enough to find my John Deere ball cap. Before leaving the creek, I looked for it and found it at the edge of the water. It was wet, but I decided to wear it, anyway. As I went to put it on, I saw that there were two large bullet holes in it.

Back at the Billings place, I quickly made myself a little breakfast, some ham and eggs. I switched on the Philco battery radio and tried to find a news broadcast, but it was Sunday, and there was nothing on but church programs and an evangelical preacher: "Beloved friends, this is Dr. E. F. Weldon, with the old-time gospel hour and back-to-the-Bible broadcast. God is still on the throne, and prayer changes things!" I turned the radio off. I knew this was Grandma Dunn's favorite radio preacher. She sent him a dollar every month, the same day she got her old-age pension check. But he wasn't mine.

Finished eating, I washed the breakfast stuff and, afterward, shaved. I put on a nice pair of clean Levi's and a black suit coat, then shined my black boots and put on my best, medium-brimmed Stetson. It was Easter Sunday, after all, and we'd be calling on the Parnells, later on. But, right now, I thought, time to attend to Leo Castor.

Just then, the telephone on the kitchen wall rang—a long and a short. It turned out to be Crystal.

"Why I'm acallin', Okie, Loretta's bad sick—not gittin' better, looks like," she said. "We have to carry her up to Crippled Children's Hospital in Oklahoma City, Mama and me. May have to miss work a few days."

"Don't worry about that," I said. "But how are you getting there? Your old car won't make it."

Crystal's husband had left her with a rusted Model-A Ford that he'd used as a kind of carryall for grease and oil and other supplies for the field. The car needed a ring job, you could tell from the way it clacked, and the old tires on it were nearly bald.

"*Has* to make it," Crystal said. "Cain't carry my sick baby up yonder on the bus."

"Listen, Crystal," I said, "hold on. I'll bring you my sheriff car and trade off with you. I can drive your Model A while you're gone."

Crystal protested, but gave up when I insisted.

To get to her place, which she rented without the farmland around it, you had to go two miles west of Vernon on the Comanche highway, then a mile and a half north on a gravel road, almost to Lincoln Valley School.

I drove out there. The unpainted old two-story, four-room house sat up on yellow sandstone rocks, as a foundation. So many of the shingles on the roof appeared to have long since been blown away that I figured the house probably leaked like a brush arbor in the kind of rain we'd had the night before.

I parked on the north side of the house. Crystal's dad, bent over with a bad back, was out in the hog pen, next to the cow lot, slopping about a dozen shoats. I knew that with a wagon and team the old man hauled food garbage from Vernon cafés and fed out hogs with it. I waved to him as I walked to the kitchen door.

Crystal let me in. Lean and gangly in a faded cotton dress, with a flowered apron over it, she pushed back a loose strand of graying hair from her plain face and said, "Okie, you know Mama, don't you? We're fryin' up some chicken to take to eat while we're gone."

The white-haired woman, as tall as Crystal, but heavyset, shook hands with me. I was careful not to squeeze hard on her arthritis-gnarled hand. "Gitchee some coffee, Sheriff?" she asked.

"No thanks," I said. "Gotta go right back to town." I turned to Crystal. "The key's in the sheriff car. Should be full of gas, too. But here's a little something to help out on that." I got four dollars from my pocket, folded the bills, and held them out toward her.

"Okie, I couldn't," she said.

I kept my hand extended. She took the money, finally, and put it in a pocket of her apron.

"Much obliged, Okie," Crystal said. "Go up with me, and see what you think about Loretta. I just know it's typhoid."

She wet a washrag in a basin of water, wrung it out, then led the way up the creaking stairs to a bedroom on the second floor.

Lying on an iron bedstead and covered with a homemade quilt, the poor little girl, a fifth-grader at Lincoln Valley, was in bad shape, I could tell—round, freckled face flushed and chapped, hair soaked with sweat, eyes vague and listless. She hardly noticed that her mother and I had come into the room.

Crystal went over and bathed the girl's face with the wet cloth, then arranged it on her fevered forehead.

"I been givin' her aspereens and sponging her off, regular, with cold water, like Doc Watson said, but it ain't helpin'," Crystal said. "Her fever goes up so high that sometimes she's out of her head. Audrey Ready said that the high fever with the regular, slow heartbeat she's got is a pretty sure sign of typhoid. And she's the one convinced me to carry Loretta up to Crippled Children's. Like you, I ain't got no faith in Doc Watson, and, besides, he don't want people in his hospital that cain't pay nothin'."

"I trust Audrey Ready," I said. "She's a practical nurse. If she thinks the girl should go to Crippled Children's, then that's what I'd do."

Crystal leaned over and kissed her daughter on the cheek, then, straightening up, patted her on the shoulder. "Hon, you just rest easy, now, and we'll take out, pretty soon," she said to the sick girl.

We went back downstairs.

"Okie, you been a great blessin'," Crystal said at the door.

Outside, I waved to her dad, still in the hog pen, then climbed into the old Model A. I adjusted the levers on each side of the steering column—the gas and the spark—pulled the choke out a little and turned the key, then pressed down on the starter pedal on the floor. To my surprise, the motor caught with the third or fourth turnover. It clacked, instead of purred, but it'd do. I headed for town—and the Luden Hotel.

*   *   *

"John Carter—the man y'all are calling Leo Castor—has done already checked out," the thin-mustached, slick-haired desk clerk at the Luden said.

Stud Wampler and I had met in the hotel lobby at just about one o'clock, as we'd earlier agreed to do—though I'd meant to get there earlier, by myself, before everything else came up. Stud looked uncomfortable in a too-tight Sunday suit, with a belt in back and slanted cowboy-style pockets. I'd given him a quick report on the preceding night's happenings—not the part about Easter at the pageant, but the part about getting shot at and having my dog killed. I told him I thought that Castor was my attacker.

"Shit for breakfast!" Stud said.

We made our inquiry at the front counter and got the disappointing report about Castor—or Carter—having already left.

"Missed the son of a bitch," Stud said. "Knowed I should have let Ethel go to church by herself and come on over here, early."

I'd had the same feeling, ever since I'd gotten up that morning, especially after what'd happened to me at the creek the night before.

"Castor'll be back," I said, wanting to reassure myself as much as Stud.

"No he won't, Okie," the clerk said, intervening. "Paid and checked out, took his suitcase. That feller's a gone goslin'."

"How'd he take off?" I asked.

"Reeves Martin's car, I reckon," the clerk said.

"You see it?" I asked. "Any damage to the front?"

"Never seen it," the man said. "He never parked at the curb

in front, last night. Somewhere else, maybe on a side street. He took off out of here with his suitcase, afoot, at eleven-thirty, thereabouts."

"Headed where?" Stud asked. "He say?"

"Not a word," the desk clerk said. "They pay the bill, I ain't carin' where they goin'."

Stud and I walked out on the sidewalk in front of the hotel. I'd parked Crystal's rattletrap Model-A Ford at the curb. Stud's yellow Dodge cattle truck was right behind it.

"Trade down on automobiles, stud?" Stud asked.

I told him about Crystal's little girl and about letting her take the sheriff car to Oklahoma City.

"I shoulda drove her myself," he said.

From the depot, a block and a half southeast, we heard two short, loud blasts of a train whistle that announced the departure of the southbound Rock Island passenger train, headed for Dallas.

"Old Try Weekly," Stud said, idly, and took out his pocket watch to check the time. "One-oh-five."

"*¡Carajo!*" I said, disgusted enough to use a Mexican cussword. "Castor's probably on that train! I'm going back in to call Earl Munson!"

As I raced up the hotel steps and into the lobby, I heard behind me the outside clanging of the train bell, then the whoosh of the great iron wheels, spinning for traction, as the train began to huff and clack away from the station.

I quickly asked to borrow the desk clerk's telephone. He put it on the counter. Stud joined me just as I got the Rock Island depot manager on the line. But Earl Munson was not one to be rushed. Before I could explain what I wanted, he said he was busy, taking down a Western Union message from the wire, and I'd have to wait a minute. When he finally came back on the line, I asked him about Leo Castor, the man Munson had earlier called a lady-killer. Was he on the train just leaving?

"No, Okie," Munson said dryly. "Not on the one-oh-five." He hung up without saying good-bye.

Stud and I walked back out to the sidewalk in front of the Luden. "What next?" I said.

"We'll catch that dude, don't worry," Stud Wampler said. "Right now, we gotta go find out about the Parnell girl. It's that time. Then, you and me chouse around, afterwards—find Reeves Martin's Packard, see for sure if Castor's the one ran through the fence and shot at you, last night."

Good a plan as any, I figured. Behind us, Em Hoffer emerged from the front door of the hotel and came out to the sidewalk, where Stud and I were standing. "You still going to drive me over to the Parnell place, Okie?" she asked.

Stud frowned. It was clear that he had increasing doubts about Hoffer.

"Sure," I said to her. "Come on." Hoffer recoiled a little when we got to the rusted Ford.

"We going in this thing?" she asked.

"It'll keep you humble," I said. I let her in the passenger side and explained that the car belonged to one of my deputies, and the reason I had it. It took two slams on the tinny door, after Hoffer got in, to make it stay shut.

Stud pulled out in his yellow Dodge truck.

I started the Model-A motor and let out the clutch. We lurched forward. I had to raise my voice a little to talk over the car noise. I told Hoffer about how we'd missed Leo Castor, and how I thought he'd stalked me and tried to shoot me the night before. Killed my dad's dog, too.

"No doubt Castor's the enforcer for Elmo Kraker Junior," Hoffer said. "My guess is that when Tobe Satville went to try to shake Kraker down, Kraker got worried and immediately put in a call to Leo Castor, down in Mexico. Sent him up here to find Lily Morgan's daughter and get her out of the way, so she can't make a claim on the oil millions. This thing's getting rough."

"May get rougher, the amount of money involved," I said. "Worth millions to young Kraker not to have to split up things."

I drove west to the railroad tracks, then south toward the depot. "I want to whip by the train station, right quick," I told Hoffer. "See if Reeves Martin's car that Castor's been using might be there."

I saw at once, as soon as I pulled in to the depot, that it wasn't.

"Castor must still be in town, then," Em Hoffer said.

"Hope so," I said. "Got a personal score to settle with that son of a bitch."

I backed the car out and drove to Main Street, jogged north to Ice House Street, then headed east on it to the Parnells' two-story stone house at the end.

TWENTY-ONE

Good Lord, look what the Easter bunny's brought!" Mrs. Parnell said, cheerfully, when she answered the doorbell and opened the front door of her house to find Stud Wampler, Em Hoffer, and me standing together on her porch. "Come in, y'all."

Stud had gotten to the house first, but waited in his truck so that the three of us could go up on the porch in a group.

Mrs. Parnell was still dressed in the blue linen suit that I figured she'd worn to church that morning and was carrying a small, embroidered handkerchief in her chubby left hand.

She ushered the three of us into a blue-theme living room—blue overstuffed couch and chair, pastel-blue wallpaper, a blue-and-white rug of Chinese design. Over the brick fireplace was a great mirror with an ornate gilt frame and, opposite, behind the couch, a large still life of flowers and fruit in an old master's style.

"Have a seat, won't y'all," she said, then turned toward the kitchen and shouted in a hoarse voice, "Mr. Parnell, we've got company. Put on some more coffee." To us, she said, apologetically, "I've taken a little cold." She touched the small handkerchief to her slightly red nose.

Nobody sat down.

"No, ma'am," I said. "Thank you for the offer of coffee, but we don't want to be any bother. We'd just like to talk with you and Mr. Parnell, and Janeaster, too, for a moment, if we could, please."

"There's something we need to get cleared up," Stud said.

Mrs. Parnell's plump face took on a slightly quizzical expression. Her husband came from the kitchen, still wearing his tan Easter Sunday suit, with a pink tie and pink pocket handkerchief—both accessories, it struck me, about the same shade of pink as the man's smooth face.

"What is it, my dear?" Mr. Parnell said to his wife. His voice was sort of high-pitched. He turned to us visitors. "How are all y'all?" I thought he meant this last as a larger question: What are you all doing here?

I introduced Em Hoffer to the Parnells, and everybody shook hands.

"Could you ask your daughter to come down, Miz Parnell?" I said. "This concerns her, too."

"I'm sorry, Sheriff, but y'all just missed Janeaster—or Easter, now; it's her professional name," her mother said. "What's this about?" Her quizzical expression had become a worried one.

"Will she be back soon?" I asked.

"She's on her way to Dallas, right now, and her father and I are so proud for her—aren't we, Mr. Parnell?" the woman said. "A wonderful man, Mr. John Carter, from the Connor Model Agency, was already here in the house, talking with her, when Mr. Parnell and I got back from Sunday services, this noon.

We'd agreed that our daughter stay home from church. She was catching a cold, too."

"Uh-oh, rattlesnake done struck," Stud said, sort of under his breath.

"What?" Mrs. Parnell said.

My heart had sunk when Mrs. Parnell said that Easter had gone off with Castor, but I didn't want to flush the covey, yet, until I got more details. "Well-dressed guy, blond-headed, was he, Miz Parnell?" I asked.

"That's the man, Sheriff—Mr. Carter," Mrs. Parnell said. "And, oh, what a cultured man he was! So smooth. So suave, if I may use that word. I thought as soon as he introduced himself, it was no wonder he's working for a modeling agency."

It looked to me like the man probably could have gotten Easter's mother to run off with him, too, if he'd have wanted. "And what did he say he'd come to Vernon for—to see Easter?" I asked Mrs. Parnell.

"Exactly, Sheriff," Mrs. Parnell said. "He said that he had been extremely—extremely!—impressed with our daughter's written application and the photograph that she sent to the Connor Model Agency, but that her outstanding—that's the word he used, *outstanding*—appearance at the Easter Parade program at the high school, last night, was the frosting on the cake, as he put it. He was present, at the program, just to observe her, he said."

"Why come to get her on a Sunday—and an Easter Sunday, at that?" I asked. "What was the hurry?"

"Well, Sheriff, that did seem odd to me and Mr. Parnell, at first," she said. "But, then, Mr. Carter completely explained it. He said that they were thinking about putting Janeaster on a fashion-show runway in Dallas, right away, and, as a matter of fact—listen to this!—might, instead, take her on down to Mexico, where a big *international* fashion show is set to take place, very soon. Mr. Carter apologized for the great rush, but 'Time is of the essence,' he said—those were his exact words, isn't that right, Mr. Parnell?"

Standing at her side, Mr. Parnell said, "That's right, Mother."

"Where in Mexico?" I asked.

"Let's see, what did he say, Mr. Parnell?" she asked her husband.

"Veracruz," he said.

"Veracruz, that's it!" Mrs. Parnell said. "Thank you, Mr. Parnell. And let me see, Sheriff, he even said the name of the hotel . . . Something like Mogumbo."

"Mocambo?" I asked. I'd had two prizefights in Veracruz.

"Mocambo—that's the hotel," she said. "We're so very proud of Easter! She's dreamed of this, becoming a model, practically since she was in grade school—and now it's coming true. It's all so wonderful!"

"So, Easter packed and went with him?" I asked.

"Packed one suitcase," Mrs. Parnell said. "Mr. Carter said they'd send for the rest of her things, later. And he wanted to see her birth certificate, said he wanted to be sure that she was eighteen, legal age for a girl. We got out one of our two copies of it and gave it to him. Put it in his pocket. He seemed especially impressed, looking at her birth certificate, that she was born on Easter. He repeated her birthday twice to himself—April twenty, 1919."

"What about Easter's teaching responsibilities?" I asked. "She think about that before leaving?"

"Oh, yes, she called Mr. Hulbert, the principal, at his home, and he said he'd get Mrs. Grimes, who substitutes, to take care of Easter's classes," Mrs. Parnell said.

Stud spoke up then. "This John Carter, as you call him—man show y'all a card, Miz Parnell, to prove he was from the Connor Model Agency, for sure?"

"Why, is something wrong?" Mrs. Parnell's forehead wrinkled. She looked at each of us and got no reassurance from our expressions. She put the little handkerchief to her nose.

"A card, Miz Parnell?" I asked. "Did the man show you any identification?"

Mrs. Parnell didn't answer. She began to twist the handkerchief in her hands.

Her husband filled in for her. "No card," he said in his high voice. Pausing, then, obviously beginning to see the potential problem, he added, almost under his breath, "Jesus, Joseph, and Mary!"

"You know Janeaster—Easter," Mrs. Parnell said. "She was so excited. The man looked ... substantial. He was well-dressed. Oh, my God, have we done something terrible?" A sob came from her throat.

Mr. Parnell put his arm around his wife's ample waist. "Sit down, Mother," he said soothingly.

"Let's all sit down," I said. "Time for serious talk."

Stud Wampler, Em Hoffer, and I arranged ourselves on the blue couch, me in the middle. Mr. Parnell steered his wife to the matching overstuffed chair to the right, then dragged over an antique-looking cherry-wood chair for himself. Placing it next to his wife, Parnell sat down, then reached over to take her right hand in both of his.

I leaned forward, toward the Parnells. "We've got to ask you both a very blunt question—and I need a straight answer," I said. "Is Easter your own natural child, your flesh and blood, or is she adopted?"

"Oh!" Mrs. Parnell cried out. She put the little handkerchief to her eyes.

Her husband withdrew a pink hand from hers and patted his wife on the shoulder. "Now, don't get upset, Mother," he said. Then, to me, he said, sounding a little put-upon, "What does that have to do with anything, Sheriff? If you want to see the other copy of our daughter's birth certificate, you surely can."

"Yes, please," I said. "We'd like to." That would be a good starting point, I thought.

Mrs. Parnell stood up, Mr. Parnell, too. "Well . . ." he said. He took his wife by the arm and guided her from the room. They were back after only a couple of minutes. Mrs. Parnell had the document in her hand. She handed it to me.

"You'll see that Mr. Parnell and I are shown as Easter's natural parents," she said.

Stud, Em Hoffer, and I huddled on the couch to look at the birth certificate, together. The Parnells reseated themselves.

"Askew was the doctor, all right," Em Hoffer said. "And the girl was born April twentieth of 1919—Easter Day." She was talking to me and Stud more than to the Parnells.

"That's why we named her Jan*easter*," Mrs. Parnell said.

"But, Miz Parnell, this birth certificate doesn't tell the real story, does it?" I said, looking sternly at her, first, then her husband.

Neither of them could meet my gaze for long. They turned to look at each other, briefly, then both dropped their gazes to Mrs. Parnell's hands, twisting in her considerable lap. Their actions were answer enough to my question, I thought.

"Let me tell you what we already know, folks," I said. "The real name of the man who introduced himself to you as John Carter is Leo Castor. He has nothing whatsoever to do with the Connor Model Agency of Dallas. That was just a dodge."

"Not with the Connor agency?" Mrs. Parnell asked, her voice breaking.

"No, ma'am, not at all," I said. "I think Castor went to the Easter Parade program, last night, just to observe Easter Parnell and find out more about her, that he heard the Connor agency's name for the first time during the program and learned that Easter was expecting a call from them. He showed up, here, this morning, then, claiming he was a Connor agency representative as a way to get Easter to go off with him."

"Oh, my heavens!" Mrs. Parnell said.

I continued. "We suspect that Castor was sent to Vernon to try to track down the long-lost daughter of an Oklahoma City woman, Lily Morgan, and that, one way or another, he decided that Easter was the young woman he came to look for. Castor's a tough customer, Miz Parnell. I hate to alarm you, but it looks likely that he's now run off with Easter to get her out of the way."

"Why would he do that—run off with Janeaster, as you put it?" Mrs. Parnell asked, her voice unsteady. She turned to her husband. "Oh, my God!" she said.

Em Hoffer answered. "Because the right girl could make a claim on millions, Mrs. Parnell. The mother is Lily Morgan—but I'm sure you know that. She's a friend of mine, a beauty-parlor operator in Oklahoma City. Doesn't have a dime, and I'm afraid the poor thing has only a short time to live, too. The father—and I doubt you know this—was Mr. Elmo Kraker Senior, now deceased, the founder of Kraker Oil Company."

The Parnells turned toward Hoffer, wide-eyed, seeming too stunned for the moment by what Hoffer had said—and what she appeared to know—to respond. But there was a quick reaction from Stud Wampler. He snapped around to look at Hoffer, first, then at me.

"First time I heard about old man Kraker bein' the daddy," he said, clearly irked.

"I was going to tell you, Stud," I said. "Em just told *me* that, last night."

Hoffer leaned out around me to address Stud, directly. "I'm a friend of Lily Morgan, as I told y'all," she said. "Lily told me that she was working for Elmo Kraker Senior in his Oklahoma City office when he got her pregnant. He wouldn't marry her, but did transfer her down here, to Vernon, for her last months— the company had an office, here, in those days, of course—and he arranged for Dr. Askew to deliver the baby, where nobody in Oklahoma City would know about it. She was too far along for him to do anything else. Old man Kraker was, sure enough, the father of Lily Morgan's daughter. I've got his own letters that he wrote Lily, as well as her affidavit and some pictures that prove it. I admit, Mr. Wampler, that I wanted to avoid telling you and Okie as long as I could about the Kraker inheritance angle. I didn't want you to think that I was like Tobe Satville, just trying to make myself some money out of this."

"So, Miz Hoffer," Stud said, "when Satville found out that Lily Morgan's long-lost daughter was rich, he thought he'd found a bird nest on the ground, easy pickin's."

"Exactly," she said. "The old man died intestate—without a will—and the younger Kraker, held to be his only heir, got everything."

"You think, then," Stud went on, "that this pretty-boy, Castor, who, I suddenly remembered last night, used to work—probably still does—for Kraker Oil Company, was ordered up here from Mexico by Elmo Kraker Junior?"

"I do," Hoffer said. "That calendar of Tobe Satville's that you and Okie found showed he'd met last Tuesday with young Kraker. That alerted Kraker, I think, that Lily Morgan's daughter, a new heir he was going to have to share his father's fortune with, might be about to be found. I think he immediately summoned Castor up here to—"

Stud interrupted her. "To somehow get the Parnell girl out of the picture, so she can't claim her inheritance, her part of the old man's estate and the oil earnings? Is that it?"

"I'm afraid that's it," Em Hoffer said.

"Do what with her?" Stud asked.

Mrs. Parnell gasped.

"He's sure not just taking her to Dallas," I said. "That wouldn't get her out of the picture, as you put it, Stud. To me, it's suddenly clear as can be that Castor's gonna take Easter back to Mexico—get her out of the country altogether, and permanently."

"Oh, my God!" Mrs. Parnell said. She began to cry.

"The truth, now, Mr. and Miz Parnell," I said to the alarmed and increasingly distressed couple. "The time for covering things up is over. Was Castor right in picking out Easter as the daughter of Kraker Senior and Lily Morgan?"

Easter's father began, hesitantly, in his high voice. "The truth is—"

"Let me tell it," Mrs. Parnell said, recovering her composure a little, and interrupting.

"Yes, go ahead, dear."

She dabbed at her eyes with the small handkerchief. "Well, here's what happened. Mr. Parnell and I were living in Archer City, Texas—south of here, across Red River, you know. We had a dry goods store there. We lost a baby. A beautiful little girl. Cord wrapped around her neck, poor little thing. Cesarean— but it was too late. The baby didn't survive, and I wound up unable to have any more children. We heard about Dr. Askew, up here in Vernon. People said you could pay him and get a baby, which we were desperate to do. We drove up to see Askew. We didn't like him, personally, but we were delighted when he said he'd call us the next time he had a baby that the mother didn't want. He said it'd cost us three hundred dollars. We went home and put aside the cash in an envelope, to be ready. Pretty soon, he called us, just like he said he would. We drove up and stayed in Vernon, that time, for two days, but, unfortunately, the baby we were going to get didn't live. So, we had to go back to Archer City, empty-handed. In the meantime, Mr. Parnell and I, from our trips here, began to see a lot of potential in Vernon. The oil boom was on. Archer City, we thought, was dying on the vine. We decided to relocate here, if we could find a store to buy. Before long, we did. We approached the Markhams, an older couple—y'all might have known of them—and they sold us their dry goods store and agreed to let us pay it out. We started closing down our store in Archer City and also found this house to buy, up here in Vernon."

"And that's when—" Mr. Parnell cut in.

"And that's when," his wife continued, raising her voice a little to override his, "Dr. Askew called and said he had a baby for us, or would have, in a short while. Said the mother was, like you know, a young unmarried woman from Oklahoma City,

Lily Morgan. We never met her. We laid out baby clothes from the store we were closing. And on Easter Sunday of that year, which was 1919, we got a call early that morning from Mrs. Askew, the doctor's wife, and she told us to come to their clinic, as soon as we could, with three hundred and fifty dollars in cash. They'd raised the price fifty dollars. Mr. Parnell and I decided not to argue about that. We were dying to get a baby. So, we arrived at the clinic a little after noon, and Mrs. Askew handed the baby right out the clinic door to us. We gave her the money. She said that she would fill out the birth certificate form, showing *our* names, as if we were the real parents, and using the address of this house, here, as our residence, although we hadn't moved in, yet. We told Mrs. Askew to put down 'Janeaster Mae' for the baby's name. We thought it up on the spot. My own first name is Janice."

I looked at Em Hoffer, then at Stud. "Now I get it," I said. "That's why the county clerk's records made it appear that so many people came from out of town to have their babies, here in Vernon. They didn't come to *have* their babies here, they came to *get* them here—and the out-of-towners were falsely shown as the natural parents. That's why, too, Janeaster—Easter—herself, didn't show up in the court clerk's records as adopted. There was no adoption."

"Baby-selling!" Stud said with disgust.

"It's a crime," I said.

"Oh, my God!" Mrs. Parnell said, again.

A broken record, I thought. "We're not after you two," I said. "But what we've got to worry about is finding Easter and this man Leo Castor—and quickly. Castor came here to do young Elmo Kraker's dirty work—I'm more and more sure of it.

Elmo Kraker Junior thought he'd inherited everything. Knows it'll cost him millions, now, if Easter turns up and presses a claim."

"What are you saying?" Mr. Parnell asked. His high voice had become as shaky as his wife's. "Do you think they might . . . do harm to our daughter?"

I stood up from the couch. "Not if we can help it," I said.

Hoffer and Stud quickly got to their feet, too.

The Parnells rose slowly. "What are we going to do?" Mrs. Parnell asked plaintively. She was very distraught. "Can y'all do something?"

"We've got to go after them—bring Easter back," Hoffer said. "I certainly am. Promised Lily Morgan I'd find her daughter. Now we have, we can't just stand still and let her be kidnapped."

"But how'd they leave—train? Car?" My question was directed to Hoffer, but Mrs. Parnell answered.

"Airplane," she said.

"Airplane? Whose?" I asked.

"His own, he said," Mrs. Parnell answered. "Flies all the time for his company, he said. Said he was an ace in the war."

"Castor is an aviator," I said to Hoffer and Stud Wampler. "It was an aviator that murdered Tobe Satville."

"Yes, he said he was an aviator," Mrs. Parnell continued. "I was impressed that he had an airplane. Said he'd left it, out at the airstrip at Moreland's Dairy."

Mr. Parnell spoke up in his high voice. "Sheriff, I pray that you can bring our little girl back, safely."

"We're going to die trying," I said.

"Hope not," Stud said.

TWENTY-TWO

I jumped up from the Parnells' couch. Stud Wampler and Em Hoffer, too, were ready for action. The Parnells got up more slowly.

"We don't have any time to lose," I said to the Parnells. "Where's your telephone?"

Mr. Parnell pointed toward the door that led off the dining room to the study. Hoffer, Stud, and I followed him there. Mrs. Parnell came along behind.

The upright telephone was on a heavy oak desk. I sat down and jiggled the earpiece cradle to get central, then asked her to connect me with Jeff Moreland's home, next to the dairy. The Parnells, Stud, and Em Hoffer hovered near me, in a standing semicircle.

Jeff Moreland answered, right away. "Hey, Okie, I was about to call you," he said after we said hello. "That little yellow Piper Cub took off, not too long ago. You said to call you, if it did, but

I got busy puttin' some raw eggs down the throats of a couple of calves of mine that've got the scours. Sorry."

"That's all right, Jeff," I said. "You see who it was that left in the plane?"

"Man and a young woman," he said. "I was over at the barn, so I couldn't make 'em out too well."

Turning away from the telephone mouthpiece for a moment, I said to Stud and Hoffer, "Castor took off in Tobe Satville's Piper Cub, just as I kind of figured."

Back to the mouthpiece, I said, "Jeff, the girl seem to be pulling back, or the man dragging her or forcing her to get in the plane?"

"Naw, Okie, I couldn't say that," Moreland said. "She looked like she was right friendly with the man, matter-of-fact, what little I saw of the two of them. He didn't push her in the plane. She got in on her own, crawled in the backseat. I don't know if he set the brakes, or she held 'em with her feet. Whichever, man cranked the propeller, then ran around and hopped in the front seat—and off they went, headin' southeast."

"Castor put any gas in the plane, out there?" I asked Moreland. "He make it to Dallas, you think? I figure that's where he's headed, right now."

"No gas," Moreland said. "If he wants to get to Dallas, I reckon he'll have to stop, first, over at Wichita Falls, soon's he crosses Red River, and fill up."

"Know the fixed-base operator at Wichita Falls?"

"Guy named Cutler," Moreland said.

"Telephone him, long distance—I'll pay the charges," I said. "Find out if the yellow Piper set down there."

Moreland said he would.

"You see what kind of car the man and woman came out there in?" I asked him.

"Black, old model," he said. "Packard, I think."

I turned to my audience. "Reeves Martin's car." Back to the mouthpiece, and Jeff Moreland, I said, "Front end of that car boogered up?"

"Couldn't tell from a distance," he said. "Want me to run look?"

I said I did.

Our little group stood idle, quiet, as I held the earpiece of the telephone and waited.

Jeff Moreland was breathing heavily when he came back on the line. "Boogered up like a son of a bitch!" he said. "Fresh dents, grill bent in, lots of bad scratches. What'd he run into?"

"Barbed-wire fence, I figure," I said. I turned to Stud and Hoffer. "Castor's the no-good bastard that tried to shoot me last night, and did kill my dog!" I said. "I'm not about to let him get away with that. I'm going to hunt him down, wherever he goes, even if it's Mexico, and when I find him, I'm gonna drag his sorry ass back here. I'll bring Easter back in the process."

I turned back to the telephone, then, and popped a question to Jeff Moreland that I'd had in my mind, all along, ever since Mrs. Parnell'd said that Castor was leaving Vernon by airplane. "Jeff, what about me using your Waco?" I asked. "County'll pay you rent—or I will, if they won't."

I glanced over at Stud and Em Hoffer. Both of them looked surprised by my question on the phone.

"Where you aimin' to go?" Jeff Moreland asked. "I can't leave here, myself, right now. Worst thing about a dairy. Gotta be here for milkin', twice a day. You know that, Okie."

"I want to fly the Waco myself," I said. "Gotta go after that guy that took the Piper Cub. A murderer and a crook—kidnapper, too."

"How far you looking to go?"

"Maybe down into Mexico—far as Veracruz," I said.

"Mexico?" Jeff Moreland said hesitantly. "Okie, I don't know about that."

"Look, Jeff, it's a matter of life and death," I said. "And not like when people say that in a picture show. This is real! That girl's life could depend on us finding her and getting her away from that man. And I aim to put him on trial, back here in Vernon, for trying to kill me and for some other bad things he's done."

"You mean, you planning, yourself, to fly the Waco?" Jeff asked. "You up to that?"

"I'm not checked out on it, of course," I said. "But you, yourself, say how easy that plane is to fly, and I flew it a little that day with you, remember, from the right seat. You said I was a natural."

"You *are* a natural, Okie," Moreland said, then paused. "Well," he said after a moment, "I'm gonna do it, against my better judgment—if that guy's as awful as you say and things are as scary as you say they are for that girl. Just hope I'm doing the right thing."

I told him he was and thanked him, then asked him to top off the Waco's tank with gasoline, said I'd be there as soon as I could.

I hung up the receiver and turned to Hoffer and Stud, angry and worried. I said, "Smooth son of a bitch—Castor—talked Easter into going with him in Tobe Satville's plane—stole it!"

"Really think you can fly that plane, Okie?" Hoffer asked. "My thought was that we'd go after them in my car."

"Take too long," I said. "God knows what Castor's up to, but we've got to hurry if we're gonna get there before it happens."

The Parnells were in such a distraught state when we left that neither of them could hardly talk.

Outside at the curb, Stud Wampler expressed some skepticism about my plan to go after Castor. "Stud, you won't have no more authority, down there in Old Mexico," he said to me, "than General Pershing did when he chased Pancho Villa across the border. Another thing, where's the kidnapping at, if that girl's went on her own? What's Marsh Traynor gonna say? County commissioners gonna pay your way down to Old Mexico?"

"For sure, we gotta go see Traynor," I said. "But whatever he says, I'm after Castor—out of my jurisdiction as sheriff or not. No telling what the man's got planned for Easter—even white slavery in Mexico, I hate to say." I not only hated to say it. I hated to think it.

"How can you be sure Castor's headed to Veracruz?" Stud asked.

"Castor told Solly, the Mexican tamale guy, that he'd come up to Vernon from Veracruz," I said. "Told him in Spanish. No reason to think anyone else would ever find that out. Veracruz makes sense for Kraker Oil's operations, too. It's in the heart of Mexico's oil patch. And, then, there's the fact that Castor mentioned Veracruz to Mrs. Parnell. I know that hotel—the Mocambo. Kind of a luxury place for the American oil crowd."

"What if he's just going to Dallas?" Stud asked.

"No doubt he'll *stop* in Dallas," I said. "Has to gas up, again, there, if nothing else. But he won't stay. Jeff Moreland's Waco's faster than that Piper Cub Castor's flying. We can get to Dallas not long after he does. So, maybe we can tree him there—and won't have to go to Mexico. Let's hope."

"I'm going with you, Okie," Hoffer said.

"Figured you would, Em," I said. Then to Stud, I said, "You drive Em to the Luden Hotel, so she can get her suitcase. Then take her on over to Marsh Traynor's house—on East Kansas. I'll grab some things together at my place and meet y'all there." As an afterthought, I said to Hoffer, "Bring an Oklahoma/Texas map from your car, if you've got one."

"Stud, I'll carry her to Marsh Traynor's and meet you there, like you said," Stud Wampler said, "but I can't guarantee you Traynor's gonna agree for you to go."

"I'll go anyway," I said.

"What about my car?" Hoffer asked.

I told her to leave it at the hotel. She and Stud took off in his Dodge truck. I crawled into Crystal's Model A and headed for the Billings place.

I went into my bedroom to pack. I put a second pair of Levi's and a matching jacket in my accordion-style briefcase from law school. Back in the kitchen, I got down an old Roitan cigar box from the cabinet. It held half my dad's stash of money. I'd given the other half, after he died, to my sister, Alene, who lived in Long Beach. I took out some folded bills—something over a hundred dollars—and a copy of my birth certificate. The money went in my billfold, the birth certificate and the shaving stuff that I scooped up from the side of the sink into the briefcase.

Then I cranked up central on the wall telephone and had her connect me with Audrey Ready's house.

"Happy Easter, Okie," Audrey said when I said hello. "Sorry we didn't see more of each other at the Easter Parade, last night."

"Me, too," I said. Then, I gave her a brief report about Easter Parnell and how she'd been carried off by Leo Castor—a murderer who'd tried to kill me—and that I was, myself, about to take off after him, perhaps as far as Mexico.

"I wish you wouldn't do it, Okie," she said. "I'm really afraid for you, going after that guy by yourself."

"Don't worry," I said. "I'll have some help."

"Stud going?"

I didn't say anything, right off.

"Not that Oklahoma City lawyer woman?" Audrey said. "She's not going with you?"

"She's a friend of Easter's real mother," I said. "On the case, with us."

"Traveling alone with a woman?" Audrey said. "You think that's wise?"

"Don't worry, Audrey," I said. "I'll be careful—in all ways. And I'll see you when I get back."

Out the door, I jumped into the Model A, only to find that I'd earlier left the key on. The battery was as dead as last year's cotton stalks.

I got the crank from the car trunk. I turned on the key and moved the spark and gas levers on the steering column to the start position, pulled the choke out, put the gearshift in neutral and set the emergency brake, then went around in front and fitted the crank into the hole under the radiator. Well, here goes, I thought. Probably break my arm! That was about the only bad thing that hadn't happened to me, lately. A lot of people, I knew, did break an arm, or a thumb, at least, trying to crank a Model-A or a Model-T Ford. The kick, as people called it, could make the crank suddenly twirl back in the opposite direction, when the motor backfired instead of starting.

I gave the crank a hard turn. No kick, thank goodness. No start, either. I cranked again. Then again. Not even a belch out of the engine. I began to smell gasoline from the motor. I'd choked it too much—and flooded it!

I got in under the wheel, and pushed in the choke. I cut off the spark and the gas. There was nothing to do but crank away until the extra gasoline in the carburetor was gone. I did that. When I thought I'd cranked as much as I should have—as much as I physically could, nearly—I crawled back under the wheel and turned on the spark and gas and pulled the choke a tiny bit. Around front, again, I gave the crank a hard whirl. The motor caught and came alive.

On my way, at last. I headed toward Marsh Traynor's house, hoping to get his approval for the chase to Mexico.

TWENTY-THREE

Hoffer was sitting in the cab of Stud Wampler's yellow Dodge truck when I pulled up behind it at the curb in front of the white frame house with green trim. Stud and Traynor were on Traynor's front porch.

I got out of Crystal's Model A and walked to the passenger side of Stud's truck.

The window was rolled down, Hoffer sitting inside. "This won't take long," I said to her.

"I'll wait here," she said.

I walked up the sidewalk toward the house. A couple of large, bright-green junipers stood on each side of the front steps. The Bermuda-grass lawn was neatly mowed. Purple irises crowded a flower bed to the right.

A verandah stretched across the front of the house. Stud sat in a porch swing there; my boss, Marsh Traynor, in one of two wooden recliners painted green. Traynor'd apparently been working in the yard, lately, without a hat. His plump face and bald head were sunburned. The banker/county commissioner who'd been a great old friend of my dad's shook hands with me without getting up, then folded his heavy arms back across a wrestler's chest.

"Glad to see you, Okie, son," Traynor said. He didn't *look* especially glad. Going on, he didn't *sound* very glad, either. "You makin' us a good sheriff, but what's this shit, now, about you flying off down to Old Mexico? You tryin' to be 'Mr. Keen, tracer of lost persons'?"

"Stud told you the details, I guess?" I said.

"He did," Traynor said. "But I don't see how this is county business. You badge don't amount to a hill a beans, son, down in Old Mexico. And from what Stud, here, tells me, that Parnell girl wasn't kidnapped, went with this guy Castor willingly. And looks like we got a murder, right here—that man Satville— that's got to be solved. What you say to all that?"

"Castor's the man we want for Satville's murder, Marsh. It was a pilot that killed Satville, hit him in the head and dropped him out of his own plane, and Castor's a pilot. He tried to kill me last night. That's two crimes, and he's planning another one, with this flight to Mexico."

"Saying that's right, Okie, we gotta depend on the Mexican law to nab him and send him back," Marsh Traynor said. "We don't have no jurisdiction down there."

"That'd be the same as just letting a thug like Castor go, Marsh—and leaving poor Easter at his mercy," I said. "Besides, I've got a personal score to settle."

"I'll tell you something else," Traynor said. "I'm not about to allow no prosecution of Doc Askew, either, no matter what y'all say he done. Anything happened, it was a long time ago. And Doc's been a solid citizen in this town."

"Suit yourself on that, Marsh," I said.

"I aim to," Marsh Traynor said. "You sweet on this Parnell girl, Okie?"

"Naw, I'm not," I said emphatically. Actually, I thought she'd probably tried to use me. I did feel a little ashamed about going with her to the Easter Pageant and for what had nearly happened between us there. Maybe that was one reason I thought I owed her a rescue from a hard guy she didn't realize was a mean predator. "Easter's in a mess, now, she can't get out of, not on her own," I said to Traynor. "If I don't go try to help her, she's lost."

"And what about that woman out there in the truck—the one you carrying with you down to Old Mexico?" Traynor asked next, nodding his head back toward the street. "Got something going with her?"

"Great heavenly shit, Marsh!" I said. "She's an Oklahoma City lawyer, as Stud must have told you. She's trying to find the long-lost daughter of a client, a daughter that's turned out to be Easter Parnell. Heir to all that Kraker oil money. And it's a Kraker henchman that's running off with Easter to Mexico, not for any honest purpose, by God! I feel like it's my duty, Marsh, to go with Mrs. Hoffer, free the girl, haul Castor back here."

"This Hoffer woman, her own self, mighta committed some crimes, Okie," Traynor said.

I looked at Stud Wampler. He was studying his nails, looking down. I knew he was suspicious of Hoffer and must have said so to Traynor. "I can't prove it, yet, Marsh," I said, "but I swear to you that that's not so." I thought I was right in saying that, but I wasn't as totally sure of it as I sounded. I didn't want to show any doubt to Traynor, right then.

"Cain't approve no county money, Okie, for you to go to Old Mexico on a wild-goose chase," he said. "That's all she wrote."

I stood up. "Gotta go on my own, then."

Stud Wampler got out of the swing and spoke up for the first time. "Take care, stud—and see if you can get my little thirty-eight police special back, while you're down there, whoever took it," he said.

"I'll call you, Stud, when I get to Veracruz," I said.

"Yeah, let me hear from you," Stud said. "I'll be worried about you." He said it like he meant it. I shook hands with Stud, then with Marsh Traynor.

"You look after my stock, out at the Billings place, Stud?" I asked.

"Like my own," he said.

At the curb in front of Traynor's house, Em Hoffer climbed out of Stud's truck with her satchel purse over one shoulder and carrying her soft leather bag and Army Air Corps raincoat. She got into the passenger side of the Model A, and we took off for Moreland's grass airstrip.

"How'd that meeting go?" Hoffer asked when I'd gotten back to Main and was turning south on it.

"Charmed my boss with my closing argument," I said.

Hoffer changed the subject. "Before I left the hotel, Okie," she said, "I called Lily Morgan's house in Oklahoma City. Had to talk with her sister. Lily was in bed, bad sick, didn't feel like talking on the phone. The sister, Caroline, cried when she told me that Lily's getting worse. I asked the sister to call Mr.

Wampler, here at the sheriff's office, if anything happens to Lily while we're gone, and she said she would. I filled her in on the facts about Easter Parnell, told her to tell Lily we'd found her daughter, for sure, and that we were on our way to Mexico to bring her back. Caroline said she knew that'd make Lily rest easier. After we get to Mexico, Okie, we have to telephone Mr. Wampler and check on any bad news about Lily. I hope there won't be any, but her sister sounded pretty blue about things."

"That's a shame," I said. "I hope she lives to see her daughter."

"Me, too," Hoffer said.

After a while, I changed the subject. "You bring a road map?"

"Texaco one," she said. "It's in my purse. Brought a couple of hamburgers, too, from the hotel coffee shop—our Easter dinner."

We rattled into the area outside the gate that led into the grass airstrip at Moreland's. We pulled up beside Reeves Martin's old Packard that Castor'd abandoned there. I got out of the Model A and went around to look at the front of the Packard. The grill and front bumper were as badly scratched and dented as Jeff Moreland had said.

"This is what happened when Castor ran through the fence, coming after me, last night," I said to Hoffer, pointing out the damage to the front of the car. "I'm gonna make him sorry he ever heard of me."

We went back and got our bags out, then headed for the white-and-red Waco, inside the gate. Jeff Moreland'd brought it around in front of the tin hangar. He was just finishing gassing it up with a hand-cranked pump, stuck in a fifty-five-gallon barrel on the back of his blue Jimmy pickup. He waved as we walked up, then got down and backed the little truck out of the way.

"You'd have thought," I said to Hoffer, "that Easter would have been more suspicious about Castor taking the plane that she knew Satville landed here in."

"He probably had a slick explanation for her," Hoffer said. "And she had stars in her eyes, believe anything."

Jeff Moreland came back to where Hoffer and I were waiting on the left side of the airplane, just in back of the lower of the two wings. He was hatless, wearing black-and-white-striped overalls, and his tousled red hair was blowing in the wind.

"I was right, Okie," he said. "George Cutler in Wichita Falls told me on the telephone that your man and the girl landed there in the yellow Piper Cub and filled up with gas, just like we figured they'd have to do. Man told Cutler they were headed to Love Field at Dallas."

"They'll spend the night in Dallas, then," I said.

"Love Field's on the north side of Dallas, about seven miles," Moreland said. "If I was you, I'd fly to Wichita Falls, turn southeast and follow the highway to Fort Worth, then go around it on the north until you see Love. Waco's got enough gas to get that far, all right. And you should make it, just before dark."

Carrying the briefcase and bag, I stepped up on the lower wing and opened the Waco's door, on the left side, just back of the front seat. I threw the bags into the back, then motioned Hoffer to come on up. From the wing, she bent her head and entered the cabin, dropped her raincoat and purse next to the bags in the backseat, then moved forward. She slipped sideways between the two front seats and crawled into the one on the right. I followed her and settled into the seat on the left. Jeff Moreland came up and closed the door securely behind us, then stepped back down and started around, outside, to my window.

EASY PICKIN'S

The Waco had dual controls so that it was flyable from either front bucket seat. Separate sets of two big, hinged pedals, on the floorboard in front of each seat, were connected through a system of cables and pulleys to the vertical rudder on the plane's tail and moved the rudder left or right, depending on which pedal was depressed, causing the nose of the plane to veer either left or right. Between the two seats and forward of them, there was a movable, black-metal yoke, like a large and hollow "Y," with another set of control cables running inside it. The base of the yoke descended through the floor. At the top of each of the two upraised arms a separate black, automobile-size wheel was mounted, one in front of each seat. Either wheel, turned left or right, banked the plane in that direction by moving the ailerons on the trailing edge of the wings, alternatingly up or down. Pulling back or pushing forward on either wheel moved the whole yoke and both wheels back or forward, and lowered or raised the horizontal elevator on the tail assembly in back, causing the nose of the plane to go up or down.

Hoffer and I buckled in. I rolled down the glass on my left. Jeff Moreland came up close. "You've watched me start this bird, Okie," he said. He reviewed the procedure. The Waco had an inertial system. First you flipped a switch to start a battery-powered flywheel, then, when it was up to speed, you turned on the magneto and pulled a knob on the instrument panel to engage the motor with the flywheel. Moreland paused a moment after running through all this. "You right sure you can fly this thing?" he asked.

"You bet," I said. I was nervous, though. My palms were sweating. I rubbed them on my pants legs, hoping that Hoffer wouldn't notice.

Jeff Moreland went on. "There's a lot more prop torque on this Waco than you're used to, Okie, more power," he said. "Take off west. You're gonna have a little crosswind from the north. When you get the tail up, the plane's gonna try to drift south on you, with the torque. So, you'll have to hold a lot of right rudder. Good luck!"

"Much obliged, Jeff," I said. "Let's have at it!"

Moreland walked away and stood at the tailgate of his pickup. I set the brakes on the plane by pushing down the tops of the two rudder pedals with both feet. I switched on the inertial, and there was a whir as the flywheel started and whined up to high speed. Then, I turned off that switch, flipped the other one, pumped the fuel primer three times, and pushed the throttle in about halfway, then pulled the knob that engaged the motor with the inertial. The big radial engine barked, belched a little blue smoke, and roared to life. I quickly eased out on the throttle, and the engine dropped down into a loping idle.

From my open window, I gave Jeff Moreland a particularly energetic thumbs-up signal because he looked so worried, standing at the back of his pickup. I pushed in the throttle a little to accelerate the engine. The plane rumbled slowly forward through the grass for a few yards, until I was at the east end of the strip, ready for takeoff. I carefully went through the checklist, as my friend in Norman had taught me to do. It was on a card at the side of the instrument panel. With the brakes locked, I ran up the engine, while watching the RPM indicator, then slowed it back to idle. I tried the controls in every direction. I set the altimeter to one thousand feet, Vernon's elevation, I knew, then rolled the side window closed and looked up through the windshield, left and right, for any oncoming planes. There were none.

Glancing at Hoffer on my right, I said, "Wanna go to Dallas?"

"Anywhere with you, Flash," she said.

I set the brakes and began to push in the throttle. The motor revved up. I came off the brakes, then shoved the throttle all the way to the wall. The Waco leaped forward in a roar and rapidly built up speed as we headed down the grass runway. I began to push forward on the wheel. The tail wheel came up in back, and, with more speed, the front tires started to lose hard contact with the ground.

Then, I was in trouble—just as Jeff Moreland had warned. The torque of the propeller began to cause the plane to drift to the left, off the main line of the strip and toward a clump of mesquites, up ahead. I was holding right rudder with that foot, but apparently not enough because the Waco's leftward drift continued. My throat tightened with alarm. Then, suddenly, I felt my right rudder pedal go down farther and realized that Hoffer was helping me by pushing the one on her side. It worked. The plane's direction stabilized. I steadily brought the yoke back toward me with the wheel, and we were in the air.

I banked the Waco to the south and climbed out to about five thousand feet. I leveled off, there, then eased back on the throttle, some, lowered the RPM, and came off the red fuel knob to lean out the fuel mixture of gasoline and air.

"Thought you weren't a flier," I said to Hoffer.

"Lord, a person didn't have to be an aviator to know you needed to hold more right rudder, back there—like the man told you," Hoffer said.

We flew on in silence and, within a few minutes, crossed over Red River into Texas. Down below us, we could see the scanty stream of water, the color of the river's name, meandering left and right in the wide sand of its southeastward course. Soon, I recognized Wichita Falls, way off to our right. When I was even with it, I banked the Waco left, above the highway that led out of town, southeast toward Fort Worth.

"Want a hamburger?" Hoffer asked.

I said I did. She leaned around the seat and dragged over her satchel purse, then took a brown paper sack out of it. She brought out the burgers and gave one to me, first rolling back the greasy white paper from it, keeping the other burger for herself.

"Happy Easter!" she said.

We chomped away, high above the native Texas grasslands and scattered mesquites below. We were quiet, both our minds, I'm sure, on what lay ahead for us in Dallas.

TWENTY-FOUR

I had no trouble finding Love Field, north of the Texas city. First, I came to Fort Worth, at the east end of the highway from Wichita Falls. The stockyards and the big coliseum, where the annual Fort Worth Fat Stock Show was held, were plenty of identification for me. I'd once hitchhiked to the Fort Worth Fat Stock Show with Dub Ready, when we were in high school. The funny Fort Worth motto we'd seen, back then, had stuck in my mind: "Where the West begins, and the East peters out."

I flew on east, around the north side of Fort Worth, and soon spotted the blacktop runway and hangars of the Dallas airport that we were looking for. I could see the city, itself, just to the south.

Love Field was below us. I circled. The airport windsock showed that the wind was out of the west, where the sun was getting low on the horizon. I began my descent, turned downwind, parallel with the strip, turned base, then banked again and headed west into the wind, on final approach.

I was edgy. The guy at Norman who'd taught me to fly had said that any fool could take off and fly a plane in the air. The difficulty, he said, was in the landing.

But things went okay. I brought the Waco in a little high and hot, as pilots put it. On a short strip, I might've had to pull up and go around again. But the Love Field runway was long enough—Ford Trimotors and a couple of other airline planes were flying out of there, by then—that I was finally able to touch down, safely, on the asphalt, if not exactly in a three-point landing.

I taxied over toward the area where nine or ten other private planes were tied down on the blacktop apron in front of the hangar/office of Lone Star Aviation—and saw, right away, that one of the airplanes, there, was the yellow Piper Cub we were looking for. Call letters: "November Charlie Triple-three Niner." Ride and lesson advertising was stenciled in black on the fuselage.

Motioning toward it, Hoffer said, "You think maybe we ought to wait out here, stake out the Piper Cub, until Castor and Easter come back?"

"They won't come back until morning, if then," I said. "But, same as them, we can't stay at the airport all night. Better to try to run them down in town. Failing that, we'll sure come right back here tomorrow."

Between the group of planes and the hangar, a blue Bellanca passenger plane, with the cowling off, was pulled up under a corrugated-metal canopy. A skinny guy in gray coveralls got down off a ladder/scaffold where he'd been working on the plane's engine, pitched a couple of hand tools onto a wooden workbench, there, and stepped out to motion me toward a spot where we could tie down our Waco.

"You want me to top off your tank?" he asked as Hoffer and I got out with our bags and he came around toward us.

"Much obliged," I said. "You see the man and woman who flew in here in that yellow Piper Cub, over there?" I pointed.

"Yeah, wadn't too long ago," the man said. "Well-dressed dude and a tall, good-lookin' young woman."

"Know where they went?"

"Downtown Dallas," he said. "Said they was goin' to a hotel. Don't ask me which one. I told 'em to hoof it over to the terminal, yonder, and they could get a taxicab. And that's what they done."

I took a dollar bill from my pocket and gave it to him. Pretty heavy tip, but I thought it might pay off. "I'd appreciate your tying down for us," I said. "And keep your eyes peeled for that Piper Cub guy. We're gonna go get a taxicab into town, too."

Hoffer and I started to walk in the direction of the little brick terminal building, next door to Lone Star Aviation.

The skinny guy called after us. "That man in the Piper, you know?"

"Yeah."

"Said him and that girl was going to go nightclubbin' before they went to bed—that interests y'all."

"Thanks," I said. "Appreciate the information."

Walking on beside me, Hoffer said, "Castor's trying to ingratiate himself with the girl, show her a good time."

"That's worrisome," I said. "I can't imagine that Easter'd be used to drinking or nightclubs."

A lone taxi sat at the curb in front of the terminal. We got in it. I asked the driver what the names of the main downtown Dallas hotels were. The Travis and the Houston, he told me, right close to each other.

"Take us to either one," I said.

In about twenty minutes, he let us out at the Houston, a big redbrick place with limestone trim. Hoffer and I went in. I took the sheriff badge from my jacket pocket and flashed it to the desk clerk, a little banty rooster in a coat and tie, his dark hair parted in the middle. To my question, he said that neither a John Carter nor a Leo Castor was registered there.

At the nearby Travis Hotel, we got the same response.

"Time to get some local police help," I said. "Let's find out where the station is."

"Why don't we check into a hotel, ourselves, first," Hoffer said. "That way, the police will know where to get in touch with us."

She'd noticed a smaller, less-expensive-looking hotel, the Tarrant, around the corner and a block down from the Travis. Bags in hand, we walked in that direction.

"Okie, what were you going to do if we'd found Castor, by ourselves?" Hoffer asked on the way. "You're not even carrying a gun, are you?"

I said I wasn't. "Dazzle him with my footwork, then punch him in the nose."

"I'm serious," Hoffer said. "And I *do* have a gun."

"What?" She had a gun?

"Castor'll put up a fight," Hoffer said.

"Guy's a mean customer, that's for sure," I said. "But I'm not afraid of a gun. Took a pistol away from a tough thug, myself, not too long ago. Castor killed Satville. Shot my dog. And probably broke into Doc Askew's office. We find him, we'll arrest him, one way or another, I guarantee you. And I don't think you'll have to pull your gun. I thought we might surprise him, but, now, we'll get the Dallas police to help. We'll throw him in the Dallas jail until we can carry him back to Vernon."

The old woman behind the desk at the Tarrant hadn't registered a Castor or a Carter, either. But she was glad to check Hoffer and me in—as Mr. and Mrs. Ray Lee Dunn—even though I was afraid I looked pretty nervous, and guilty, to her as I reached over to sign the register that way.

The husband-and-wife arrangement had been Hoffer's somewhat surprising suggestion. She'd made it just as we'd arrived in front of the Tarrant, saying, "Okie, don't get the wrong idea, but to save money, we can share a room, if you want to."

We told the old woman at the desk that we'd carry our own bags, climbed the stairs to the second floor, and with the skeleton key let ourselves into the musty room. Each of us freshened up a little in the bathroom down the hall, then went back downstairs.

The desk woman told us how to find the police station, five blocks away. And, while she was at it, she also recommended the City Steak House, a block west of the Tarrant, for supper. We thanked her and started out on foot.

At the station, up a flight of stairs, the heavyset, red-faced police sergeant looked bored behind his high desk. It was still early evening, and things were slow, I figured. I showed the man my sheriff badge and introduced myself, and Hoffer.

"What can we do for you, Sheriff?" the desk sergeant asked, helpful.

"We've come after a Leo Castor, alias John Carter, wanted in

Oklahoma on suspicion of murder and assault with intent to kill," I said. I thought about adding that the son of a bitch had killed my dog, too, but decided against it. "Young woman, Easter Parnell, we think is with Castor under false pretenses and that he's carried her across state lines for immoral purposes."

I went on to give the sergeant the pair's descriptions and the details of their arrival and said that the two would probably be found at some local hotel. I told him that I wanted the Dallas police to arrest Castor and hold Easter until Hoffer and I were contacted and showed up to take over—that the two of us'd be at the City Steak House, for a little while, and at the Tarrant Hotel, later, for the night. "He's a tough customer, this Castor," I said, finally. "So, tell your people to be mighty careful with him."

"Sheriff Dunn, we're used to tough customers, here in Big D," the man said. "I'll put my two best night officers on him, right away." Hoffer and I turned to go, but the desk sergeant stopped us. "Sheriff, y'all know why all them Okies stayed put, up north of the Red River?" he asked.

I felt that I had to bite. "Why was that?" I said.

"When they come down to the river and saw the sign that said, 'Texas, this way,' them that couldn't read stayed right where they was."

Hoffer and I joined, ingratiatingly, in the man's laughter.

We left and walked on back, then, to the City Steak House whose motto, painted on the front window was: "Our customers are choosy—our beef is choice!" The food lived up to its billing.

We thought, briefly, about going to the corner picture show afterward. There was a double feature, *Double or Nothing*, with Bing Crosby and Martha Raye, and *Born Reckless*, with Brian Donlevy. But Hoffer and I agreed that it'd be best if we went on back to the hotel, where the police could contact us if they needed to. And we hoped they'd need to, soon.

Upstairs in our shared room, Hoffer said, "Remember, Okie, we're just doing this to save money. I mean it." She turned back the chenille bedspread. "Cut off the light, now," she said.

I stepped over and twisted the switch on the wall, next to the door. The overhead globe went dark. Back at my side of the double bed, I slipped off my boots and pulled off my Levi's and shirt, leaving on my shorts and cotton undershirt. There was some faint light through the blowing curtains from a neon sign, outside at ground level. I got under the bedsheet and turned away as Hoffer took off her khaki slack suit.

The springs squeaked when she lay down at the far opposite side of the bed and pulled the sheet over her. We both laughed at the noise, then got quiet. Hoffer soon began to breathe heavily. I lay there, wide awake, as long as I could stand it, maybe ten minutes. Then, I quietly rolled over under the sheet and snuggled up close to her. She was on her side, facing away. I moved my right arm across her body and gently hugged her to me.

Without moving, she said, "Okie," her voice low and sweet, "I like you."

"I like you, too, Em," I said. My own voice, I knew, was huskier than usual.

"A lot," she said.

"I like you a lot, too, Em," I said.

"I really appreciate your coming down here with me, to find Lily Morgan's daughter and bring her back," Hoffer went on.

I could tell that the little talk we were having was not going to wind up with a favorable ending. "But?" I asked. "I'm guessing there's a 'but.'"

"But, after my ex," Hoffer said, "I just don't want to get involved with another man, right now. There may be a time for us, Okie, but this isn't it. All right?"

"All right," I said, lying. I rolled back over to my own side of the bed.

TWENTY-FIVE

The next morning, Monday morning, about the first thing Hoffer said to me, directly, was, "You're mad, aren't you?" There was a teasing tone in her voice.

I didn't say anything to her, right then. It was early Monday, and we were sitting at a table in the City Steak House. We'd gotten up at daylight, taken turns bathing separately, down the hall, and put on the same clothes from the day before. We'd checked out of the Tarrant Hotel and gotten the names and locations of three other hotels in the downtown Dallas area. My plan was that Hoffer and I would eat a quick breakfast, then walk around and make inquiries about Castor and Easter at those three additional places before checking in at the Dallas police station.

Our bags and Hoffer's purse and air corps raincoat in the booth between us, waiting for my ham and eggs and Hoffer's toast and tea, I figured that I didn't look all that good. The light down the hall in the Tarrant Hotel bathroom had been kind of dim, and I knew that I'd made a poor job of shaving, even nicking my chin and making it bleed. I was a little out of sorts, too, and not much in the mood for conversation.

"I can tell you're mad," Hoffer said.

"I'm not mad," I said. I was, I guess. Woman gets in the same bed with you in her underclothes, you've got a right to expect something's going to happen.

I wished that I'd had the opportunity for my morning devotional exercise. That might have made me feel better.

"You *are* mad, but I hope you'll think about it and be a little more understanding."

"I'll make a stab at it," I said.

I went to work on my full breakfast, Hoffer on her customary little dab. She finished first and lit a cigarette, dragging on it greedily. She hadn't been smoking in the plane because she knew I didn't like it. When I was about to wind up, we saw a black police car pull up out front and two blue-uniformed officers get out. They came into the café, looked around a moment, then stepped back to our table. In size, the officers could have been Mutt and Jeff of the funny papers.

"You Sheriff Dunn?" the Jeff guy, the taller one, asked me. The name on his shirt said "Muldrow."

I said I was.

"This is Officer Higgins," the taller man said, nodding toward his short partner, the Mutt guy. "I'm Muldrow."

I introduced Em Hoffer. "Any luck, finding our fugitive?" I asked.

"Yessir, we found him and the girl," Muldrow said.

"You did?" I asked, galvanized.

"Well, we found where they spent the night," the officer said. "Gone, now?" I asked.

Officer Higgins spoke up. "'Fraid so," he said. "Took off this morning, the two of them, desk clerk told us."

"Stayed last night at the Dallas—nice out-of-the-way hotel, close in, but off the beaten path, a little," Muldrow added. "Registered as Mr. and Mrs. John Carter. Matched your descriptions perfectly. It was them, all right."

"Husband and wife?" I asked. "Registered as husband and wife?" This hit me pretty hard.

"Yeah, so the hotel desk clerk told us," Muldrow said. "Man winked at me and Higgins, here, and said, 'If I do say so, myself, Officer, Mr. Carter has married a much younger woman than himself, mighty cute, too.'"

"How long since the happy couple left the hotel?" Hoffer asked.

"Maybe an hour and a half ago," Muldrow said. "Paid out and took a taxicab from out front of the Dallas, clerk said."

Hoffer and I jumped up from the booth and gathered our things. "Look," I said to the officers, "if we hurry, we might catch them at the airport. How about running us out there, right now?"

The officers agreed. I rapidly paid us out of the café, and the four of us rushed out and climbed into the police car. I told Officer Higgins, who was driving, to get us out to Love Field, adding, like in a James Cagney cops-and-robbers picture show, "And step on it!"

"Son of a bitch has already seduced her!" I said to Hoffer in the backseat as we zipped through the north-Dallas streets. "I heard that's the first step of a pimp who wants to turn a young woman into a prostitute."

Hoffer was reassuring. "Now, Okie, don't jump to conclusions," she said, under her breath, so the officers in the front seat wouldn't hear. "You and I took a room as a married couple, and nothing at all happened in our case."

"Thanks for reminding me," I said.

At Love Field, Higgins turned into the Lone Star Aviation gate and, with me directing, drove right out onto the blacktop apron toward the tied-down planes. Before we even got close, we could see that the yellow Piper Cub was gone.

Hoffer, the two officers, and I got out of the police car. The same skinny guy in coveralls was back working on the Bellanca plane's engine. He got down from the scaffolding and walked with the four of us into the office, warily eyeing the two police officers all the way. I didn't explain their presence, but paid the man for filling up the Waco with gasoline.

"Oh yeah, sir," the man said to me, before I had a chance to quiz him, "that yellow Piper Cub you was interested in done left, 'bout an hour ago. Same man and woman. Dude seemed pretty talky. Said he normally flew a company plane, not the Piper Cub, but it was being worked on. Bragged he was an ace pilot in the war."

"Say where he was going?" I asked.

"Not a word," the guy replied. "Did ask for a Mexico flight map, if that's any help to you."

"Got another one?" I asked.

"Nawsir, and didn't have none for him, neither," the man said.

Finished inside, Hoffer and I and the two officers all started for the door.

"You friends of his, I reckon," the guy in coveralls called to me.

We all stopped and turned. "Not exactly," I said. "Why?"

"After the dude went out to his Piper Cub, he musta saw your Waco. Come back in here, then, and asked about it—and you. Said y'all was friends, and he needed to get something out of your airplane that you was bringin' him. I told him we couldn't allow that, without you was here."

"No friend of mine, that guy," I said. "Where was the girl all this time?"

"She was already getting in the backseat of the Piper Cub," the man said. "I watched out that window, here, as the dude left, and he looked like he stopped a second at my workbench at the Bellanca. Then, before he got in his own plane, he opened the door and climbed in yours. I started to go out there to tell him to get out of it, when he come right out on his own."

"He leave then?" I asked.

"After he come out of your Waco, I didn't pay him no mind for a while," the man said. "But when I looked that way again, he was back around the tail of it—doing what, I ain't got no idea. I thought about hollerin' at him or something, but he soon went to his own plane, and they left."

"Any tool gone from your workbench?" Officer Muldrow asked the man.

"I thought about that," the skinny guy said. "Could be my little file missing, but I ain't sure it was there, before."

I asked the Lone Star attendant to come help and, together, he and I and Hoffer, with the two Dallas police officers looking on, examined the white-and-red Waco carefully, inside and out and all around, but we could find nothing at all amiss.

"Hell was Castor after, you think?" I said to Hoffer as we went over to the left side of the Waco and got ready to load up.

"Key, maybe," she said. "Thought he might take off with this plane instead of the Piper Cub."

"Maybe so," I said. "Next time, I'll damned sure lock the door."

I was anxious to be off, and after Castor. I thanked the officers and the Lone Star Aviation guy. Hoffer and I climbed into the Waco. I got the engine started, and we were soon down the runway and in the air. It was a little before ten. I climbed out to about five thousand feet, then eased off the throttle, reduced the RPM, and leaned out the fuel mixture.

Spreading Hoffer's Texaco map in the cabin, we could see that, flying pretty much due south, we'd hit the Gulf of Mexico coast at about Corpus, then keep straight on south from there to Brownsville, just this side of the Rio Grande and the border. I told Hoffer that we'd land and refuel in Brownsville, then wind up for the day in Ciudad Victoria.

"That's the next Mexican town big enough for us to get gas, again, and find a place to spend the night—before we head on down the coast tomorrow morning," I said. "Don't want to fly at night."

"How come you know so much about Mexico?" Hoffer asked when we'd refolded the Texaco map and put it away.

"Spent six hard months prizefighting all through there, before I figured out that college and law school would be easier," I said.

"Make any money as a prizefighter?" she asked.

"More than I could fighting up here in the US of A," I said. "In Mexico, they called me 'the Gringo'—and that was when they were being nice. Mexican fans're rougher than Mexican prizefighters. But there's a promoter I know in Veracruz, if he's still there. Tough little guy. Doesn't operate totally within the law, you might say. But, we find him, I think I can get him to help us."

The Waco droned on. There was no rough air to bump us or to cause me to have to work the controls much. Hoffer leaned her head against the right window, with her eyes open. I began to sing to myself, like I'd done all my life. It was a habit of mine that'd sometimes driven my dad crazy.

When I was a kid, riding with him in his old truck, to buy cattle from a farmer or to take a load up to Oklahoma City, I'd start singing and whistling to myself without thinking about it, sometimes the same song, over and over. One time like that, when my dad was drinking a little, he'd yelled at me, "God dammit, Okie, if you *have* to sing, could you sing something different, ever now and then?"

Flying along in the Waco, the song that came to my lips was one of the old, sad ones: "Give my love to Nellie, Jack, and kiss her once for me. . . ."

Em Hoffer waited until I'd sung and whistled it about three times before she straightened up and spoke. "Okie, I've decided I should call you 'Flash' for a different reason than my first one," she said.

"What's that?" I said, still feeling a little cranky, not in the mood to be teased.

"Flying this airplane and the sunlight hitting you from your left side, you remind me of Flash Gordon—in the picture-show serial," she said.

"Flash Gordon went to the planet Mongo," I said. "I can't even get to first base."

"You're as good-looking as Flash Gordon—or, more accurate,

Buster Crabbe, playing him—though your hair's dark and you've got a better suntan than his."

"You trying to cheer me up?" I asked, looking over at her.

"Maybe," she said.

"It's working."

A little before one, we caught sight of the ocean to our left and passed over Corpus Christi. It was a good-size place, and we saw, below, its modern airport, apparently built to handle airline planes. But we weren't stopping. It would be another dull and uneventful hour and a half, farther on for us, to Brownsville.

To fill the time, Hoffer talked about how she missed her father, and how she didn't miss her ex-husband. I asked her about her experiences as a woman law student. Hoffer said she'd been the only female in her whole law school. There'd been a lot of discrimination, a lot of teasing and snide remarks—even from some of the professors. A criminal law teacher had always called on her in class to brief the cases dealing with rape or some other sexual matter. He'd perversely delighted in making her discuss the facts of those cases in detail and had done nothing at all to curb the resultant snickering from her male counterparts. More recently, as a woman practicing law in Oklahoma City, she'd had it just as rough, she said. Other lawyers sometimes made off-color comments in her presence. Judges found it difficult to treat her seriously. One judge had refused to permit her to appear in court in slacks. "You may be a woman in a man's profession, girlie, but you can't dress like a man, not in my courtroom," she said the judge had told her.

After it was quiet again, for a while, I began to sing an old cowboy song to myself: "I won't see my mother when the work's all done this fall. . . ."

I whistled some verses, sang others—a good many more than once.

After a while, I stopped singing and pointed out Brownsville, Texas, to Hoffer, when it was just off our nose. She helped me pick out the airstrip, and I set the Waco down in a pretty good landing, smooth and straight south down the runway, with no gusts or crosswind to give me any trouble. I was getting better.

TWENTY-SIX

I told the chunky blond kid at the fixed-base Brownsville hangar to fill the Waco's gasoline tank as hurriedly as he could. Got a Mexico map—it was a highway map—from him, first.

Up against the south wall of the hangar, there was a little stand that sold tamales and Coca-Colas. I stepped over there and bought two drinks and four tamales from the tiny Mexican woman who was running it.

Hoffer and I more or less gulped everything down while the blond kid finished filling the tank. I asked him if he'd seen a yellow Piper Cub and described its occupants for him.

"Cain't believe you didn't see it, yourself, when you was on downwind," the boy said. "He taken off just almost as you was fixin' to land."

I paid the kid for the gasoline and asked him if he would carry our bottles back to the stand. I cranked up the Waco, took a quick look at the map, and we were quickly down the runway and airborne. I began to climb out.

"Showdown's coming—faster than we thought!" I said to Hoffer. "Ciudad Victoria's southwest of here a couple of hundred miles, a ways back from the Gulf Coast. Only place Castor can get gas. That's where we'll catch him." I could feel the tension in my body mounting.

Down below us was the Rio Grande—Rio Bravo, as it was called in Mexico. We quickly passed over it, then above Matamoros, the Mexican town that was a border twin to Brownsville.

"My God, Okie!" Hoffer suddenly shrieked.

I saw the yellow Piper Cub at the same instant. Two hundred yards away, it was coming straight at us from the southwest, a little to the right of the Waco's nose, a little south from the sun.

"He's going to shoot at us!" Hoffer yelled. "Dive!"

Castor had the top of the fold-down door open on his right side, and his hand was out, pointing a pistol toward the Waco, and us.

"That son of a bitch!" I said, at the same time turning the control wheel to the left and shoving it forward while vigorously stomping my left rudder. I wanted to make a rapid diving bank to the left, to get out of Castor's way—and out of his pistol sights. Instantly, I felt a snap under the left rudder pedal, and it went totally slack, useless. The rudder cable had busted, and the fact that Castor'd been in and around the Waco, earlier, leaped into my mind. He'd done something. The plane was in a tight left spiral.

"Give me some help, Em," I yelled. "My left rudder pedal's gone."

She braced herself in her seat and jammed her feet on the pedals on her side. "Mine, too!" she shouted.

Of course. Both sets of rudder pedals were connected.

Hoffer put her hands on the wheel on her side. "We can level, Okie, with the ailerons," she said. She was right.

I pushed in the right pedal to neutralize the rudder, in back. With the wheel, we leveled the wings and pulled up the nose. By then, the yellow Piper Cub was long gone. We couldn't see it anywhere around us.

"We've gotta put this thing on the ground, the best we can, and get the rudder cable fixed," I said.

"You can turn by banking, you know, without the rudder," Hoffer said. "The plane'll be sluggish, but you can do it."

She was right, again. It was clear that Hoffer knew a good deal about flying.

"It's gotta be Matamoros," I said. We'd seen its grass strip, just earlier.

Grimly focused, heart pounding, turning the wheel to the left, I used the ailerons to bank the Waco toward my side, causing the plane's nose to come around mushily in that direction, too. By that method, I managed a wide turn, back to the north, and, descending, worked the ailerons until I had the plane lined up with the Matamoros runway. Luckily, there was virtually no crosswind. I brought the Waco in for a passable landing and rolled out close to a little shack in what appeared to be about a two-plane Mexican airport.

When the Waco was stopped and the motor killed, Hoffer and I jumped out and went back to the left side of the plane's tail. We both saw at once that the cable had snapped, just a little back of where it emerged from the fuselage. Looking closer, I noted that about half the break in the cable was smooth, the other half ragged.

"Castor filed this thing through," I said to Hoffer.

"My God!" she said. "He meant to kill us, for sure."

"Must've thought the cable'd break and we'd crash on take-off from Dallas," I said. "Losing rudder control on takeoff would have been fatal.

"But the cable held for a while," I said. "So, then, I guess Castor figured he had to push things along. That's why he made that head-on run at us, here. Probably wasn't going to shoot us. Wanted me to stomp a rudder so hard the cable'd bust, and we'd lose control."

Hoffer and I both were a little shaky. We embraced out of a sense of relief, then stepped back and began to look around. Nobody was to be seen. But just when we thought we were probably going to have to walk into town and find some help, an old-model, faded-red Chevrolet pickup came bouncing and rattling down the dusty road to the airstrip and pulled up near where Hoffer and I were standing, in front of our airplane.

A middle-aged Mexican man in a dirty gray shirt and a pair of brown trousers with two buttons missing at the fly jumped out of the pickup and hurried over to pump my hand, first, and, then, Hoffer's. He proved to be the airport custodian.

"*Bienvenidos, señores,*" the Mexican said, cheerfully. "*José María Anaya Gil a sus órdenes.*" Welcome. At your orders.

I spoke back to him in my best high school and prizefighter Spanish. "*Permítame mostrarle algo, Señor Anaya,*" I said to the man. Let me show you something.

I led him to the left side of the plane's tail and showed him the rudder-pedal cable break. The man grasped the problem at once. "*¡Se le rompió el cable!*" The cable broke on you.

"*Más o menos*," I said. More or less. "*¿Puéda usted arreglarlo, reconectarlo?*" Can you fix it, reconnect it?

The man took one last look at the break. "*¡Cierto, jefe!*" Sure, chief!

The man hurried over to the shack and went in. Soon, he was back with a bunch of stuff—pliers, small wire cutters, a strand of near-matching cable, and some other things.

"*Con permiso*," he said to me.

I gave permission, and he went to work.

"We're in luck," I said to Hoffer.

That didn't prove to be entirely true, because at that moment a black Model-A Ford roadster, missing its fabric top, rolled down the road in a cloud of tan dust and came to a brake-squeaking stop not far from where we stood.

The mustachioed man in a worn khaki uniform who stepped out of the car introduced himself as an official of Mexican immigration and customs. He asked in Spanish if we were "*del otro lado.*" From the other side. I acknowledged that we were. He asked for our documents, passports, and airplane title.

I stepped up into the Waco and, rummaging around in my briefcase bag, dug out my birth certificate, then got the airplane document from the cellophane pocket on the dash. Back down on the ground, I handed these to the all-business immigration official. I knew that my birth certificate was as good as a passport in Mexico. But I also knew that Hoffer had neither. We'd discussed this briefly, back in Vernon. I'd said we'd cross that bridge when we got to it. We were now to it, I thought.

"Give him your Oklahoma driver's license," I said to Hoffer under my breath.

Her satchel purse was slung over her shoulder. She got out a billfold from it, extracted the license, and handed it to the man.

"*Se requiere permiso especial por el avión,*" the immigration official said to me.

"*Sí, lo comprendo,*" I replied. I knew that a separate tourist card of some kind had to be made out for the airplane, like for a car that was brought into the country.

Bending over the passenger-side door of the Model A, the official gathered up a manila folder from the front seat. He shuffled through the forms in it and took out the one he wanted. He said in Spanish that it was for an automobile, but he assumed that it would work for an airplane, too. He lay the paper on the hood of his car and, with a pencil from his breast pocket, began to fill in the blanks, looking repeatedly at my birth certificate and the Waco title.

When he was finished, he signed the form, went to the car, again, picked up an ink pad and stamp from the seat, and made my entrance legal with the black-inked likeness, inside a circle, of an eagle holding a snake in its mouth. He handed me the official form and my documents. I thanked the man, and he turned his attention, then, to Em Hoffer's driver's license.

He looked up and, to her, said, "*¿No tienes pasaporte o partida de nacimiento?*" Passport or birth certificate?

I answered in her place. "*Desafortunadamente, no, jefe. Pero nos importa mucho entrar a México.*" Unfortunately not, but it's very important that we enter Mexico.

"*¿A dónde van?*" the official asked.

"*A Veracruz, jefe.*"

"*Tu puedes pasar, la mujer, no,*" the man said to me. You can pass through, the woman, no.

Hoffer looked at me with concern, getting the drift of things. "Okie, don't go off and leave me here," she said.

"I can handle it," I said to her, under my breath.

I turned sideways, reached into the right-hand pocket of my Levi's, and took out two dollars. I folded them carefully, then passed them discreetly to the official's waiting hand.

"*Jefe, le agradeceremos mucho su consideración,*" I said to the Mexican. We will greatly appreciate your kindness.

He slipped the folded bills into his shirt pocket and, without a further word, began to fill out another form, in the same manner as before, consulting Hoffer's driver's license from time to time for information. Finished, he signed the form with a flourish, stamped it, as before, and handed it to Hoffer.

"*¡Pasen ustedes!*" the official said. He saluted briskly, then went around and got into his Model-A Ford, and was off.

Not long after, our Mexican repairman and airport caretaker came over to us, a triumphant smile on his brown face. He said in Spanish that the cable was repaired. Like new, he said. The man motioned for me to come take a look. I did. He'd done a terrific job of splicing the rudder cable. We were ready to go.

I gave the Mexican two dollars and thanked him. He was most grateful. "*Que le vaya bien, señor,*" he said. May it go well for you.

I said, under my breath, "I hope so," and, to him, "*Igualmente para ti.*" The same for you.

I cranked up the Waco. At my run-up before takeoff, I did a very vigorous check of the controls. Perfect. We were soon down the grass strip and in the clear air of a bright afternoon.

From above, I followed the highway, south out of Matamoros. Off to our left, we could see the green waters of the Gulf, whitecaps topping the waves as they broke into shore, one after the other. Down below and to our right, toward the sun, was the dry, overgrazed, and overworked Mexican countryside, much of it taken over by scavenger vegetation like short palmettos and thorny bushes. The dry season was still on, in those parts, and I knew that the rains wouldn't come for another month. Here and there, we saw Mexican farmers plowing their hilly fields, some with horses, some with teams of oxen, in preparation for eventual sowing, just in advance of the rains.

After about an hour in the air, I saw, below, the fork in the highway that I was looking for. I took the main arm that led toward the southwest—away, some, from the coast. It would take us to Ciudad Victoria.

Another hour and we came in sight of the town itself. I circled it and readily found the little grass strip. But after I lost some altitude, Hoffer and I could see that the yellow Piper Cub was not anywhere on the field. In fact, there appeared to be nothing, or nobody, there except for a tattered cloth windsock.

"We're going to have to buzz town, to get somebody to come out," I said to Hoffer.

"That work in Mexico?" she asked.

"Worth a try," I said.

I buzzed Ciudad Victoria's main street twice from about five hundred feet. It caused a stir, each time. We could see people run out of the stores and houses to look up at us, many waving.

"Probably think we're Charles Lindbergh," I said.

I banked, then, and headed back to the grass strip, hoping I'd roused someone who'd come for us. On downwind, the nose of the Waco pointed north, we saw an old Model-A pickup coming along the road toward the airstrip. A barrel and pump were in the back. Someone'd gotten the message.

EASY PICKIN'S

By the time I'd set the Waco down and taxied back toward the middle of the strip, then pulled off the runway, two old cars had joined the pickup there. Hoffer and I got out of the airplane with our things. I locked the door with the key.

Stepping down from the wing, I shook hands with the young Mexican who'd emerged from the pickup. He wanted to know if we needed gas. I told him we did, and gave him three dollars in advance—for the gas and for looking after the Waco, overnight. I asked him whether a little yellow airplane had been there. He said it had, but had taken off, again, immediately after he'd gassed it up.

I turned to Em Hoffer. "Dammit to hell!" I said. "Looks like Castor's decided to try to make it on to Tampico before dark. I don't want to. We won't catch up before Veracruz, now."

Five people had gotten out of the other two cars, four men and a woman. They were quite friendly, very interested in the airplane. I asked about a place to stay for the night. There was a little hotel, downtown, they said, and the man and woman agreed to drive us there.

The small, two-story place was on the main cross streets in Ciudad Victoria. The sign out front identified it as the Vista del Mar, a strange name since you would have had to use an impossibly powerful set of binoculars to view the sea from that far inland.

Hoffer and I checked in as husband and wife, again, without even discussing it. The hotel man changed some of our dollars for pesos. I didn't figure he gave us a very good rate. After putting our stuff in the upstairs room, Hoffer and I walked up and down the few blocks of the town's business district, curious and killing time. It didn't take too long. We found a restaurant that looked good. It was, though it must have looked good to the flies, too. They'd beat us there. I ate a big plate of beef enchiladas, Hoffer some tacos. I told her not the eat the lettuce and tomatoes that came with her order, but she ignored me. We each drank a couple of cold Bohemia beers, Mexico's best. Afterward, as we left the place, we were still its only customers. Mexicans didn't eat their evening meal, I knew, until much later.

Up in our hotel room, things were pretty dreary. We followed the same routine as the night before—turning off the ceiling light, getting undressed in the dark, taking our accustomed positions, each on the far, opposite side of the bed. I lay down and tried to think of nothing but sleep and was grateful when I soon began to feel drowsy.

But our first night in Mexico proved to be a surprise for me. After only a few minutes had passed from the time we'd both gotten under the sheet, Em Hoffer quietly rolled over to my side of the bed and affectionately put an arm around me. Delighted, I turned toward her and raised up on an elbow. Our lips met.

In a little while, when we drew apart, some, I spoke first. "I thought you said you didn't want to get involved, right now."

"I meant right *then*."

"What changed?" I asked.

"Your singing in the airplane won me over, I guess, Flash," Hoffer said.

"My singing?"

"You want to try a few more verses?" she asked.

"Maybe later."

TWENTY-SEVEN

I woke up before Em Hoffer did on Tuesday morning. The sun was just coming up. I could see it, out the east window of our hotel room. Quietly, and still in my shorts and undershirt, I stepped over to the open window and spread my arms wide, to catch the bright rays.

"Thank you, Lord, for letting me live another day," I said, in whispers. I made a short prayer, especially mentioning Easter Parnell, then recited my Spanish-language psalm, afterward dropping my arms and stepping back a little from the window.

"What's this?" Hoffer said, behind me.

I turned to see that she'd been watching from the bed. I was embarrassed.

"Nothing but a sort of morning routine," I said. "Took the idea from an old Comanche Indian man I know."

"You're a more serious guy than you seem, Flash," Hoffer said.

Without shame or modesty, she got out of bed, fished a

217

white knit shirt from her bag, and slipped it on. The shirt hung down a little past her hips.

Her tall, full body and long, shapely legs were shown off to great advantage in the makeshift costume, it seemed to me. With long fingers, she fluffed out her red hair.

I went over to her. We embraced warmly, and kissed.

I was the one who stepped back first. "Time to get moving," I said.

"In what direction?"

I knew what she meant, and the prospect was tempting. But duty called. "Toward Veracruz," I said.

The bathroom was down the hall, a type of hotel arrangement that we were getting used to. She and I took turns. Afterward, we both put on fresh clothes. For me, it was pretty much the same kind of outfit as before—a long-sleeved white shirt, a fresh pair of Levi's, and black cowboy boots. But Hoffer switched costumes. Out of her leather bag, she took and unfolded a long royal-blue cotton skirt and a white cotton, low-necked peasant blouse, then quickly slipped them on. It was the first time I'd seen her in a skirt. The effect was magical. But I was a little puzzled by the change from slacks.

Hoffer looked up, apparently catching my quizzical expression. "Decided it wouldn't be smart to shock the natives too much," she said, by way of explanation for wearing a skirt rather than pants.

I'd told the Mexican guy at the airport to meet us back there, early. After my *huevos rancheros* and Hoffer's boiled egg and toast at a hole-in-the-wall café next to the Vista del Mar, we got a guy in a beat-up old taxi to drive us out to the strip. Our man was already there, standing at the side of the Waco, ready to help us aboard. Loaded up, I saluted the Mexican out my window, then cranked the plane, and we were off.

The eight or so hours it took us to get to Veracruz were uneventful and boring. I felt a growing anxiety, though—Hoffer, too, I sensed—about what awaited us. How would we find Castor and Easter? How would we get Easter away from him? What if she didn't want to leave? What would we do with Castor, once we'd caught him? Hoffer and I talked very little about any of this. She dozed, from time to time. I sang and whistled.

From Ciudad Victoria, I'd pointed the nose of the Waco southeast toward Tampico and the Gulf Coast. We'd touched down there at about eleven, gobbled down some quick tacos from a nearby stand, and had the plane gassed up. I'd asked the attendant whether he'd seen the yellow Piper Cub, but he'd only just come to work and knew nothing about planes that might have landed there, earlier.

We were soon off, again, headed straight down the coast. We passed over Tuxpan at close to three-thirty and finally arrived at Veracruz, just as the sun was about to go down. I flew over the harbor and the palm-treed downtown section of what was Mexico's main coastal city, then continued on to the southwest edge of town, to where I knew the blacktopped Veracruz airstrip was located.

There were about a dozen private planes in the tie-down area. I taxied to them, and the little yellow Piper Cub was not hard to spot. Hoffer and I got out of the Waco. I gave an attendant three dollars, American, and asked him to fill up the tank and tie us down. I walked over, then, and put my hand on the Cub's cowling. It was barely warm. Castor and Easter had been in for a while.

I spotted a *red* Piper Cub that I knew, too. "Come look at this," I said to Em Hoffer. She walked with me to the little plane. Its door wasn't locked. I opened it to show her how the rudder pedals for the front seat had been specially extended, to be in reach of short legs, and how the seat, itself, had been built up with two fat pillows. "Belongs to my tough little Mexican friend, Margarito," I said. "Gave me rides in it, when I was down here."

We got a taxi into town and took a room at a little hotel off the Plaza de Armas, called the Posada del Cafeto.

"Let's go over to the telephone office and call Stud Wampler," I said.

"Won't they be closed by now?" Hoffer asked.

I explained that Mexicans closed down and took off work at about two every afternoon for *comida* and a little rest, then opened up again from about four until eight, or so.

We walked east from our hotel and crossed the streetlighted Avenida de la República to the white stone, several-columned post office building that also housed the Mexican telegraph and telephone agency. We went up an entrance stairway that was flanked by two great stone lions.

I gave Stud's home number in Vernon to the matron behind the telephone-agency desk and asked her to place the long-distance call. Hoffer and I waited on a couch, next to a row of three phone booths, while the woman went about making the connection. Fifteen minutes or so later, she called out to me and pointed me to the booth on the end, nearest her desk.

Hoffer and I got up and went over to it. I stepped in and picked up the receiver, then put it to my ear. Hoffer stood just outside the booth's open door to listen.

After we said hello and I briefly told Stud where we were and how the trip down had gone, he said he was glad to hear that Hoffer and I'd made it okay. "Any sign, yet, of Castor and the girl?" he asked.

"None yet, here," I said. "But, as soon as we hang up, Em Hoffer and I'll search out a Veracruz friend of mine and get him to help us find them."

Stud said that Jeff Moreland had been anxiously calling him for word about our flight—and his Waco. I asked Stud to call Moreland back and reassure him.

Stud said he'd take care of it, then added, "I'm afraid I've got some bad news about Lily Morgan, Okie. I got a call from her sister in Oklahoma City this morning, to say that Lily Morgan passed away Monday night."

"Oh, my gosh!" I said. "How sad! But Em Hoffer was pretty much expecting that."

At the open door of the booth, Hoffer apparently heard my end of the conversation and marked my tone. She took hold of my arm and asked, "What is it?"

I turned away from the telephone mouthpiece and told her that Lily Morgan had died.

"What a shame!" she said. Tears came to her eyes.

I patted Hoffer on the shoulder, then returned to my conversation with Stud.

He said, "Okie, stud, you won't be surprised to know, I reckon, that the crowbar we found under the driver's side of Tobe Satville's rented car fit exactly the booger marks on the busted courthouse doors."

"You're right," I said. "I'm not surprised."

"Nother thing," Stud went on, "old lady Askew called to say

that, after all, whoever broke into the Doc's office and conked me on the head didn't get away with any whole file. Doc Askew'd made two copies of everything, she said."

"You get the copy on Easter Parnell?" I asked him.

"Got it," Stud said. "I went over and hotboxed the Askews, in person. They finally admitted everything the Parnells told us—about Askew delivering Lily Morgan's baby and turning her over to the Parnells as their own. Wouldn't say that any money changed hands, though. Made 'em show me the file on the Parnell girl. Somebody'd taken the original, but the copy was there, just like they'd said—old man Kraker and Lily Morgan, her natural parents. I took the copy."

"Find your little revolver, too?" I asked.

"Naw, but I hope *you* do," Stud said.

I said I'd try.

"Be careful, now, stud," he said.

I said I'd make a good try on that, too.

"'Nother thing, stud," he said. "Audrey Ready's been calling me. What you want me to tell her?"

"She knows that Hoffer's with me," I said. "But tell her that everything's going okay."

Stud said he would. I thanked him and told him I'd call again, soon, when I had more to report. I hung up, went to the desk, and paid for the call.

Hoffer and I started back out of the building. "It's such a sad thing, isn't it, that Lily Morgan's never going to see her daughter?" she said. She looped the long strap of her satchel purse over one shoulder as we got down the front stairs to the street and began to retrace our earlier steps.

"It is, but I sure hope *we* do," I said. "Shame, Easter's never gonna know her real mother." We walked west awhile. "We've got to catch a streetcar," I said.

"Where we going?" Hoffer asked.

"South end of Veracruz—to Boca del Río," I said. "Great modern hotel, there, the Mocambo. Possibility we might corner Castor, if he's checked into the hotel with Easter. Also, that's where my Mexican friend, the promoter I told you about, the guy named Margarito Fuentes, hangs out—in the bar. He's got connections that can help us find Castor and Easter, if they're not at the Mocambo."

We crossed over to the west side of Zaragoza Street and waited. The trolley came down the mid-street track and clanged to a stop. We stepped over to it and climbed on. It started on south, again. The evening breeze through the open windows of the car was humid, but it felt good, anyway. The Plaza de la República was on our left, the big white-washed Municipal Palace, or city hall, on our right.

The streetcar crossed the east-west Insurgentes and clacked on south. Zaragoza became a street of low shops and stores, with lots of white-washed walls, flaking stucco, and a number of old redbrick buildings—shoe stores, dry goods stores, restaurants—many with wrought-iron balconies along their second stories. Oleander and bougainvillea bushes and tall, blowing palm trees lined the sidewalks. Families came and went, in and out of the retail establishments and eating joints.

"This place is New Orleans on sleeping pills," Hoffer said.

I thought, with her mention of it, that Veracruz *was* something like New Orleans, a place I'd been, once. Colonial architecture, languid pace, a feel of quiet decay. A Negro population in Veracruz, too, like in New Orleans, first brought in as slaves by the Spaniards. Veracruz was more tropical than the Louisiana city, sleepier, too, as Em Hoffer had meant by her comment. There were other differences. The Mexican port city had its own unique, enveloping and rich smells of hot tortillas and piquant chile, its own bouncy and melodious harp and marimba music, its own Cuban-rhythm *danzón*, its white-washed walls, and the unique *huasteca* heritage of the local Indians that the Spanish *conquistadores* had found when they'd arrived in the 1500s. No other place was *really* like Veracruz. That was my view. Not New Orleans, or anywhere else.

Boca del Río, at the south end of the trolley line, was a little fishing village and the site of a well-known beach, Playa Mocambo. It was getting dark when Hoffer and I got off and walked the half block farther toward the beachside Mocambo Hotel, as, behind us, the streetcar reversed and started back into Veracruz.

We climbed the stairs and entered the hotel.

"This place is a sight!" Hoffer said, looking around in wonder.

"Like something in a picture show, isn't it?" I said. "A Hollywood musical."

The expansive, high-ceilinged lobby featured tall, stained-glass windows and a jungle of plants, gently curved walls of floor-to-ceiling mahogany-wood paneling, great flower-stalk pillars throughout, and a profusion of Art Deco electric light and other fixtures.

We stepped over to the mahogany registration desk. The clerk, a Mexican guy in a red vest, hair slicked back like Valentino, looked up.

"*Perdón, maestro,*" I said. "*¿Está aquí un tal Señor Leo Castor, por favor?*"

EASY PICKIN'S

The man looked me over carefully, without speaking.

I flashed him my sheriff badge. "*Una mujer joven está con el,*" I said. A young woman is with him.

The clerk glanced toward Em Hoffer. Is this the wife of the man you are seeking? he asked in Spanish.

No, I answered. We are law officers. The man we seek is wanted in a criminal matter. He is blond, well-dressed, speaks Spanish with a North American accent.

"*No, señor, ellos no están aquí,*" the man said, abruptly. Too abruptly, I thought. But before I could question him further, he turned away and went into a connecting office, out of sight.

"He lying?" Hoffer asked me as we turned and stepped away from the registration desk.

"I wouldn't be surprised," I said. "We'll get my friend Margarito to find out. But, first, let me quickly walk you through this place." In Veracruz for prizefights, I'd been to the Mocambo, more than once. "Built only about four years ago, when the oil rush was strong and a lot of Americans hung out here," I said. "Apparently not too busy, now, since Mexico expropriated the private oil companies."

Through double doors to the right, we entered an immense, and empty, ballroom, with the same lavish mahogany paneling and pillars as the lobby. The sound of our heels on the parquet floor echoed as we passed through to a huge adjoining room that housed a giant indoor swimming pool. Three teenage boys were playing in it. An older couple sat in deck chairs against a wall. We went around to the far side of the pool and stepped outside, through glass doors, to a covered balcony that stretched along the entire north-south wall at the back of the hotel building.

Off to the left and down a level, we could see two lighted

tennis courts. A couple of pairs of older men and women played mixed doubles on one court, their movements slowed, I figured, by a combination of age and the coastal humidity. Mocambo Beach was straight ahead and down five levels of well-lit, staired terraces, each crowded with an exuberance of blooming plants and bushes: red bougainvilleas, white oleanders, yellow birds of paradise, red gingers and heliconias, pink hibiscus—and, on the lowest level, a variety of flowering trees—white angel's trumpets, red African tulips, and lavender jacarandas. Coming from fairly dry Oklahoma, I'd been much impressed by all the greenery and flowering plants of Veracruz, and it'd taken me two trips to learn some of their names. I took pride in saying them to Hoffer.

"The hanging gardens of Nebuchadnezzar," she said.

"Before we go back in to look for Margarito Fuentes, let me tell you about him," I said. We leaned on the balcony banister, the lights of the hotel reflecting on the gentle Gulf breakers, out past the beach, below. "Bright and generous little guy. Shoot you quick, though, I think, if you messed with him. Promotes prizefights, but mainly deals in Mexican colonial art and stuff. Sells mostly to rich American women. Probably does a few other things, on the side, that we don't want to know about."

"You met him, fighting down here?"

"Treated me right," I said. "Got to know him. He liked me because I was scrappy—and because I was an American. He likes Americans, so he latched on to me. Took me a couple of times to art sales and flea markets. Speaks excellent English. Went to school for a while at Ohio State, but couldn't stand the cold, he said."

"Why Ohio State?"

"Sister living up there, or something like that," I said.

I took Hoffer's arm, then, and guided her north along the balcony to a different door from the one we'd come out of. It led directly into the roomy and dimly lit Mocambo Bar—with the same kind of mahogany paneling, pillars, and Art Deco light fixtures we'd seen in the rest of hotel, though the ceiling in the bar was much lower than in the other public rooms.

The bar was fairly crowded, but I saw Margarito right away. He sat at one of the many mahogany tables, against the right wall. He was talking in a serious manner with two gray-haired women in tennis clothes who were sipping large martinis.

Hoffer and I crossed to a table on the opposite wall. Margarito nodded almost imperceptibly to me as we passed his table. Seated, Hoffer and I both ordered a Bohemia beer. We were only about half through them when we saw the two women at Margarito's table stand up and leave. He came right over, then, walking with a silver eagle-headed cane, an affectation, I knew. I got up and bent over to embrace the tiny Mexican. He was about the size of a healthy U.S. thirteen-year-old.

"The return of the nonnative!" Margarito said. "And you look very hardy." He tilted his head back and laughed. I'd always figured that Margarito was in his fifties, but it was hard to tell, for sure. He died his hair crow black.

"This is my friend Em Hoffer," I said.

Margarito took Hoffer's hand, tilting his head back to look up to her eyes. "Ah, *señora*, what a pleasure!" he said. He kissed the hand with a flourish, then released it and pulled himself into one of the heavy mahogany chairs, his slipper-shod feet not reaching to the floor. He leaned his cane against the right arm of his chair. "Don Ray," he said. He made my name sound like the Mexican word "*rey*," king. "*Amigo*, you have returned, you know, like the swallows. And, speaking of swallows . . ." He twisted around and motioned to the bartender for another drink.

Margarito was wearing, outside his nice gray lightweight trousers, a tailored short-sleeved, white linen jacket/shirt that in Mexico was called a *guayabera*. His clothes were specially made for him, I figured. When he turned in his chair, his loose shirt flap came open a little, and I saw a big pistol tucked in the waist of his slacks. It looked to me like a German Luger, the kind you saw Hitler's storm troopers carrying in the newsreels. I glanced at Hoffer. She'd seen the gun, too.

Margarito turned back to us and straightened his shirt, then took a silver cigarette case from one of its pockets. He held the case toward Hoffer. She took a cigarette. With a silver lighter from another pocket, he lit it for her. He put another cigarette in a long silver holder and lit it for himself.

After a drag and a puff of smoke, Margarito said to Hoffer, "*Señora, yo soy jarocho. Margarito Fuentes González a sus órdenes.*" He threw his head back and laughed, heartily.

I knew that "*jarocho*" meant a *veracruzano* of mixed African and Indian blood, and I figured that Margarito was probably at least partly correct in calling himself that. He had tightly curled black hair, cut close, and his skin was sienna, with a slight tinge of chocolate.

"How's business, Don Margarito?" I asked him.

"Beesness ees a leetle slow," the Mexican said, showing one of his peculiarities. He normally spoke largely unaccented English, but, now and then, fell into a teasing kind of stereotypical Mexican-accented English, like a comic Latin figure in an American picture show.

EASY PICKIN'S

Was it self-mockery? I'd always wondered. Margarito had an odd aversion to almost anything Mexican—food, customs, music, and even Mexicans themselves, I'd sometimes thought. The tough little man dealt in Mexican colonial art and artifacts. But he really didn't like them, not for himself, at least. He personally favored something like the naively colorized print he'd once found at a flea market and bought as a gift for me. It was a large, framed, black-and-white print of the image of Our Lady of Guadalupe that some unknown and untrained Mexican artist had tried to improve upon by painting over it with pastel oils of red, green, yellow, and red.

Margarito was an Americaphile. His drink came. It was a manhattan.

I quickly filled him in on what I'd been doing, back in Oklahoma, in the years since we'd seen each other, how I'd become a sheriff. I asked about Margarito's mother. He'd taken me for dinner at her house, once. She was fine, he said. I was well aware that, in the Mexican way, it was not proper for two people to get down to business until after the preliminary courtesies had been dispensed with.

Those finished, Margarito asked, "Now, *amigo*, what brings you back to our humble country?"

"Don Margarito, we need your help," I said. "We're looking for an American who works for an oil company, here. Name's Leo Castor. Company's Kraker Oil."

Margarito took a sip from his manhattan. "President Lázaro Cárdenas, you know, has taken over the private oil companies," he said. "These gringos got, you know, too arrogant, tried to crush the union, the *petroleros*, who were only fighting for an eight-hour day. Now, it's the gringo companies that are getting crushed." He tossed his head back, long cigarette holder clenched in his teeth, and laughed.

"Yes, but this guy Castor's still down here, somewhere," I said. "He's brought an American girl with him—kidnapped her, pretty much. Mrs. Hoffer, here, and I have come to rescue the girl. We need your help, Margarito."

"What's the man, you know, look like?"

"Fancy dresser, a blondie, speaks gringo Spanish," I said. "Dangerous, antiunion muscle man. Carries a pistol."

"Good-looking, you know, the girl?"

"Yes, tall, black hair—a model," I said. "Her name's Easter."

"*Pascuala*." Margarito said the equivalent, kind of rare, woman's name in Spanish.

"Correct," I said. "We think the girl's in serious trouble."

"Veracruz is a place where pretty American girls have been turned to prostitution," Margarito said in a serious tone. "Sailors, here, like them." Then he added, more teasingly, "You interested in her personally, *amigo*? Why aren't you, you know, satisfied with this beauty, here?" He nodded toward Hoffer, then threw back his head and laughed loudly, his small feet dangling out in front of him.

"Mrs. Hoffer is a lawyer," I said. "Hired by Easter's mother to find the girl. Can you help us, Margarito?"

The little Mexican took another drink of his manhattan, then fished out the cherry and offered it to Em Hoffer. She thanked him, took the fruit with her fingers, and popped it into her mouth. He puffed on his cigarette holder, then blew the smoke out slowly.

"I have thees associate, you know," Margarito said, finally, dropping into his teasingly accented English. "Who knows, you know, the evil that lurks in the hearts of men? The Shadow knows." The Mexican laughed after the recitation of these last lines from a popular American radio series—not his usual laugh, but the famous, sinister laugh of the radio character, the Shadow.

He went on, then. "Thees associate not only knows, you know, the evil that lurks in the hearts of men. He has a leetle of it in hees own heart." Margarito again laughed the chin-uptilted laugh. "He can find anyone, especially those, you know, with evil connections. No? But, first, you know, we must find my associate. Come, we will go, now, to his office, Los Portales."

I loved the place, Los Portales. But I also knew it was not a favorite of Margarito's. Too Mexican and too *veracruzano* for him.

Margarito took up his cane, slid down from his chair, and stood. Hoffer and I got up, too. I left some pesos on the table for the check, and the three of us exited to the lobby of the hotel, then started out the front door and down the steps. Hoffer and I walked a little more slowly than usual so that Margarito could keep up.

"*¿Cuéntas con coche, amigo?*" Margarito asked.

"No car," I said. "Came down by airplane."

"*¡Por avión!*" he said, impressed. At the curb, he turned and motioned with his cane. A black Buick pulled up in front of us. A large man got out and opened the rear door for us. All three of us climbed into the backseat, Margarito on the right-hand side. He told the driver where we were going.

TWENTY-EIGHT

Los Portales was a famous block-long stretch of adjoining open-air cafés—some Mexicans called it the world's longest bar—all under the same lengthy, overhanging porch roof. The place faced south, toward the white-washed, buff-trimmed Municipal Palace and the Plaza de Armas, or *zócalo*, as Mexicans called it.

Margarito's driver let us off on the street, nearby, at about eight-thirty that Tuesday evening.

"This is the right time of day, you know, for us to find my associate," the little Mexican said as we walked to the open-air front, then along it. We passed by two side-by-side cafés. Margarito chose the third, and we turned in and picked a table, two rows back from the walk.

It was cool beneath the overhanging roof, whirling ceiling fans stirring a nice breeze. A waiter came at once and took our order—for me and Hoffer, two cold beers, or *frías*, as they were called there, with salt and lime on the side, and for Margarito, a glass of white wine. Soon, a four-member marimba group, wearing typical *huasteca* dress—matching white cotton *guayaberas* and trousers, white shoes, little peaked white straw hats, and red bandanna neckerchiefs—came along and set up on the sidewalk in front of our café. I knew that several rotating bands moved continuously down the line of cafés, then back again, playing for tips. This one struck up a lively coastal tune, one man beating a little drum set like he was killing ants, the other three band members, a kind of six-armed spider, synchronously plinking away at a beautiful hard-wood marimba.

Hoffer patted her foot, in time. "This music could get in your bones."

"We passed my associate in the second café," Margarito said. "He'll come over."

A grizzled and toasted old man in a frayed straw hat and sandals, badly faded blue shirt, and a pair of dark brown shorts shuffled into the café area from the out-front walk and stepped up to our table. He was selling spiced, steamed shrimp from the large woven basket that he lugged. I bought half a kilo, a little too much, but I was feeling hungry. The peddler spread a newspaper on the table and mounded up the pink-hued cooked shrimp, throwing in a few lime wedges for free.

An old woman in a black shawl and a worn, blue-figured cotton dress appeared, right on the heels of the shrimp man, offering hand-patted corn tortillas from a newspaper-lined fishnet bag. I bought a quarter of a kilo of these. She stacked them, warm and fresh, in the center of the table, next to the spiced shrimp. Margarito seemed to withdraw a little from all this, but Hoffer and I thought it wonderful. We peeled shrimp and, with the warm tortillas, made our own *tacos de camarón*, as Mexicans said, squeezing lime juice and sprinkling table salt and hot salsa on the shrimp for flavor, and washing everything down with swigs of cold beer. The thumping melody of the marimba band vibrated, out front.

I felt a twinge of guilt about letting the serious reason for why we'd flown down to Veracruz—finding and rescuing Easter from what could be a terrible fate—recede a little in my mind.

Just then, a dark Mexican with slicked-back hair, a big, droopy mustache, and furtive eyes pulled out a chair and quickly sat down across from Em Hoffer, to my left, Margarito's right. He was wearing nicely pressed dark blue gabardine trousers and a pale blue *guayabera* shirt.

Margarito greeted him. They shook hands. "This is my associate, Fernando," Margarito said to Hoffer and me. To Fernando, he said, "*Son mis amigos—Don Rey y la Señora Hoffer.*"

"*Mucho gusto,*" I said, reaching to shake the man's hand.

Em Hoffer smiled across the table and nodded to the new arrival. "The same as he said," she offered, nodding to her left, toward me.

"Fernando and I, you know, have worked together," Margarito said to Hoffer and me. "We have known each other for many years."

There was silence for a moment. To fill it, I asked the man called Fernando an idle question. "*¿Cuál es su ocupación o profesión, señor?*" I knew it was an inappropriate question as soon as it'd left my mouth.

The man, who spoke only Spanish, looked momentarily disconcerted. He paused, as if he were trying to decide which of several possible answers to give, then declared that he was an "importer of tractors."

Such an odd answer produced another brief moment when nobody said anything. Then, Margarito spoke up to explain to the other Mexican that Hoffer and I urgently wanted to know the whereabouts of a Kraker Oil Company man, Leo Castor, just back from the United States, and a young American woman, named Easter—*Pascuala*, Margarito added, in Spanish—whom Castor had brought with him. Margarito gave a description of the pair and said that they had probably arrived in Veracruz that early afternoon. "*Te pagarán mis amigos por la información.*" My friends will pay you for the information.

We will? I thought. I said, "We will."

The man—Fernando—asked a couple of quick questions, which Margarito fielded. Fernando wanted to know the location of Kraker Oil's office in Veracruz and whether the company's affairs had already been handed over to the Mexican government. Margarito told him that he figured that the office was somewhere south of Veracruz, on the highway to Coatzalcoalcos, and that he imagined that the transfer was virtually complete.

The man stood and spoke directly to me. "*Señor, aquí mismo nos vemos mañana a la hora de la cena,*" he said. We'll see each other, right here, tomorrow, at the time of the *cena*, supper time.

I figured that he meant around nine or ten.

The Mexican turned to Em Hoffer and bowed slightly. "*Con su permiso,*" he said. With your permission. He turned quickly and walked back the way he'd come—and out of sight.

"If your two people are in Veracruz, you know, Fernando will find them," Margarito said.

"What does he *really* do for a living?" I asked.

Margarito took a slow sip of his wine. "*Amigo*, you know, it's like the code of the North American West," he said. "Never ask a man where he comes from or what his business is. Right?" He went on, then, in his teasing Mexican accent. "We did a lot of crazy theengs, you know, Fernando and I. We had an old truck that looked like sheet on the outside. No? Nobody suspected us. Once we brought back from Houston all the equipment of a dentist who was remodeling—the chair, the dreels, every-theeng—and sold them in Mexico Ceety." Margarito paused and looked at his expensive gold wristwatch. "And, now, kind friends, I must take my leave. I have an appointment, you know, at the Mocambo."

He slipped out of the chair and stood, taking up his cane. He asked where we were staying.

At the Posada del Cafeto, I told him.

"I hope, you know, that you enjoy your stay in Veracruz," the little Mexican said. "I would like for you to be my guests for *comida*, tomorrow at two, in a decent and modern restaurant, La Alhambra."

I knew the place, over on Avenida Montero. It served paella and other Spanish, not Mexican, food. I said Hoffer and I would be honored.

When Margarito had left, Hoffer and I each had another *fría*, then headed to our nearby room.

We were in Veracruz. So were Leo Castor and Easter Parnell. Hoffer and I went to bed, thinking about how soon we'd find the pair we were looking for and what we'd do when we did find them. We went to bed thinking about other things, too.

TWENTY-NINE

Wednesday morning, Em Hoffer and I were slow to leave our room at the Posada del Cafeto. Both of us woke up feeling frustrated that we had so much extra time to kill before we could get information about the whereabouts of Easter and Castor. But we tried to make the best of the delay.

Later, we walked to Los Portales, again, for a kind of combination breakfast and lunch, duplicating what we'd enjoyed so much, there, from the night before—*frías* and the self-constructed *tacos de camarón*, with ingredients for them bought from the same strolling vendors. The marimba band was back, too, plinking and bonging away, melodiously.

Sitting under the overhanging porch, ceiling fans whirring, Hoffer said she was afraid we were having too good a time. She felt that we should be doing something more, looking for Easter and Castor in some other way and not depending, totally, on Margarito's associate.

I said that I had the same feeling, exactly, but that I couldn't imagine what else we might be doing. Veracruz was too big a town to try to find somebody, without leads.

"What about going to the local police?" Hoffer asked.

I didn't think that was a good idea. "Police may be on the take," I said. "On Castor's take."

We decided to look around Veracruz. It was a beautiful spring morning. We got up and walked east to the harbor. I pointed out, for Hoffer, the old fort, San Juan Ulúa. We went south, then east on Insurgentes, to the Carranza Lighthouse and Naval Headquarters, with its two white-uniformed Mexican sailors standing guard at the arched entrance. Inside was a little historical museum, which didn't take long for us to walk through.

Back outside in the bright sun, we strolled farther east, along the waterfront, to the end of the street, then turned around to retrace our steps. Suddenly, across the pavement from us, on the harbor side, there was a screeching of brakes.

Hoffer and I glanced in that direction. At the wheel of a late-model, black Chrysler, staring at us, was Leo Castor, himself. He looked as much like he couldn't believe his eyes as we must have. Then, glaring at Hoffer and me intensely, he stuck his left hand out of the window, aimed the forefinger of it at us, and snapped down his thumb, like a hammer. Before she or I could do or say anything, Castor put the Chrysler in gear and, making the tires squeal, sped off. He turned right at the first corner, and was out of sight.

Hoffer and I stood, transfixed for a moment. We hadn't even thought to look at the license tag.

"We saw him, but we still don't know how to find him," she said.

"He'll put somebody on us," I said. "We're going to have to be careful."

We started walking, again, toward Avenida Montero and the restaurant known as La Alhambra.

Margarito's black Buick was at the curb, his heavyset driver standing nearby. We went in and told the man in front that we were joining Señor Fuentes. He led us toward the back of the large room, which was decorated with wall paintings of the Alhambra and other scenes of Spain.

Margarito slipped out of his chair at our approach, gave me a Mexican *abrazo*, or hug, and kissed Em Hoffer's hand.

We immediately told him the news about seeing Castor.

"Be patient and be careful, *amigos*," he said, "and everything will work out. Nothing to do until we get the report from Fernando. In the meantime, try to relax a little, enjoy yourself."

It didn't seem right, but what else could we do? Margarito shared my view, when I asked him, that it was not a good idea to try to get the local police to help us.

It was a long *comida*, in the Mexican way. And a delightful one, as it turned out. Sautéed calamari to begin. Cold gazpacho, next. A wonderful Spanish paella for the main course. And a good deal of wine from Rioja, from start to finish. Dessert was something like peach melba.

Margarito told us that there was to be an outdoor musical program, in the early evening, some kind of anniversary performance. It was to take place on a stage set up in the Plaza de Armas, the *zócalo*, right near our little hotel.

"A kind of *jarocho* festival," Margarito said, by way of explanation. "Celebrates the African and Indian blood of us *veracruzanos*. It's not, you know, my cup of tea, but the *señora* might like it." He motioned toward Hoffer. "We'll meet, afterward, at Los Portales. No?"

Hoffer and I agreed. Margarito paid, and, outside, we left him at the curb, by his big car. She and I walked to the Posada del Cafeto and took a little nap.

A quarter past seven that evening, freshened up and rested—and with time to kill—the two of us were out on the plaza. We heard the music before we saw it. A temporary stage had been built, and wooden folding chairs set up in rows in front of it. The crowd was large.

We kept a sharp lookout as we searched for seats, trying to see if anybody was watching or tailing us. There was no one, so far as we could tell. We found vacant chairs, about a third of the way down toward the stage, just as one Cuban-sounding musical number—with strumming guitars, shaking gourds, and pounding bongos—ended and another began.

A dozen dark-skinned young *jarochos* danced onstage—men in fluffy red shirts and sashes, women in flouncy, frilly red skirts and white blouses—stamping their heels, clapping their hands, and whirling feverishly in the *danzón*. In Spanish, they sang, flapping their elbows like bird wings: *"¡Vuela sin tardanza! Mientras que la vida dure lugar tiene la esperanza."*

I whispered a quick translation for Hoffer. Fly without delay. While there's life, there's hope.

The time went quickly, though not quickly enough for me. I was restless, anxious to get on with our search. As soon as the program ended, Hoffer and I walked to the nearby Los Portales and were both glad to find that Margarito had already arrived, ahead of us. We ordered drinks, all three of us the same as we'd had, there, the night before—Margarito, white wine, Hoffer and I, two *frías*.

"Would you like a leetle tacko?" Margarito asked us, teasingly, while the waiter was still at our table. We ordered some of pork, some of chicken.

"How much should I pay Fernando?" I asked Margarito.

"Pay him in dollars," the Mexican said. "Twenty, if he's got something, five if not. But I am sure he'll have the information you want."

Fernando, the Mexican with the big, droopy mustache and the furtive eyes, showed up at Los Portales about thirty minutes after Hoffer and I had.

We'd left a vacant chair for him, as before, across the table from Em Hoffer. Fernando pulled it out and sat down. He answered Margarito that, no, he did not want anything to eat.

"*¿Y la información?*" I asked him.

The man looked suspiciously to his left and right, as if what he was doing might be illegal, then spoke in a low voice. Yes, the man Castor had arrived in Veracruz the preceding afternoon, Tuesday. He and the young woman with black hair had checked into the Mocambo Hotel. One room, with a single *matrimonial* bed.

I translated for Hoffer. "So, the desk clerk *was* lying," she said to me. "They *were* there."

"Sleeping together," I said. "They were obviously at the Mocambo, yesterday, when we were all there." To Fernando, I asked, "*¿Y entonces? ¿Todavía están allí?*" Then, what? Are they still there?

The man and woman swam in the hotel pool, late yesterday afternoon, Fernando said, then went to their room, where they spent the night. They had checked out of the Mocambo, that very morning.

"*¿A dónde fueron?*" I asked. Where did they go?

Fernando said that he'd talked with the bellman who'd carried the luggage to the car, which, he said, was a late-model, black Chrysler sedan with a U.S. license, state of Oklahoma tag, in fact. The driver of the car had told the bellman that he was taking Castor and the young woman to a house in Veracruz that belonged to Kraker Oil Company.

I asked why the pair had stayed Tuesday night in the Mocambo Hotel if Kraker Oil owned a residence in the city.

Fernando said that he didn't know, but, maybe, the house had to be cleaned up, first, or somebody else moved out.

Where was the residence?

The bellman got nothing from the driver about the location, Fernando said. But Fernando had found out from another source, a man who'd earlier worked for Kraker Oil, that the company owned a house, a residence, in southeast Veracruz, close to the corner of Avenida Simón Bolívar and Bulevar Ávila Camacho and near a beach area called Villa del Mar. Fernando went on to report that he, himself, had driven around the area that afternoon, looking for a house with the black Chrysler in the drive, but he'd had no success. One more thing, he said. The former Kraker employee had said that the Kraker house had a long driveway down to it from the street, lined by bougainvilleas. That was the best Fernando could do.

It was pretty good, I thought, though I wished that he'd found the actual whereabouts of the house.

I translated everything quickly for Hoffer, then asked Fernando whether the young woman, Easter, appeared at the

Mocambo to have been forced in any way to accompany Castor to the car.

The Mexican said that the hotel bellman indicated nothing like that. He'd said she seemed happy, even. Then, Fernando added a warning. Castor is a dangerous man! He is known to have hired Mexican judicial police officers as his accomplices—to beat up local union strikers, maybe even kill some.

I took from my Levi's pocket two ten-dollar bills, which I'd previously folded, discreetly handed them to Fernando, then thanked him for his help. The Mexican quickly took his leave.

Margarito spoke up. "Too late, tonight, *amigo*—too dark. I'll bring my car around for you in the morning, if you want, and we'll drive through that area, you know, together, until we find your people."

I thanked the tough little Mexican and said that we *did* want.

"We meet in front of your Posada del Cafeto, then, at ten," Margarito said.

I knew that he had an apartment, somewhere nearby. I agreed to the time, though it was a later start than I would have liked.

"You have a peestol, *amigo*?" Margarito asked. "You may need one, with thees man, Cahstore."

"No, no pistol," I said.

"I do," Em Hoffer said and patted the satchel purse in her lap.

An image of Stud Wampler's little .38 police special flashed into my mind. I couldn't help what I was thinking.

THIRTY

I had time Thursday morning for a harbor-side sunrise devotional exercise, with Em Hoffer looking on, and, finally, participating. She even added a little prayer at the end of mine—for Easter and for the soul of Lily Morgan. The two of us had jogged north of the *centro* to a beach called Playa Norte. No one was around, that early. So, when we'd finished the devotional, and after I'd talked her into it, Hoffer and I peeled off our clothes and went for a refreshing swim in our underwear.

Afterward, as we quickly pulled our clothes back on, I noticed that we weren't as alone as I'd thought. There was a black Ford sedan parked at the curb, a half block east, as Hoffer and I came back up to the street from the beach. Two men sat in the front seat, seemingly engrossed in their own conversation and paying no attention to the two of us.

A little damp and sandy, we jogged back to the Posada del Cafeto. Every now and then, I looked back and saw that the

Ford was slowly, but certainly, following us. Upstairs in the hotel, Hoffer and I showered—in our own private bathroom, a welcome change—and dressed, wearing the same outfits of the day before, except that Em Hoffer put on a blue bolero jacket over her white cotton, low-necked peasant blouse, the matching piece for her blue cotton skirt.

We walked over to Los Portales, then, for sweet rolls and *café lechero*, as it was called there—coffee with milk—and, afterward, went back to the Posada del Cafeto to wait for Margarito. Nobody we could detect followed us, going or coming.

Margarito's black Buick pulled up to the curb in front of our hotel, almost exactly at ten. My friend jumped out, embraced me and kissed Em Hoffer's hand. I thought she was beginning to like that. We all climbed in the backseat. Margarito instructed the driver, and we sped off.

South, on Independencia, we went to Simón Bolívar, then east to its intersection with Ávila Camacho. After that, it was up one nearby street and down the other. Back and forth.

Nothing. No sight of a black Chrysler sedan of any kind, much less one with an Oklahoma tag.

It got to be a little after one—with still a third, or more, of the streets of the area not yet driven out.

"Detective work, you know, makes a man hungry, *amigo*," Margarito said to me. He told the driver to go back to Hidalgo Street. Then, he spoke again to me. "There's a telephone on the corner. I'll call my mother. She is a *funcionaria*, you know, at the customs house. We'll go to that restaurant you like, *amigo*, and she'll join us."

I knew at once the place the little Mexican meant. It was my absolute favorite in Veracruz. La Joya del Mar—the Jewel of the

Sea—was above a corner fish market on Xicotencatl Street, a small upstairs restaurant with blue-tiled interior walls.

The three of us had already ordered Bohemias and a white wine when Margarito's mother came up the narrow stairs to join us. She was a patrician-looking woman who, I thought, might have descended directly from some Spaniard who'd landed at Veracruz with Cortés in the 1500s—thin-nosed, olive-skinned, straight black hair slightly graying. She was dressed attractively in a long black skirt, white blouse, and black vest. She kissed her son on both cheeks, then did the same with Em Hoffer and me, having to go up on her toes with us.

Señora Fuentes spoke English well, though with more of a Mexican accent than her son—at least, when he wasn't teasing. "*Hijo*, I did not think you liked this place," she said to Margarito after she was seated.

"These gringo tourists like it," he said, meaning Hoffer and me, and threw back his head and laughed.

"And, Señor Dunn, you have returned," Mrs. Fuentes said. "We are happy."

With everybody's agreement, Margarito's mother ordered for all four of us—spiced shrimp and fried calamari, to begin. Then, a great fish stew, with crab, shrimp, and fish in a piquant red sauce. *Huachinango estilo veracruzano* for the main course—a whole red snapper, fried in garlic and smothered with a salsa of tomatoes and green chiles. Flaming bananas for dessert.

I told Margarito's mother about Lily Morgan, who had died, and about the long-lost daughter, Easter Parnell, an heiress who didn't know she was one and whom Em Hoffer and I were trying to find. I told her—and some of this was news to Margarito, too—about the man Tobe Satville being shoved out of his own airplane, and killed, about someone, after Easter's birth records, breaking into the doctor's office, knocking the deputy in the head, and stealing his gun. I told her about the man Leo Castor bringing Easter to Mexico, said that Em Hoffer and I were deeply worried about what sinister plan Castor might have in mind for the young woman.

"*¡Que horrible!*" Mrs. Fuentes said when I was finished. She shuddered and crossed herself, as if to ward off the evil eye. "*Mi tío*—my uncle—is a judge. The brother of my husband, God rest his soul, who died of blood poisoning when Margarito was young. He has told me of instances where young American girls have been enticed into the bad life, here, in the city of Veracruz. You should hurry!"

A look of dismay clouded Em Hoffer's face. She would have crossed herself, too, if she'd been Catholic, I thought. "We have to find Easter, before it's too late," Hoffer said. "We've driven through most of the streets where they say Castor and she are staying." Hoffer described the area near Villa del Mar.

"I have a house in that area," Margarito's mother said. "You can all stay with me until you find the man and girl."

I thanked her for her kindness, but politely demurred, saying we were already well taken care of.

"Do you have a description of the house you are looking for" Mrs. Fuentes asked.

We told her about the long driveway and the bougainvilleas.

Mrs. Fuentes was suddenly excited. "I think I know that house!" She said there was a private drive like the one we described, hard to notice, in the second block west of Ávila Camacho, on Simón Bolívar. "There are two big araucaria trees, like big Christmas trees painted an unnatural dark green, at the curb. Go in between them."

EASY PICKIN'S

Em Hoffer and I were as excited as Mrs. Fuentes was. We finished eating as fast as we could. All four of us then loaded up in Margarito's Buick. We dropped his mother off at the customs house, then proceeded at once to Simón Bolívar.

Soon, exactly as Mrs. Fuentes had said, two blocks back from Ávila Camacho, we saw the two dark green araucaria trees, and the private lane between them that we hadn't noticed before.

Hoffer yelled out the news. "There's a house down there, down that lane."

She was right. Margarito ordered his driver to stop, back up a little, and turn into the narrow private driveway, which was unpaved, but hard-packed with a mix of crushed oyster shells and gravel. There was heavy vegetation on each side of the lane—large oleander and bougainvillea bushes and, here and there, *hule* and magnolia trees. The tops of some of the trees on each side touched in places and almost made a kind of arch, overhead.

About fifty yards down the driveway, surrounded by tall beech trees and more araucarias, was a two-story stucco house painted a pastel green. Wooden steps in front of it led up to a porch that stretched across the width of the residence.

On the west side of the house sat a late-model, black Chrysler. We all saw it at the same time. "Bingo!" I said.

"And it's an Oklahoma tag!" Hoffer cried when we were a little closer. "We've found the right house. Easter's in there."

Margarito told his driver to turn around. Fifteen yards or so short of the porch, the man wheeled around on a loop and drove back up the packed surface of the lane toward Simón Bolívar. At Margarito's instruction, the driver pulled over to the right, close to the bushes, and stopped, a little way before we got back

251

to the paved street. A black bird with a long tail—the Mexican name was *tordo*—leaped into flight from a high branch.

"Now what, *amigo*?" Margarito asked.

Hoffer echoed the Mexican. "Now what?"

"We watch," I said. I really wasn't sure what our next move should be. I needed to think. Maybe Easter would come out of the house, alone, for some reason, and we could grab her. Was there some way we could do what was needed without violence?

"We want this car out of sight, *amigo*," Margarito said. The three of us got out. Margarito directed his driver to park the Buick up on Simón Bolívar, where it couldn't be seen from the house. Hoffer opened the back door again and pitched her purse in on the seat.

The car pulled away from the pavement, turned right, and disappeared. All three of us pushed into the bushes, watching the house, with its window blinds and curtains all drawn, waiting for something to happen, not knowing exactly what.

Suddenly, Margarito said, "I think, you know, we have been spotted, as they say."

He was right. The front door of the house opened slightly, and a person peered out in our direction. We couldn't tell whether it was a man or a woman. The door soon closed, again. We moved farther back into the bougainvillea and oleander bushes.

Another fifteen minutes or so passed. Margarito and Hoffer lit cigarettes, turning their heads with each exhale, so as not to be so noticeable to those in the house.

Then, we saw the front door of the green stucco open, completely. The three of us tried to keep out of sight while still carefully keeping watch. An old Mexican woman came out. She closed the door behind her, pulled a black shawl over her head, and descended the porch steps. She walked heavily up the hard-packed lane in our direction.

When she was near, the three of us stepped out of the bushes. She stopped, startled, putting a hand to her mouth as if to block a cry. She was as wrinkled as a raisin and looked nearly as dark.

"*Discúlpenos, Señora,*" Margarito said to her in a reassuring voice. Then, continuing on in Spanish, he said that "for the authorities," he and his two companions, here, were conducting an important investigation. That was not altogether untrue.

I have done nothing wrong, the old woman said in Spanish. She said this somewhat defiantly. I whispered translations for Em Hoffer.

We know you haven't, Margarito said. He asked the woman for what purpose she had been in the green stucco house.

The man sent for me, she answered.

What man? Who was it that sent for you?

"*Señor Castor,*" the woman said.

For what reason?

I am a *curandera*, the Mexican woman said with a kind of proud shake of her head. I have been that for forty years, she added. No one has ever complained about me.

I continued to translate for Hoffer, the best I could. A *curandera* is a native doctor of folk medicine and remedies, I said.

No one is complaining about you, now, *señora*, Margarito told the woman. Is someone sick in the house?

I simply gave the young woman some of my special tea, yesterday, the Mexican woman said.

Is the name of this young woman *Pascuala*—Easter?

"*Sí, señor. Así es.*"

Is the young woman sick?

"*No, señor. No es enferma.*"

What is the tea that you gave her?

At its base is *ruda*, the Mexican woman said.

Margarito turned to Em Hoffer and me and said in English, "It's a plant, or herb, you know, that in English is called 'rue,'" he said. "It has several medical uses. Was your young woman, you know, pregnant?"

"Yes, " I said.

Hoffer was shocked. "What?"

I didn't respond.

Margarito turned back to the Mexican *curandera*. How does the young woman—*Pascuala*—feel, now?

"*Pascuala ya está de luto,*" the old woman said. Easter is mourning.

Margarito thanked her and stepped back to allow the Mexican woman to go on her way.

"The *curandera*, you know, did not want to say so," Margarito said to me and Em Hoffer, "but she has just caused your young woman, you know, to have a miscarriage."

"Lord, what next?" Hoffer said. "What do we do, now?"

Before anyone could answer, a black Ford sedan suddenly wheeled off Simón Bolívar and into the private lane. I recognized it, at once, as the same car Hoffer and I had seen earlier, when we'd gone for a swim. The car's tires slid to an abrupt stop, next to where the three of us stood. Two men in street clothes, *guayaberas* outside their trousers, leaped from the car, each with a pistol in his hand. One man grabbed me by the arm, the other, Hoffer. Hoffer appeared quite frightened. I was alarmed.

"*¿Ustedes son gringos, verdad?*" the taller of the two men, the one with a Zapata mustache, demanded of me.

We are, I said in Spanish. He's not. I motioned toward Margarito.

What is the problem? Margarito asked, appearing somewhat calmer than Em Hoffer and I. Perhaps there is a way to work this out.

Not you, the shorter man said to Margarito. You are a Mexican, right?

Margarito said he was.

We don't want you, the man said. We want these two. "*Se prohibe la entrada ilegal.*" Trespass is prohibited. That, apparently, was the trumped-up reason for seizing us.

The two men began roughly to jerk Hoffer and me toward the black car. They opened the back door and shoved us in, Hoffer first, then me.

Where are you taking them? Margarito asked.

"*A la cárcel municipal.*" To the city jail.

Margarito spoke English to me, in a low voice. "These men must be judicial police on Castor's payroll," he said before the door on my side was shut. "I'll get you out."

"*No les hable inglés,*" the tall man said sternly to Margarito. Don't speak English to them. "*¡Vayase!*" Leave!

The back door was slammed shut. The two men jumped into the front seat, the short one under the wheel. The driver rapidly backed and turned the car around, then sped up to Simón Bolívar and swerved right onto it, toward the *centro*.

Perhaps, there is some way we could compensate you for your trouble, I said in Spanish, leaning forward, toward the taller of the two men, the one seated on the passenger side. I'd heard plenty of bad things about Mexican jails.

"*¡Silencio!*" the man ordered.

THIRTY-ONE

It was a long night. Not until about nine on Friday morning was my name finally called, back in the cells, and I was brought out to the booking desk. I was delighted when I saw that Margarito was waiting for me. We embraced. I had slept in my clothes, on a stone floor—what little I'd slept, at all—in a big, barred pen with a dozen other men, most of them looking like pretty tough customers. I had a headache. My dark hair was sticking up every which way, I could tell. I needed a bath and a shave. A sour jail smell was all over me.

At the desk, I was about to ask anxiously about Hoffer when she, too, showed up, escorted by a matron. Her clothes were as wrinkled as mine, her red hair just as tousled. We hugged.

"Not as bad a night as it might have been," Hoffer said.

"Bad enough," I said.

Margarito told the police officer behind the desk to get our things, Hoffer's and mine. The man stepped back to a cabinet.

"How'd you get us out, *amigo*?" I asked Margarito. "What did it cost you?"

"A friend of mine, you know, is the *delegado* for the presidency, for President Cárdenas, here in the state," Margarito said. "All I had to do, you know, was to tell him that Castor, who had you two put in here, was a North American oilman. That was enough to get my friend, the *delegado*, down here, you know, this morning. He wouldn't stay after he commanded that you be released."

The desk officer returned and handed my things across the counter to me—billfold, comb, and some Mexican coins. I checked, and the money in my wallet seemed to be the same as when I'd given the wallet to the police, the preceding night.

Margarito and I looked to Hoffer. "I didn't have anything for them to take," she said. "I left my purse in Margarito's car." I took her by the arm, and the three of us headed toward the front door of the Municipal Palace. Hoffer turned back for a moment toward the desk officer. "Thank you for your hospitality," she called.

Margarito's black Buick was at the curb. The driver jumped out and opened the back door. We piled in. Hoffer retrieved her satchel purse from the floor.

The driver turned to look over the seat toward us. "*¿A dónde, jefe?*" he asked Margarito.

The tough little Mexican looked at Hoffer and me. "Time to storm the bastille, *amigos*!" he said. "Your man, Castor, won't be expecting us, so soon. You two ready?"

"*¡Santiago—y a ellos!*" I said. I knew that was the battle cry of the Spanish *conquistadores* before they charged. Saint James— and at them!

"Whatever *he* said," Hoffer said.

To the green stucco house, Margarito commanded the driver. West, we roared in the Buick, to Independencia, then south until we could take a left on Simón Bolívar. We neared the twin araucaria-tree entrance. Margarito reached under his *guayabera* and dragged out the Luger. It looked huge in his small hand—and as dangerous as his dark eyes had become.

"Time to get out your pistol, too, *señora*," he said to Hoffer. Then, to me, he said, "The car stops at the end of the drive, we're out and on the porch. No knocking. *Amigo*, you kick the door in—and all three of us are inside in a rush!"

Hoffer reached into her purse. I almost wanted to close my eyes, to avoid seeing what kind of gun she'd come out with. Not a .38 police special, I hoped!

She jerked out a little .32 automatic. I let out my breath.

Hoffer caught this reaction at once. "You thought I'd have your deputy's gun—that I'm the one who broke in at Dr. Askew's? You bastard!"

We swerved into the narrow driveway and sped to the green stucco house. The car slid to a stop.

"Let's hit it!" I yelled.

We were all out of the car immediately, and rapidly up on the porch. I was in the lead. In a full charge, hardly changing stride, I raised my right foot and crashed it against the front door. The lock burst loose from the facing, and the door swung wildly around on its hinges, banging against the wall behind with a blast.

Margarito ran in, first, the Luger pointed ahead, Hoffer next, with her little .32. I was in back, with no weapon, but focused and ready for whatever might come.

Nobody was in the living room. We all stopped a second and looked warily left and right, and up a stairway. Suddenly, Leo Castor rushed at us from a straight-ahead archway that led from the dining room. He came, shooting. Twice, the pistol in his hand boomed, and, in between those two shots, Margarito's Luger exploded, once.

Once was enough. Margarito's big bullet slammed into Castor's chest and drove him back against the dining room table, which broke in the middle and collapsed under his weight. With a shocked look in his eyes, Castor, who was in his pajamas and barefoot, settled to the floor in a sitting position, his legs sticking out oddly in front of him. A red stain began to spread under a hand that he held to his chest.

Everything became eerily quiet, except for the ringing in my ears. The harsh smell of gunpowder filled the room, and there was still some haze from the shots. Hoffer, Margarito, and I quickly looked each other over. Castor's two bullets had both apparently missed all of us, and dug into the front wall. Hoffer, behind Margarito, hadn't fired her little weapon at all.

The shooting was over. Leo Castor was breathing, but heavily. His eyes were wide as he silently watched us.

A couple of feet from Castor's outstretched right hand, I saw the gun he'd used, then apparently dropped to the floor when shot. The pistol was a .45 automatic, I could see—definitely not Stud's little revolver.

I stepped over to Castor's slumped body and yelled at him, as if he were hard of hearing. "You shove Tobe Satville out of his airplane?"

Castor nodded his head up and down, then slumped more, making no sound.

"We gotta get a doctor, here, right quick," I said.

Margarito stepped over and put a small hand to Castor's throat. "Too late," he said. Margarito didn't sound sorry.

Rapidly surveying the living room, I saw a tooled-leather briefcase on the dark-wood coffee table. I went over and undid the latch, then turned the case upside down.

Some papers spilled out. I picked them up and hurriedly leafed through them, extracting one. "No copy of Doc Askew's file, but here's the birth record for Easter Parnell that Satville got by breaking into the county clerk's office," I said.

"Sounds like you're surprised, Okie, to see the clerk's page in Castor's briefcase," Hoffer said. "Thought to accuse me of that crime, too?"

I didn't answer, but I was making rapid calculations. Satville, of course, had broken into the county clerk's office and taken the birth-record page, then Leo Castor had grabbed it from Satville's car, after he killed Satville. But, if Satville or Castor, not someone else, had broken into Doc Askew's office, why weren't Askew's records in Castor's briefcase, too? And where was the blackjack Castor'd used on Satville in the airplane—the same one he, or somebody, had used on Stud at Askew's office?

Suddenly remembering where I was, I thought of Easter. "Up the stairs!" I yelled.

Hoffer bounded after me. On the landing, we saw three doors, one closed. We chose the closed one. It was the correct one.

Easter screamed as we rushed into her room. She was sitting up in bed, looking nearly disabled with fright, sheet up to her face. She was wide-eyed, her usually olive-toned face flour white.

The young woman recognized me at once. "Okie?" she cried.

Hoffer and I hurried to the bed. I put my hand soothingly on Easter's shoulder. Hoffer sat down by her and began comfortingly to brush the black hair back from her face.

"Don't be afraid," I said. "Everything's going to be all right."

"What's happened?" she asked, very scared. "What in the world's happened? I heard crashes and shots. I was too weak, too frightened, to go see." She began to cry.

Margarito called from downstairs. "*Amigos*, time we got out of here!"

"Who's that?" Easter asked.

"A Mexican friend of ours," I said.

Margarito yelled again. "None of us wants to be here, you know, when the police come. You must get the girl and grab her things, you know, and let's get out of here."

"What?" Easter said.

"Get up and put on some clothes, girl, as quickly as you can," Hoffer said sternly. She jerked the covers off Easter, revealing her in a peach nightgown, and, taking her by the arm, assisted her out of bed. "Put this on!" Hoffer said, grabbing clothing items from various parts of the room and pitching them in Easter's direction—underwear from an open suitcase, a white blouse and a purple linen suit from hangers in a corner closet, black slippers from the floor. "Put these on!"

I closed and buckled up Easter's suitcase, then grabbed it and headed downstairs. In the living room, I stuffed the loose county clerk page inside my shirtfront and rebuttoned it. Margarito was at the door, watchful.

"Hurry up, y'all!" I yelled up to the two women.

They soon appeared at the head of the stairs. Easter looked as if she might faint, and Hoffer was having to support her, with an arm around the young woman's waist. The two rapidly descended.

"Oh, my God!" Easter screamed as she suddenly saw the slumped and lifeless body of the man she knew as John Carter, with all the blood on his chest. "Oh, my God!" She tried to jerk away from Hoffer and run to where Castor lay. Hoffer held on to her, wouldn't let her. She practically dragged Easter toward the open door.

"But what's happened to John?" Easter cried. "He was so good to me!"

"No, he wasn't," Hoffer said. She insistently jerked Easter along, and out to the porch.

"I can't leave him like that," Easter said.

"Yes, you can," Hoffer said. "We've got to get out of here." She guided the young woman down the stairs and to the car. The driver held the door open. They got into the backseat.

We put Easter in the middle, Hoffer and I on each side of her. Margarito jumped into the passenger seat in front.

Easter seemed almost in shock. I didn't feel much better.

Margarito commanded the driver, "*¡Al aeropuerto!*"

THIRTY-TWO

At the Veracruz airport, Margarito ordered his man to drive the Buick right out to where the planes were tied down, and just to the rear of Jeff Moreland's white-and-red Waco.

We bundled a compliant and dazed Easter Parnell into the backseat, where she curled her thin, lanky body under the air corps raincoat that Em Hoffer spread over her. The three bags we pitched on the floor behind the front seats.

Hoffer and I turned back, then, to say good-bye, and thanks, to Margarito. He kissed Hoffer's hand, then embraced me.

The tough little Mexican waved away my attempt to express appreciation for all his help. "You owe me, you know, Gringo, another prizefight, down here—for no pay. Eh? *¡Que te vaya bien, amigo!*"

After we'd untied the plane and pushed it back, Hoffer and I climbed in, closing the door behind us, then settled into the front seats. The Waco cranked up with no trouble. At the end of the runway, I hurriedly ran through the checklist, then shoved in the throttle and we were down the runway—and off. I banked the plane and pointed the nose toward the north.

For the first hours, nobody talked. My own mind was on getting out of Mexico as soon as we could. We touched down in Tuxpan for gas. From a nearby stand, I bought a great quantity of tacos and tamales, as well as four Coca-Colas, paying to take the bottles with us, and an opener. We were rapidly up and away, again, northeast toward Ciudad Victoria.

In the plane, Hoffer kept herself turned sideways between the front seats, her hand extended to pat Easter's shoulder and, now and again, smooth the black hair back from the troubled young forehead.

"You're safe, now, Easter," Hoffer said occasionally. "Everything's all right."

Easter seemed only half conscious. I turned to check on her, myself, from time to time. The young woman's eyes stayed shut, as if she was in a trance. She drowsed, seemingly almost unaware of her whereabouts or what was happening. Now and then, she would rouse and whimper a little, like a child waking from a bad dream. Then, comforted by Hoffer's warm attentions, she would drop again into what appeared to be a kind of dazed numbness.

I buzzed Ciudad Victoria, and, again, the guy in the pickup came out to fill our tank.

"We're pressing on," I said to Hoffer. We'd taken turns going behind a big bush while the Mexican guy put gas in the Waco.

"In the dark?"

"Corpus's got lights," I said. "And I want to be out of this country, quick as we can."

In the air, again, as Easter continued to sleep in the backseat, Hoffer turned to face me. "I can't believe you made love to me, Okie," she said, "all the time suspecting I was the one who broke into Dr. Askew's office, and probably killed Tobe Satville."

"Forget all that, Em," I said. "I'm sorry. I really am."

"Saying you're sorry doesn't seem like enough," she said. "Told you I wasn't in this for the money. Just trying to help Lily Morgan. Now, poor thing, Lily'll never see her daughter." Hoffer began very quietly to cry.

"I know," I said. "I know."

She wiped the tears away with the fingers of both hands. "I feel so grimy, dirty, inside and out," she said. "Gotta get a hot bath and some clean clothes before too long or I'll die."

She did look awful. Her hair was a mess, her white blouse and blue skirt and jacket soiled and wrinkled. I assumed that I looked no better.

I spoke soothingly to Hoffer. "I'll find us a tourist cabin, soon as we get to Corpus. Close to midnight, I figure. Take baths, get a few hours' sleep, all three of us. We'll feel better." I hoped that would be true.

In the air, again, we droned on toward the Rio Grande, Hoffer dozing, off and on, in the passenger seat, Easter still quiet in the back. About three hours later, we passed over the lights of Matamoros and, then, across the Rio Grande, the lights of Brownsville, Texas.

I felt for a moment like singing the "Star-Spangled Banner." Instead, without thinking about it, I started whistling and singing a cowboy song to myself, not loud enough to disturb the other two, I thought: "As I was out walking, the streets of Laredo . . ."

I went through the song several times. And it was only when I stopped that Easter sat up in the backseat—my dad would have said, "Sittin' up, ready to take nourishment."

"You want a Coca-Cola and something to eat?" I asked her, glancing back.

"Yeah, thanks, Okie," Easter said. She rubbed her eyes and pushed her hair from them.

Hoffer roused quickly and picked up a Coca-Cola from the floorboard in front of her, then opened it and passed it back to the young woman. Hoffer rummaged around, then, in one of the two sacks at her feet and assembled a taco and a couple of tamales for Easter, handing these back, too.

Easter ate and drank. She seemed to regain some of her strength in doing so, some of her old assurance, too. When she spoke, it was angrily and with a little of a prosecutor's tone. "Why did you two come down here, anyway, Okie?" she asked, leaning forward, toward Hoffer and me. "Who killed John Carter? I can't get it all straight, can't believe all that happened, back there."

The Waco's engine made quite a bit of noise. The airplane cabin wasn't the best place for a conversation. But there was no help for it.

"It's time we talked, Easter," I said, looking back at her and talking loudly enough to be clearly heard. "There's a lot you need to know."

"But John was so sweet and nice to me, so helpful," Easter said. At that, her manner melted, some, and she looked like she might cry. "I fell a little in love with him. The Connor agency was going to take me on as a model, my dream."

"Easter, I'm an Oklahoma City lawyer, Em Hoffer," Hoffer

said. She'd turned to look directly back at the young woman. "First off, I should tell you that the man's name wasn't John Carter. Second, he had nothing whatsoever to do with the Connor Model Agency."

"What?" Easter was incredulous. "I don't believe you."

I took over. "It's true. The man's real name was Leo Castor. He worked—mostly as an antiunion enforcer—for Kraker Oil Company, headquartered in Oklahoma City."

"How could that be true?" Easter asked. "He was so solid, so . . . what? So reliable, and charming, too."

"It *is* true, though, Easter," Hoffer said. "Not the slightest doubt. The man was a complete fraud—and totally evil."

"John Carter?" Easter asked, shaken.

"Leo Castor," I said. "Back in Vernon, you weren't suspicious when you found that he was flying you away in the same airplane that you saw Tobe Satville land in?"

Easter thought for a moment. "He said it was actually his company's plane, and I believed him."

"Easter, Castor killed Satville, then stole his plane," I said. "You weren't alarmed, later, when he tried to kill Em Hoffer and me in the air by aiming the airplane you were in at us?"

"Told me in advance that he was just going to scare you off, make you go back and leave us alone," she said.

"The man was a liar and a killer, Easter," I said, then paused for a moment. "And, now, for the rest of what we've gotta make you see," I said.

"What else, for God's sake?" Easter asked. It was almost a cry.

"Just as I tried to tell you when we were on the way to the Easter Pageant—was that nearly a week ago?—the Parnells are not your real parents," I said.

"I sure don't believe that!" Easter said emphatically. "I told you so back then, Okie."

Hoffer intervened. "Yes, what Okie said is the truth, Easter," she said. "I know this is all hard for you to accept, hard to take. But a wonderful friend of mine, Lily Morgan of Oklahoma City, is your real mother. I knew her well."

"*Knew* her?" Easter asked. "Past tense?"

"She died, just after Okie and I took off to Mexico after you," Hoffer said.

"What of?" Easter asked.

"TB."

"First, you're telling me that my mother's not my mother, and, now, you're telling me that my real mother's dead," Easter said.

The young woman took a while to think all the new, and shocking, information over. "Then, how come I was born in Vernon?" she asked, finally.

"The owner of Kraker Oil Company, where Lily Morgan worked when she was a girl, was a man named Elmo Kraker Senior," Hoffer said. "He got Lily pregnant—with you—and, at his insistence, she came to Vernon, to Dr. Askew, to have you. The doctor gave you to the Parnells and registered your birth as if you were the Parnells' natural child. Before Lily Morgan died, she sent me to Vernon to discover your identity, to find you. She was always so sorry she'd given you up. She loved you, Easter, and she always wanted you back."

"If that's true—"

"It's the gospel, Easter," I said. "I've got the Cash County clerk's birth-record page, right here, to prove it." I patted the belly of my shirt. "Back home, my deputy Stud Wampler has a copy of Dr. Askew's records that removes any doubt whatsoever."

Em Hoffer added, "And I've got pictures of Lily Morgan, your mother, with Kraker. I've got letters from your real father to Lily, and her affidavit, too."

"I can't stand this!" Easter cried. "I can't *under*stand this!" She slumped and remained quiet for a good while. Finally, she sat up and spoke, again. "My real parents . . ." It was all obviously a lot for her to have to think through.

"They're Elmo Kraker Senior, who died a few years back," Hoffer said, "and Lily Morgan—who, I'm sorry to say, has also passed away, now, as we told you."

"So, my real mother's dead," Easter said.

"She is," Hoffer said. "She so wanted to find you. Now, she never will."

"I had an induced miscarriage in Veracruz," Easter said. "That's one thing John Carter—or Leo Castor, you say—helped me with."

"We know," I said.

"I was already mourning that . . . that loss," Easter said, looking very sad. "Now, you tell me that I've got to mourn for the mother I didn't know I had." She paused. "Two generations to grieve for—in a way, my own blood that I'll never know."

"We feel very sorry for you, Easter," I said. "And I want you to know, too, neither I nor Em Hoffer shot Castor. It was a Mexican guy we know. And he did it to keep Castor from killing us."

Easter sat back in her seat.

It was many minutes before she finally leaned forward and spoke again. "Then, what was Carter—Castor—after?" the young woman asked.

Hoffer and I both turned back toward her.

"You!" Hoffer said.

"Easter, you're rich!" I said.

"Rich?" Easter asked, adding, as if to herself, "I'm rich."

"Richer than you can imagine!" I said. "Elmo Kraker Junior, who's actually your half-brother, obviously thought for some time that he was the only heir of his father's—and *your* father's—estate, the sole owner of Kraker Oil Company and all its oil millions. Kraker Junior had Leo Castor come up to Vernon from their office in Veracruz, to search out your identity and, then, get you out of the country."

"What was Castor, as you call him, going to do with me?" Easter asked.

"Don't know for sure," I said. "Several options. None would have been good for you. Wanted to make sure that you never found out who you were, that you never made a claim for your inheritance. Kraker Junior was obviously determined not to share a dime with you."

"You'll have to go to court to get your rightful part of the estate, Easter, and the oil money," Hoffer said, "but you'll win."

It was quiet, again, for a time. Finally, Easter said, "So, the Connor Model Agency never actually contacted me, then. I'm not going to be a model after all."

"Easter, listen to me," I said. "As Stud Wampler would say, 'You've found a bird nest on the ground, easy pickin's.' You're rich! You can *buy* the Connor Model Agency!"

THIRTY-THREE

Hot baths in our two separate rooms at the Yankee Courts, near the airport, in Corpus Christi, Texas—Easter and Em Hoffer sharing one room, me alone in a second—a few hours of sleep, a change of clothes, and a hot breakfast cheered us up, some. But not much.

Saturday morning, going back out to the Waco and, afterward, in the air, there was only the barest minimum of talk among us. We headed toward Dallas, where I planned to gas up the plane a last time, grab us a bite to eat, and call Stud Wampler on the telephone. There were three of us in the airplane's cabin, but I felt like I was all alone, there, too, the same as at the Yankee Courts, the night before.

Em Hoffer was almost sullen toward me. She wanted me to say that I didn't believe that she was the person who'd broken into Dr. Askew's office. I couldn't say that, because I didn't know what the truth was. I'd been happy to learn, for sure, that it was Leo Castor, not Hoffer, who'd killed Tobe Satville. But who'd knocked Stud Wampler in the head and rifled Dr. Askew's files? There were several possibilities.

Tobe Satville might have done it. If so, wouldn't Leo Castor have later grabbed that record, after he pushed Satville out of his own Piper Cub and killed him—and wouldn't I have then found the record, the same as I did the torn-out county clerk page, among the papers in Castor's briefcase?

A second possibility was that Leo Castor, himself, had broken into Doc Askew's. But, if he was the one, why, again, wasn't the birth record he took in his briefcase when I dumped it out?

Then, there was the third possibility. Em Hoffer might have broken into Askew's office—and still have that record, herself, in her satchel purse, say, just as she might have the blackjack there, or a sock full of nickels, or whatever it was that Stud Wampler'd been knocked out with.

And, of course, I had to consider a final possibility, that Leo Castor did have the Askew record, himself, however he got it, but simply had kept it somewhere other than in his briefcase, the same as the weapon he'd used on Tobe Satville.

Which possibility was it? I couldn't make up my mind. And, when Hoffer looked at me, I could tell that my doubts apparently showed in my eyes.

Easter Parnell seemed resentful of me. I thought that she'd more or less digested what Em Hoffer and I had told her about who she really was and about the evil in Leo Castor. But, somehow, although in the rational part of her mind she'd come to realize, I thought, that neither the so-called John Carter—Castor—or an offer to her from the Connor Model Agency had been real, she blamed *me* in another part of her mind, it seemed to me, for having snatched away her modeling chance, and an admiring and attractive man, too. None of that made any sense, but I was pretty clear that that was the way things stood. What was the old Chinese proverb? "Why do you hate me? I never did anything for you."

At Love Field, in Dallas, while Hoffer and Easter went to buy us some food, for the last leg of the flight, I stepped into the office of Lone Star Aviation and, with permission, placed a long-distance call, collect, to Stud Wampler, at his home in Vernon. When Stud came on the line, I gave him a really brief rundown of what'd happened, told him that Leo Castor was dead, and that Hoffer and I were bringing Easter back home in the Waco. I said that we'd be at the Moreland's strip in Vernon at five, and I'd appreciate his coming to pick us up.

Stud said he'd do it.

"I'll reimburse you for this call," I said.

"Don't worry none about that, stud," he said. "This is business. The county'll foot the bill. Marsh Traynor's had a change of heart."

"Would you call Easter's folks, too, Stud?" I said. "Ask them to meet us at Moreland's. Easter's not feeling the best in the world, and I'm sure she'll want to go directly home with them."

"We'll all be at the airstrip," he said. "Might could get the Blue Devil band to come out to meetcha, too, stud."

There was a pretty good-size welcoming party at Moreland's strip, when I set the Waco down, there, and taxied over close to the tin hangar. The Parnells had come in their maroon Buick Roadmaster; Stud Wampler, with Crystal, in my blue sheriff car. Jeff Moreland had walked over from the dairy.

The cars emptied out. Everyone let themselves through the wire gate and came over to greet Easter, Em Hoffer, and me. We got out of the plane with our bags. Jeff Moreland seemed like the happiest of the bunch to see me—and his Waco.

We shook hands all around. The well-dressed Parnells—the chubby Mrs. Parnell, the pink-faced Mr. Parnell—both at the same time hugged Easter, laughed and cried awhile, then hugged her some more.

"Things have been so awful for you, Mama," Easter said, when she'd stepped back a little. "I'm sorry I caused so much worry and trouble."

"The main thing is that you're here," Mrs. Parnell said. "Nothing else is important." She put her arm around Easter, again, and kissed her on the cheek.

"I've been shocked to death, though, to find out you're not my real parents, but it doesn't change anything between us," Easter said.

"We wanted to shield you, dear, from the sordid details," Mrs. Parnell said. She took a little handkerchief from her sleeve and dabbed at her eyes. Then, she took Easter's face in her plump hands. "Poor thing! You look so pale, so weak."

"I love you both," Easter said. "You're still Mama and Daddy to me." The three Parnells all hugged again, and cried.

Stud Wampler, Crystal, Hoffer, and I had been standing to the side while the Parnell family reunion was taking place. Em Hoffer helped me, and the two of us rapidly filled in everybody on what'd transpired since we'd left Vernon to find Easter in Mexico. Leo Castor was dead. Castor'd been the one who'd dumped Tobe Satville out of the Piper Cub, killing him, in order to get Satville out of the picture and to get his hands on the county clerk's birth-record page that must have led Castor, ultimately, to Easter. We felt sure that Elmo Kraker Jr. had sent Leo Castor to Vernon, to find Easter and get her out of the way. Castor had tried to kill me, had killed my dog. Neither I nor Hoffer said anything about the break-in at the office of Dr. Askew or about Easter's caused miscarriage in Mexico.

I did wind up by saying to Stud, "Sorry, we never found your little pistol."

"You couldn't have," Stud said. "It was here all the time. Old lady Askew finally found it under a desk at their clinic." Saying this, he reached into the right-hand pocket of his khakis and pulled the weapon out a ways, to show me.

Mr. Parnell spoke up, then. "Sheriff, any way to prosecute Elmo Kraker Junior, you think, his part in all this?"

"I've thought about that, and, sorry to say, I doubt it," I said. "I don't believe we could prove in court any direct tie-in between him and the actual crimes. It's a damned shame! But, Mr. Parnell, you can punish him in the way he'll hate most—taking away some of his money—by pressing Easter's claim against him and the Kraker estate."

It was Mrs. Parnell's turn, then. "We'll be grateful to you two, Sheriff and Mrs. Hoffer, to our dying day, for bringing back our little girl."

"I want to go home, now," Easter said quietly. But, instead of moving toward the Parnell car, she turned to Em Hoffer. "I'll never forget all you've done for me, Mrs. Hoffer. Will I go to court, for my part of the Kraker estate?"

"Yes, and, as I told you, you'll win," Hoffer said. "You'll have to get the probate reopened, but I doubt Elmo Kraker Junior will put up much of a fight on that, with what we know on him, now."

"I want you to be my lawyer," Easter said.

"It'll all work out," Hoffer said. "I'll call you."

"Do, please," the young woman said. "You're the only lawyer I'd have."

Hoffer spoke to Easter's parents. "Could y'all drop me off at the Luden Hotel? I want to get my car and head right on to the city, tonight."

"Of course, dear," Mrs. Parnell said.

Easter and her parents turned and went through the wire gate, toward their car. Hoffer picked up her bag and raincoat. I stepped over to say good-bye to her.

She cleared her throat. "Well, I've got to get going," she said.

"You still think there might be a chance you'd come down here to Vernon to practice law?" I asked her.

"I'd have to study some more about that, Okie," Hoffer said.

"I'll call you," I said.

"Do that."

The two of us shook hands. Hoffer went through the gate, to join Easter and the Parnells in their Buick.

I went over to the Waco, where Jeff Moreland was looking it over, shook hands with him, and thanked him. "The county'll pay you, Jeff," I said.

I turned back to Stud and Crystal, and the three of us went through the gate and loaded up in the sheriff car, me under the wheel, Stud in the passenger seat, Crystal in the back.

"Stud, was it Leo Castor or Tobe Satville," Stud Wampler asked, as I put the car in motion, "that conked me on the head and got into Doc Askew's files?"

"One or the other, I guess," I said.

"Nothing worked out with you and that Hoffer, I reckon?" Stud asked.

"Looks like not," I said.

"Audrey Ready's a lot better for you, anyhow, Okie, than that lawyer woman," Crystal said from the backseat. "Comparing them two is like chickens and eggs."

Stud spoke up in his best W. C. Fields voice. "Crystal, my dear, the Great McGonigle, himself, could not have said it more aptly."

I glanced back at Crystal and changed the subject. "What about Loretta?" I asked her.

"Thank the good Lord, Okie, my little girl's all right," Crystal said, always cheerful. "Brought her home from Crippled Children's Hospital. The typhoid run its course, look like. She'll go back in school, sometime next week, and, as they say, all's swell that ends swell."

The Billings place was quiet and lonesome when I got there after letting Stud and Crystal out at the courthouse parking lot. No Scooter, even, to welcome me home. The dog was lying in a week-old grave, down by the creek.

Maybe I'd jog over there and take a swim, I thought. Just then, the party-line telephone on my kitchen wall rang out, a long and a short.

"Yes," I said into the mouthpiece, when I'd picked up the receiver and put it to my ear.

"You don't even know the question, yet." It was Audrey Ready.

"I'm easy." I said that to be funny, but, the second the words

were out of my mouth, I thought of what they meant and felt guilty.

"Stud Wampler told me when you were getting in," Audrey said. "I called him this afternoon."

"'The hog returns to his wallow, and the dog to his vomit,'" I said. It was a phrase from the Bible, I thought, and a kind of distasteful one, too.

"Get another saying," Audrey said. "You weren't kidnapped, then, while you were in Mexico?"

"No such luck."

"You want to come over to my house and try it?" she asked.

"Getting kidnapped?"

"Well, I'd feed you, first."

"Now, you've made it sound interesting," I said.